PRAISE FOR HALLIE EPHRON'S
COME AND FIND ME

"[*Come and Find Me* is] a suspenseful tale of high-tech skul-duggery that even low-tech readers will appreciate."

—*Booklist*

"[Hallie Ephron] does a solid job of carrying the suspense genre into the twenty-first century."　　　—*Boston Globe*

"Explores the dark side of cyberspace. . . . Although *Come and Find Me* is at its core a breathless thriller, Ephron also explores the issue of personal identity in an age when we can pretend to be anything we want to be online."

—*Connecticut Post*

"Psychologically astute and emotionally gripping . . . Ephron understands that the fears we inflict upon ourselves can be more crippling than a man with a gun. . . . A unique and compelling novel to be read more than once."

—*Mystery Scene* magazine

"Propelled me from first page to last in a single sitting."

—Bookreporter.com

"A compelling yarn of deception and danger. . . . A caution-ary tale about the power of information technology. . . . And although this novel seems to be a stand-alone, readers can hope that a sequel is not out of the question."

—*Richmond Times-Dispatch*

NEVER TELL A LIE

"Lovers of classic mysteries will adore Hallie Ephron's *Never Tell a Lie*. . . . A richly atmospheric tale. You can imagine Hitchcock curling up with this one."   —*USA Today*

"Suburban noir has rarely been done with such psychological insight or plot-twisting suspense."   —*Boston Globe*

"A snaky, unsettling tale of psychological suspense."
          —*Seattle Times*

"*Never Tell a Lie* delivers a tale about obsession, relationships, and forgiveness. Ephron quickly builds a foundation of psychological terror that doesn't let up until the last surprise twist."   —*South Florida Sun Sentinel*

"A page-turner with a Hitchcockian opener."
          —*Sacramento Bee*

COME AND FIND ME

ALSO BY HALLIE EPHRON

FICTION
Never Tell a Lie

NONFICTION
The Bibliophile's Devotional
1001 Books for Every Mood
Writing and Selling Your Mystery Novel

COME AND FIND ME

Hallie Ephron

_wm_

WILLIAM MORROW
An Imprint of HarperCollins_Publishers_

A hardcover edition of this book was published in 2011 by William Morrow, an imprint of HarperCollins Publishers.

Excerpt from *Never Tell a Lie* copyright © 2009 by Hallie Ephron.

FIRST WILLIAM MORROW TRADE PAPERBACK PUBLISHED 2012.

Designed by Jamie Lynn Kerner

The Library of Congress has catalogued the hardcover edition as follows:

Ephron, Hallie.
   Come and find me / Hallie Ephron.—1st ed.
     p. cm.
   ISBN 978-0-06-185752-2
    1. Recluses—Fiction. 2. Sisters—Fiction. 3. Missing persons—Fiction. 4. Psychological fiction. I. Title.
   PS3605.P49C66   2011
   813'.6—dc22

2010037260

ISBN 978-0-06-210372-7 (pbk.)

12 13 14 15 16 OV/RRD 10 9 8 7 6 5 4 3

For Molly and Naomi, little girls who grew up to be friends

ACKNOWLEDGMENTS

THIS BOOK WAS INSPIRED BY THE IDEA THAT SOMEONE COULD SPEND her waking hours "living" in a virtual world. For orienting me to that world and showing me its possibilities, special thanks to Jeff Bardin, Olin Sibert, Char James-Tanny, Jim Freeman, Yael Even-Levy, and Michelle Chambers.

Thanks to others who shared their expertise: George Fournier, Cathy Cairns, David Cairns, Doug Lyle, MD, and Anthony Sammarco.

Thanks to fellow writers who provided valuable critiques of the manuscript: Jan Brogan, Linda Barnes, Roberta Isleib, Hank Phillippi Ryan, Naomi Rand, Donna Tramontozzi, and Barbara Shapiro.

A special thanks to Pam David-Braverman for her generous contribution to National Braille Press and allowing me to pinch-hit for the incomparable Robert B. Parker.

Thank you, Jerry Touger, my patient husband, for reading and encouraging.

There can be no smarter or warmer agents than Gail Hochman and her international colleague, Marianne Merola. For savvy and insight and patience, thanks to an extraordinary editor, Katherine Nintzel. Also, many thanks to the rest of the folks at William Morrow, especially Danielle Bartlett.

COME AND FIND ME

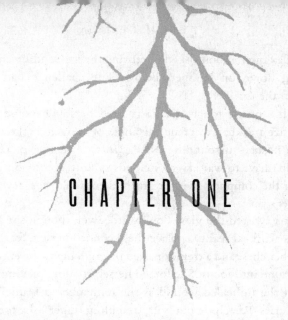

CHAPTER ONE

IF IT WERE UP TO DIANA, THERE'D BE WEATHER. RAIN, SNOW, EVEN the occasional hurricane. But climate was one of those things that were out of her control in this always blue-sky world. The terrain, on the other hand, was her choice: a replica of a spot in the Swiss Alps at the base of Waterfall Pitch with the towering North Face of the Eiger looming overhead.

Nadia, Diana's alter ego in the virtual reality of OtherWorld, was barely visible standing at the base of a cascade of frozen water sculpted against the nearly vertical slope. Diana zoomed in on her avatar, who wore wraparound sunglasses, a fitted black leather jacket with a zipper and upturned collar, slim jeans, red boots, and a red newsboy cap. In the real Swiss Alps, she'd have lasted about thirty seconds in that outfit; the bitter cold turned any exposed bit of skin pink, then red, then white. Diana re-called the stillness into which tinkling cowbells and voices from the valley below had risen like whiffs of smoke.

Waterfall Pitch had been nearly unclimbable—every placement of ax or crampon risked fracturing the ice, sending chunks crashing down on climbers below. The challenge had only added to the thrill.

With a gentle touch, Diana twisted her 3-D mouse with its oversize trackball to crane the angle of view and take in the pristine beauty surrounding Nadia. In this version of reality, you didn't have to wait days for clouds to shift. It took only seconds for the computer's vector graphics engine to rez, revealing the Eiger's tip.

Diana twisted the view downward. Even though she knew this was artificial reality, a place she'd created herself, fear flickered in her chest and a tremor passed through her as icy crevasses below came into focus. She forced herself to look, picking once again at the unhealed wound as she remembered Daniel's last echoey cries. Reaching out with trembling fingers, she touched the frame of her computer screen. It calmed her to trace the boundaries of the image.

Diana had made it back. Daniel hadn't.

She pulled up on the mouse and nudged the space bar. Nadia rose into the air, landed on a narrow outcropping near the top of the peak, and stared out at the void. At her desk, Diana crossed her arms and hunched her body to staunch the shudders of pain that rippled from her core.

With a *ding*, a text message popped into a corner of the screen.

JAKE: RU there?

Where else would she be? Diana swatted away the message with a click of the mouse. She had a timer ticking down in the corner of the screen, reminding her of their meeting with

MedLogic. It wasn't for another twenty minutes. Whatever Jake needed from her could wait.

Diana typed /pray. A single violin keened the opening of Pachelbel's Canon, and her avatar dropped to her knees and lowered her head. The somber, stately notes stepped down the scale, stepped down again, and then melodies intertwined and the pace quickened as more violins joined in, their melodies swirling and circling one another.

Diana splayed her fingers and rested them on the screen. *Rest in peace.* The words repeated themselves in her head, a chanting counterpoint to the music.

A discreet buzzer sounded a fifteen-minute reminder. With a few clicks, Nadia was home. Pixel by pixel, a virtual room resolved itself around her. It was identical to Diana's real office in the house where she'd grown up in a Boston suburb, right down to the brightly colored Peruvian weaving that hung on the wall. Nadia's "office" was much neater, though, and its plants were green instead of brown.

Diana shot a note to Jake, telling him that she'd be ready. Quickly, she put the finishing touches on their presentation and dragged files for the meeting across the screen and into Nadia's briefcase. She was scrolling one last time through her notes for the meeting when a Klaxon sounded. INTRUDER ALERT flashed in the corner of the computer screen.

Diana's heart lurched and her breath caught in her throat. She swiveled to an adjacent monitor. Live video feeds from cameras stationed outside her compact ranch house showed a brown UPS van parked out front, a hulking shadow on this bright sunny day. A uniformed man had just breached her electronic fence and was on his way to her front door with a good-size package.

Diana took a deep breath and steadied herself against the edge of the desk. The alarm continued. The doorbell rang. The meeting buzzer went off—ten-minute reminder.

"Shut up, all of you!" Diana screamed. She hit a button to silence the Klaxon. But there was no button to slow her heartbeat or erase the sick feeling that had invaded her gut.

She turned back to the video monitor. At the front door, the deliveryman peered up at the camera from under the brim of his cap. She recognized his face. Wally. She'd never caught a last name.

Through the speaker came his voice: "Package for ya."

She knew that her house appeared to be empty; every shade was drawn and the car that she hadn't driven for months, Daniel's Hummer, was locked in the garage. Soundproofing kept what little noise she made inside from leaking out. If it had been anyone else, she wouldn't have answered the ring. But Wally would know she was there. She never wasn't.

Diana sighed and pulled over a microphone. "Hey, Wally. Whatever it is, can you just leave it for me in the bin?"

"Come on, Lady Di," came his tinny voice. "This one needs you to sign."

She hesitated. Glanced at the clock. She had a few minutes yet before her meeting. But time wasn't really the issue.

"You can sign it for me, can't you? I'll never tell," she said.

"I'm not going down for forgery just so's you don't have to take a breath of fresh air. It's a beautiful day, trust me."

But could she trust herself?

She watched Wally in the fish-eye lens. He was holding the package over his head, showing it to her. "Hey, you ordered it. Did you think it was going to transport itself inside? You just let me know when you're ready."

She stood, exasperated, knowing from past experience that he wasn't going to give up. "I'm coming, I'm coming."

She left her office, pulling the door shut behind her, and continued through the living room and on to the front hall. Heart pounding, she peered through the peephole in the door. Wally's eyeball seemed to bulge back at her.

"Anyone else out there?" she asked.

"Uh, hang on, I'll check . . ." He withdrew from the eyehole for a moment. Then returned. "Nope, just me. The duke and duchess send their regrets."

A comedian. Diana swallowed a nervous laugh and patted her pocket, feeling for her Xanax, her magic tranquillity pills.

She threw two dead bolts, removed the security bar, and entered a twelve-digit pass code into the alarm. As she opened the door, she felt as if an abyss opened in front of her, like an elevator door sliding open into an empty shaft. She grasped the door frame with both hands.

Wally flashed her a crooked-toothed grin. He was well over six feet, and looked as if his arms and legs were made from the limbs of slender saplings. He touched a long index finger to his cap. "You're lookin' spruce."

Diana looked down, taking in her matted furry slippers, sweatpants, and an oversize Smashing Pumpkins T-shirt, black with a silver ZERO printed across the chest. Her face grew warm, and she tried to run her fingers through the tangles in her long dark curls.

"Here you go," he said. "For Nadia Varata." He held the clipboard out like bait, just beyond her arm's reach. "Russian?"

"Pardon?"

"Varata. Sounds like a Czech or Russian name."

"I guess it does," Diana said. What it was, was pure nonsense—Varata and avatar were anagrams, just like Nadia and Diana.

The air within the door frame seemed to quiver like the

surface of a pond. She'd have to reach through in order to sign.

"Polish?" Wally said. She could almost see the word floating toward her, the *P* and the *O* round and buoyant. He waggled the clipboard and called past her. "Yoo-hoo, Nadia! You hiding her in there?"

Diana forced in a breath, leaned forward, and swiped the clipboard from him. It was warmer outside than in, unusually so for March. Another sign of global warming?

The screech of car tires on the street pushed her back. Relief washed away the panicky feeling as soon as she recognized the gold Mini Cooper that had come to a halt behind the UPS van.

Panic flared again—wasn't Ashley in Los Angeles on business?

Wally turned to look. "Toy car."

Diana drew back into the dark coolness of the doorway and scrawled a hasty signature on the form.

Ashley climbed out of the car and clattered up the walk on spike heels, bangle bracelets on each arm, heedless of any anxiety her unexpected appearance had generated. She hugged a grocery bag, and her enormous purse swung from her shoulder. In her other hand, she carried an incongruous, corporate-looking computer laptop case.

Diana heard the Klaxon going off again. Intruder alert, indeed. Diana felt a twinge in a spot behind her right eyeball, a headache starting to bloom.

Ashley's denim skirt ended a few inches below her panty line, which, in turn, was a few inches below the ends of her long blond hair. Her western-style shirt clung to her considerable anatomy. She'd gotten breasts from Grandma Highsmith. Once upon a time, everyone said Diana had inherited Grandma H's sheer nerve, verve, and stubbornness.

"Well, look at you! You're out!" Ashley said. She set down

her computer case on the front steps and tossed back her tresses like she was auditioning for a L'Oréal commercial. She gave Diana a juicy smack on the cheek.

"Ick," Diana said. She hated to admit it, having Ashley there calmed her jitters. But it didn't keep the ache in her head from starting to throb.

Wally's gaze shifted back and forth from Diana to Ashley. "I'm guessing here, but this isn't Nadia."

Ashley smiled at him and winked. "You think?"

"Behave yourself," Diana said.

"You sure do sound alike," Wally said. His speculative glance wandered from Ashley to Diana and back again. "And except for the hair and—" His gaze drifted down a notch or two.

"The attitude," Diana said. "Not to mention the accessories."

"Sisters?" Wally asked.

"Got it in one," Diana said. Inside, the phone rang. In seconds the meeting reminder would sound again too. "Thanks." In a single move, she pushed the clipboard back at Wally and took the grocery bag from Ashley. "I gotta go."

Ashley appraised Wally, narrowing one eye. She rummaged in her purse and came up with a sleek, brushed-steel business-card holder. Opening it, she offered him a card. Wally took the card with his teeth and transferred the package into her arms. Then he reached two fingers into the pocket of his shirt and pulled out a slip of paper, scrawled on it, and handed it to Ashley. She tucked it into her purse.

"So, are you in or out?" Diana asked Ashley. With her free hand she picked up Ashley's computer case.

"Well, duh. In." Ashley stepped inside and pushed the door shut. She glanced at the label on the package and shot Diana a sharp look. "So who's this Nadia Varata?"

CHAPTER TWO

ADIA," Diana said, fastening the security bar and door
locks, "is me."

Ashley registered that with barely a blink. "What's in
here?" She sniffed at the package, turned it over, and examined
the label.

"It's my stuff. Something I ordered." Diana set Ashley's
laptop under the coatrack.

Ashley shook the package. "What stuff? A trampoline?"

Another comedian. "What's this?" Diana peered into the
grocery bag. "Prison rations?"

Ashley pointed to the tip of her nose. *On the nose!* Like when
they used to play charades.

"You shouldn't have," Diana said as she carried the bag into
the kitchen. It was sweet of Ashley to keep bringing her groceries. But Diana did shop for her own food, even if that shopping
was online. She put away eggs, sliced American cheese, whole-

wheat bread, and a bag of Granny Smith apples. At the bottom was a pint of rum raisin ice cream, Diana's favorite.

What had started as a twinge in her head was gaining strength and turning nasty. She shook out a couple of aspirin from an oversize container on the kitchen counter and knocked them back with a cupped hand of water from the tap.

When she returned to the living room, Ashley had already pried open one edge of the box.

"It's clothes, you twit. What else would it be?" Diana took the package from her. "And did I say you could open it?"

"Mail order?" Ashley made a face, like the concept stank.

"What are you doing here, anyway? I thought you were in L.A."

"I finished early and got my flight moved up. Took the red-eye. They don't expect me at work until Monday, so I thought I'd come bother you."

"Well, you're succeeding." Diana laughed. "You sure don't look like you took the red-eye."

"I'll take that as a compliment. Business-class seats recline and I slept all the way. Thank God for Ambien. Though my throat's scratchy. And my joints"—she massaged her shoulder and winced—"are really sore. The person behind me coughed and sneezed the whole way. I hope I'm not coming down with swine flu. Or SARS."

"Or the phage," Diana said.

That perked Ashley up. "What's that?"

"A virus. One of the early symptoms is joint pain."

"Really?"

"Excruciating. Then it attacks your bones and disrupts your genetic code."

"No kidding?" Ashley's wide eyes went narrow. "You *are* kidding."

"But I had you going, didn't I?"

"One day I'll get really sick and then you'll be sorry."

"I'm looking forward to it. In the meanwhile, I've got a meeting that's supposed to start in"—Diana checked her watch—"Shit. Four minutes." She started for her office door.

"You're having a business meeting in Mom and Dad's bedroom?"

"So?"

"So, I'm just asking."

"You know it's my office now."

"Yeah, but when are you going to let me see it?"

Ashley had been the one who'd convinced Diana to move back into their childhood home soon after she lost Daniel. Life in the farmhouse where she and Daniel had been living was spartan, and all she'd brought back with her were a few pieces of furniture and the computer equipment that had filled the railway container where they'd worked.

But since then, Diana hadn't let anyone, not even Ashley, into the safe space she'd created where no one could reach her unless she invited them in.

Diana began to key in her security code.

"You plan to lock yourself in or me out?" Ashley asked.

Diana paused. "What is that? Multiple choice?"

"I mean the house is barricaded enough. Why do you bother with locks on inside doors too?"

"I lock doors." Diana turned around. "I do a lot of crazy things because it makes me feel safe. Gives me the illusion that I'm in control. I know you think that's nutty." She could hear her voice rising, turning shrill, but she couldn't stop herself. "And I would agree. But I do it anyway. Okay? *Okay?*"

"Okay!" Ashley held up her hands. "You don't need to jump

down my throat. Hey, it's your life. You do whatever. It's just that, you know, it doesn't make sense."

"What's logic got to do with it? You've been in therapy. Fear's not rational. And sometimes, being rational isn't the most rational thing to be."

Ashley's mouth dropped open. She blinked and reared back. "Ouch." She reached out her hand to Diana. "I only . . ." Her eyes teared up. "I just . . ." And just like that, Ashley turned the tables and she was the aggrieved party.

Diana took Ashley's hand and squeezed it. "I know, I know. You only want what's best for me. But let me be the judge of what's best, would you?"

Diana tried to drop Ashley's hand but Ashley held fast. "You're right," Ashley said. "After all, you *never* judge me . . ." Ashley held on long enough for Diana to catch the irony.

"You're impossible," Diana said, but she was laughing.

"Sorry. I couldn't resist. You stepped right into that." Ashley bit her lip and stared past Diana at the locked door. "So, can I at least come in and watch your meeting? I'll be quiet as a mouse."

"Ha! You have never, in your whole entire life, been remotely mouselike."

"Come on." Ashley held Diana's gaze. "Sweetie, seriously, don't you think it's time you let someone in?"

This time, Diana blinked first.

Ashley gave her a look of mock surprise. "Besides, leave me out here and I might open your package. Or even worse, neaten up the place."

As Ashley glanced about the living room, still furnished with pieces they'd grown up with, Diana registered the discarded clothing, cereal bowl with congealed oatmeal, a week-old mound of clean laundry that she'd never put away. On the mantel over the fireplace was a simple brass urn that contained Daniel's ashes.

"If you're not careful," Ashley added, "I might even fold your towels and sort your underwear."

Diana turned back to her office door. She started entering the security code again. The door clicked and swung open a few inches. She could feel Ashley peering in from behind her. It really was past time to let another human being into her inner sanctum.

She held the door wide open and Ashley stepped past her and stood in the doorway.

"Wow," Ashley said. "I didn't realize you broke through the wall. This is a great space."

Soon after she'd moved in, Diana had spent days swinging a sledgehammer, venting her rage on the wall between what had been her parents' bedroom and her own. It was better than lying comatose for days on end, under a mound of Daniel's clothing. By the end, she'd been coated with plaster dust, her face streaked pink from tears. She'd patched and painted the walls and ceiling, and pieced together oak flooring to fill the spots where wall had been ripped out.

Ashley continued into the room. "Gorgeous," she said, running her fingers over the wall hanging that Diana had picked up in Peru when she and Daniel had gone there to climb Machu Picchu. "But this"—she took in the computer equipment— "looks like some kind of command central. And what are these?" She indicated the bank of monitors. "Surveillance?"

"With infrared for night vision. Plus an alarm system. Redundant Internet access. Firewalls. Motion sensors. Welcome to Gamelan Security headquarters. Aka, my office."

"How did you manage to set all this up?"

"Jake helped me."

"So all that experience hacking into other people's systems finally pays off." Ashley paused, but when Diana didn't rise to her bait, she gave a brittle smile and asked, "So, how is charming Jake?" Ashley and Jake had gone out on one spectacularly awful date during which he'd spent the whole evening texting.

"He's good. I think. We're working together, but I haven't *seen him* seen him in months."

Ashley picked her way past a dead ficus, over an empty can of Red Bull and some open boxes filled with foam packing material. She settled herself in Diana's desk chair—white fiberglass molded into a tulip shape with a red seat cushion and polished aluminum base. Daniel had given Diana that chair, a period piece from the sixties, as a Valentine's Day gift a few years earlier.

Before Diana could stop her, Ashley reached for the mouse and jiggled it. The monitor flickered to life. The replica of the room they were in came up. Nadia was frozen in the middle of it. The queue of waiting messages in the lower corner of the screen had grown.

"How cool is this?" Ashley said.

Diana closed the office door. She crossed the room and tapped Ashley on the shoulder. "You mind?"

"Sorry." Ashley relinquished the mouse and stood. She leaned forward, staring at the screen, her long blond hair falling almost to the keyboard. "OtherWorld?" she read aloud. "So what is this, some kind of game?"

"Game?" Diana choked on a laugh. "No. It's—" She paused, searching for the word. "Just like the name says, it's another world. There are stores and other offices here. You can go to parks and hear concerts. I meet with clients."

"Wow. Video conferencing with cartoon characters." Ashley snickered.

Diana massaged her forehead. "Sort of. But I don't get paid in Monopoly money." She edged Ashley aside and slipped into the chair. "And the cartoon characters are real people."

"You're sure about that?"

"Reasonably so."

Ashley gave her an astonished look. "This, from a woman who trusts no one?"

"No one but you, my dear."

Diana noticed the timer: minus two minutes, thirty seconds. She was officially late. She eyed the message-waiting flag on Skype. Probably Jake, trying to raise a response out of her.

With a few clicks, she transformed Nadia's hair from short, spiky blond to conservative brown done up in a French braid.

"Meet Nadia," Diana said as she exchanged her avatar's leather jacket, jeans, and boots for a dark tailored suit jacket, a short skirt, and ballerina flats. "She's my alter ego in-world. And this is Gamelan Security's in-world headquarters. Her office. You can think of it as my very own 3-D MySpace."

"Or Rapunzel's virtual tower?" Ashley said.

Diana remembered the green cover of the book of Grimm's fairy tales, its spine peeled away. Rapunzel had been their favorite. Over and over they'd play out the story, taking turns at being the princess who lets down her long hair so that a wicked enchantress, and later a handsome prince, can climb up to her tower prison.

"Except Nadia doesn't need rescuing," Diana said. "Business is booming. And she's late for her meeting."

Clients had been lining up ever since Gamelan exposed a young medical student as the mastermind behind the breach of a prominent health insurer. They uncovered a massive theft of patient and physician medical records, though unfortunately not before the hacker's customers abroad had used the information to manufacture thousands of counterfeit health insurance ID cards and generate thousands of phony prescriptions. After the story hit national and international papers, Diana and Jake had more work than they could handle.

Diana dragged the red cap and wraparound sunglasses back to her inventory. The gold charms that her avatar wore around her neck—just like the real pair of gold Ds that Diana often wore around her own—were barely visible.

"Okay. Here we go." She swiveled toward Ashley and put her finger to her lips. "Remember"—she lowered her voice to a whisper—"you're a mouse."

"Where do you want me?" Ashley squeaked.

Diana pointed to a chair. Ashley held her hands like paws in front of her, minced over to the chair, and sat.

CHAPTER THREE

DIANA TOGGLED A SWITCH. THE COMPUTER MONITOR WENT BLANK, and the image of the virtual room that had been on the screen reappeared, projected across the upper half of the blank wall opposite them.

Ashley's mouth fell open. "Wow."

"Shh," Diana said, suppressing a smile. She felt a little like the first time she had ridden a two-wheeler, zooming past Ashley, who watched from astride her Hot Wheels. Her glee had been short-lived. A week later, Ashley was riding a two-wheeler, too, self-taught.

Diana hooked on her earpiece and typed in some coordinates. Moments later the image of her office dissolved, replaced by MedLogic's chrome-and-glass corporate building. A box appeared in the corner of the screen and she typed in the pass code, then swiped her index finger across the fingerprint reader on the side of her keyboard. A bell sounded.

"Nadia Varata," Diana said into the microphone.

The building exterior dissolved and MedLogic's conference room materialized around Nadia. Projected across a full wall, the replica of a corporate conference room, complete with a long table and a white board, felt like an extension of Diana's office.

The suited male avatar, standing beside a window with Diana's slide show already running in it, belonged to Jake. He even looked like Jake, or at least the way Jake had looked when Diana had last seen him in the flesh, more than six months earlier when he'd been slim with thick, reddish hair that grew like straw thatch, and had a fondness for John Lennon wire rims.

Five other avatars, all belonging to employees of MedLogic, sat at the conference table. Diana recognized the CFO Michael Courtemanche and head of security Anish Chander. She'd met them at previous meetings. Both wore suits and ties. Jake had already started to run Diana's presentation.

"This is surreal," Ashley whispered. "Can they see the real us?"

Diana shook her head and shushed her. She clicked on her virtual briefcase and dropped it onto the conference table. Then she sat Nadia in a chair.

Jake continued delivering the presentation. "And here's the inventory showing every storage device that's been connected to your back-end systems for the last three months," said Jake. The presentation showed a long list of devices and serial numbers.

For all Diana knew, Jake could have been anywhere in the world where he could get a wireless connection with enough bandwidth to run OtherWorld. As he continued, summarizing the security analysis they'd done, a text message popped to the top of her queue.

JAKE: YOK?

Yes, she was fine, she texted back. Just late.

Jake's avatar explained how they'd methodically traced every connection until they'd discovered a laptop with a data file that had no business being on its hard drive. The laptop also had a little program that automatically copied its files to another location out on the Internet.

Diana typed:

NADIA: T4 TO

Thanks for taking over.
Back came:

J: NO BD

Actually, it *was* a big deal. She shouldn't have been so late that he had to fill in for her. It was unprofessional.

The slide presentation was replaced by a window with video that showed the real Jake sitting opposite the unfortunate employee who owned the laptop with the suspect files. The poor woman—the name SONYA LOCHTE floated briefly on the screen and then disappeared—looked to be barely out of her mid-twenties. She had wispy pale blond hair, down to her shoulders, perspiration glistening on her forehead, and a deer-in-the-headlights look in her eyes.

"I . . . On my computer?" Ms. Lochte touched her neck. Pink streaks ran up her pale throat, from crisp white shirt collar to her chin. "I'm in marketing. You tell me there's files on my computer that shouldn't be there? I believe you. But honestly, I have no idea what you're talking about."

"Marketing." Diana recognized the voice and the derisive snort that followed. An empty voice balloon appeared over the head of CFO Michael Courtemanche's avatar. Diana wondered if in real life the guy had hair like Matthew McConaughey too.

"It's entirely likely that she has no idea what happened," Diana said, a voice balloon appearing over Nadia's head. Outside attackers often probed until they found a vulnerable entry point, poked a hole, and then exploited it low and slow without anyone being the wiser.

"We can't afford employees in any department who don't understand security protocol." Courtemanche again. Diana didn't bother to point out that it was doubtful that any of their security protocols would have prevented this particular incursion. "We've confiscated her computer and locked her out of the system. At least it was an easy fix."

A text message from Jake streamed across.

J: F**IDIOT

Diana agreed. The guy was a complete idiot if he thought that confiscating poor Sonya Lochte's computer was all it was going to take to solve the problem. She pressed her palm into her forehead. When was that aspirin going to take hold?

"Was the data encrypted?" Diana asked, even though she knew the answer. She'd already examined the stolen spreadsheet. Its cells contained unencrypted data—letters and numbers that meant nothing to her.

A moment of silence stretched out. "Felix?" The voice balloon was over Chander's head.

"Of course it was encrypted." This bold-faced lie was from an avatar wearing a dark suit. That had to be Felix Manning, their director of IT.

"Hmm. I wonder if you were using AES." Diana feigned innocence, knowing full well that they had not used Advanced Encryption, the latest industry standard. "We've found, in some cases, that our clients think they're protected when they're not. We can run a few tests, help you troubleshoot—"

Manning cut her off. "I'm satisfied that the problem is solved. It's clearly an inside job." He sounded so smug, but she knew he was blowing smoke. There was no way to tell if the attack had come from outside or in.

Manning added, "And we triple-wiped the laptop."

Damn. Diana had baited that laptop's hard drive with a phony data file that had in it a homing device that would have enabled her to trace the hackers.

"In that case, we should be all set," Jake said. "Don't you agree, Nadia?" *I so do not,* Diana wanted to shoot back. Customers were right, except when they weren't and then they didn't want to know. "Nadia?"

"Right," she finally said. "All set except for some recommendations. Shore up your firewalls and intrusion prevention systems, stuff like that. I'll send over a report with the details. Meanwhile, we'll get started tracking down these criminals and—"

"At this point, the ball is in your court, Felix," Jake said, talking over her. "It sounds as if you're confident that you have the situation under control . . ."

"Anish?" IT director Manning asked.

"Completely," Chander said.

"But if everyone just rolls over and—" Diana started.

A text message popped up on her screen:

J: BACK OFF

Chander continued. "I'm well aware that I'm responsible for security, and I'm satisfied that our people have this issue covered. We can take it from here. We've been assured."

"Been assured?" Diana winced as she heard the shrillness in her own voice. But really, what was that supposed to mean? And who exactly had assured them? She hated it when victims simply plugged the breach and folded. That's what hackers depended upon. When victims didn't come after them, they'd go on probing for the next unguarded entry point. In fact, Daniel would have called that the hackers' greatest and most unappreciated service to industry—finding chinks in corporate armor.

There were a few uncomfortable moments of silence.

"Nadia. Jake." Courtemanche spoke up. "I appreciate the work you've done for us. Thank you so much."

Blah, blah, blah. Diana swallowed her frustration.

"It's been our pleasure working with you," Jake said. "We'll send you our final reports. And, of course, the invoice." He chuckled.

"Of course. Send it to my attention," Chander said. "And we trust you'll continue to observe the nondisclosure?"

A new text message streamed across.

J: O&O

Over and out? It was more like *Over and don't let the door smack your sorry asses on the way out.* Diana transported Nadia home.

"Know what that reminded me of?" Startled, Diana turned around. She'd nearly forgotten that Ashley was in the room with her. "Client I once had. Bugged out after I'd met with them for hours, worked up an entire ten-page proposal, then she goes, 'Sorry, the event's been canceled.' Only it's not. Turns out they're using my proposal to spec an RFP for other hotels to bid on."

"That sucks."

"Yeah, it sucks. But there's one thing I've learned. Whatever you do, don't take it personal. "

But Diana *was* taking it personal. This wasn't the first time she'd seen this happen. Neponset Hospital five months ago. Unity Health Insurance six weeks later. When she'd pointed out the similarities to Jake—two clients rushing for the exit when they'd barely gotten past *hello*—he'd told her to grow a thicker skin. Now this was number three.

"I'm not being paranoid," Diana told Ashley.

"Did I say you were? Actually, I thought you were very . . . tactful."

"I made an effort. But I don't get it. I mean why—?"

"Weren't you listening to them?"

"They didn't *say* anything. It makes no sense."

"That's the point. Trust me. This has nothing to do with you. You can bet they've got some hidden agenda, some internal thing going on."

Diana stared at Ashley. Of course she was right.

"They pulled the rug out from under you?" Ashley went on. "So? Big frickin' deal. Move on." She stood, held her hands together in prayer, and drew them up and down, slicing the air in front of Diana. "I grant you absolution. As of this moment, it is officially not your problem."

More excellent advice. But once Diana saw a pattern, she was like a terrier going after a bone. That's what had drawn her into hacking in the first place—one puzzle after another, each more complex than the last, waiting for her to connect the pieces.

Besides, it pissed her off when clients hired them to stop the hemorrhaging, then opted for a Band-Aid. Each time it happened, it pissed her off more.

"This isn't the first client who's done this," she said. "Hit the panic button and shut us down rather than track the problem to its source."

"Maybe it's easier for them to just pay someone off. They definitely wanted you to stop digging."

"Pay someone off?" Diana remembered Chander's words: *We've been assured.* If they'd been hit up for payment in return for silence, then the last thing they'd want would be for her to keep sniffing around.

"You're right," Diana said. "The publicity could have done serious damage. They warehouse data for some of the biggest hospitals and health-care companies in the country. If someone's got them by the short hairs, dammit, I'm going to find out who."

"You are, are you?" Ashley narrowed her eyes at Diana.

Diana didn't answer. But with or without their client's cooperation, she was going to find out what was going on. Otherwise Gamelan was doing nothing more than playing a glorified version of Whack a Mole. At least this time she'd anticipated the speed bump. Only time would tell if she'd baited the laptop in time.

"I know that look," Ashley said. "What are you up to?"

CHAPTER FOUR

"Come on, spill," Ashley said as Diana transported Nadia back to her virtual office.

"You like this outfit?" Diana asked as she turned Nadia's hair back to short and blond and traded her going-to-meeting clothes for leather jacket and jeans.

"Yeah, but—"

"You'd wear it?" Diana added a line of chalky black beneath Nadia's eyes.

"I know what you're doing," Ashley said, but Diana knew she had her. Ashley couldn't resist the question. Clothes had always been the perfect distraction. "Absolutely. Those business clothes are so Marian the Librarian. Does she have a Cheerleader Barbie outfit, too? Remember when we used to play Barbies?"

Diana did remember. They'd play for hours on end. They had Bride Barbie, Ballerina Barbie, Cheerleader Barbie, and

Western Barbie. Western Barbie, Diana's hands-down favorite, came with a pair of six-shooters, each with a cylinder that actually rotated. All the Barbies had lived in the Barbie house, swam in the Barbie pool, and argued over which one got to drive the pink Corvette.

"All you ever wanted to do was change their clothes," Diana said.

"Which was hard because you kept losing the shoes and hair accessories," Ashley shot back.

"Hair accessories? You lost their arms and legs."

"Those were scientific experiments and sacrifices to the gods."

"Sure they were."

"So what's this?" Ashley asked, pointing to the corner of the screen where a stack of messages had queued up. Atop the stack was a message from PWNED, a friend Diana had made in this virtual world. "E-mail?"

"Just like."

With a *ding,* a new message appeared on the top of the stack.

GROB: Hey!

"Grob?" Ashley leaned toward the screen and slowly turned her head to face Diana. "What kind of a name is that?"

Diana felt her face flush. A moment later, another *ding.*

MISSION: UP IN THE SKY 6 PM COPLEY PLACE

"Now here's something you'll appreciate," Diana said, clicking the message open.

SPONTANEOUS COMBUSTION: 2NITE

"Spontaneous Combustion? Sounds like a band. There's a Copley Place in this Fantasyland?"

"OtherWorld. Probably. There's an Eiffel Tower. A Moulin Rouge. A Taj Majal. A downtown Detroit. However, this event"— Diana indicated the message—"is right here in Boston. The real one. Spontaneous Combustion is an improv group. Like a flash mob? They'll pile into a subway car and fill it with balloons and streamers and serve cake. Or show up in a clothing store and all try on the same dress, guys, too, then walk out onto the floor and freeze like mannequins. They post videos of their events on YouTube."

"Like those people standing frozen in the middle of Grand Central during rush hour."

"This one's at the BPL. 'Meet on the front steps of the old entrance,'" Diana read from the screen. Those steps faced the west side of Copley Square. "'Six sharp. Today. All you need is a cell phone and a pair of sunglasses.'"

"What are they going to do?"

"Be there at six and find out."

"Today? But I'm meeting Aaron."

It took Diana a moment to remember. Aaron was Ashley's latest, a guy she'd met on a plane. A stockbroker, according to him. Wanted to date her but wouldn't give her his phone number or tell her where he lived. The only way she could reach him was through e-mail.

Ashley must have read her expression because she said, "You've never even met the guy."

Diana raised her eyebrows and held Ashley's gaze.

"Okay. You're right," Ashley said. "He is a shit. And on top of that, he's been weirding me out. Checking up like he's some kind of control freak."

"So why are you seeing him?"

"I'm not. I'm dumping him. Tonight." Ashley sounded determined.

"Well, dump him early. Then you can go to this. I bet the people you meet here will be far more interesting than Aaron."

"'If you accept this mission . . .'" Ashley read the screen. "So anyone can just show up and participate?"

"And there's a ring tone." Diana clicked on the link and a piano crescendo played, then horns came in: *DUM dah DUM, DUM dah DUM.* Then a man's solemn voice. "Faster than a speeding bullet." There was a *whoosh.* It was the iconic opening of the old Superman TV show. "More powerful—"

Diana laughed and turned off the player. "You're supposed to download that to your cell before you go."

"That's easy. I'm in."

Diana hit reply. "There. You're registered." She hit print and the original message rolled off her printer.

Ashley grabbed the printout and scanned it. "Nadia Varata?"

"Sorry. She got the invite, so you're registered as her. It doesn't matter. I'm sure they don't make you wear name tags or show a photo ID."

A new message popped onto the top of the queue, confirming the registration. Diana was about to delete it when there was another *ding.* This time there was a blinking star beside the message—a file attachment.

Yes! She'd planted the bogus data file in time and MedLogic's hackers had taken her bait.

A third *ding* announced a new message from GROB.

Diana turned the monitor away from Ashley, stood and clapped her hands together. "So, you want to see what came in that UPS box?"

CHAPTER FIVE

THE SHIPPING BOX LAY OPEN ON THE FLOOR OF THE LIVING ROOM. The only thing that remained, nestled among the tissue paper, was a red cap. Ashley's white hobo bag lay like a deflated dirigible beside the box. From down the hall, the toilet flushed. Boot heels sounded on the wood floor. Then silence.

Ashley peered around the doorjamb. "Ready or not." She stepped into the room, and pirouetted in front of the fireplace. "You're going to look so great in these."

Ashley looked pretty great herself in the skintight black jeans and elaborately hand-tooled red cowboy boots. The fitted leather jacket hung open over a T-shirt emblazoned with the fractured word HACKER.

Ashley sniffed the arm of the jacket. "Leather, right? Because I'm allergic to latex and polyester."

"No vinyls were killed to make any part of that outfit. We're talking sheepskin. Cotton. Wool. Well, maybe a little Lycra in the denim."

Ashley pulled at the crotch of the jeans. "I had to lie down to squeeze into them." Then she twisted, straining to look over her shoulder and down her backside. "Wish there was a mirror in this place . . ." Her voice trailed off.

Diana offered her the red newsboy cap.

"Hang on." Ashley rummaged in her purse and came up with a hair clip. She pulled back her long hair, formed it into a figure eight, and anchored it with the clip on top of her head. Then she put on the hat, setting it on her head at a jaunty angle. She zipped the jacket and turned up the collar.

"You look great, Ash."

"Great pretty? Great sexy? Great . . . big?"

"Great in a don't-mess-with-me kind of way."

Ashley tugged the jacket smooth. "I can live with that." She stood tall, her feet apart, arms folded over her chest. *Wonder Woman*. "Don't mess with me." She delivered the words with a snarl.

"It all fits you so perfectly," Diana said.

"As if they were made to order. So, when I give them back, are you going to wear these clothes or what?"

"Or what, what? Of course I'm going to wear them."

"I meant *out*. Otherwise, what's the point?"

"The point is . . ." Diana took a deep breath. Because if she barely left her own property, then what *was* the point of gorgeous hand-tooled boots and a butter-soft leather jacket?

"I'm sorry," Ashley said. "Forget it. I should mind my own business." She slipped on the wraparound sunglasses. "These are perfect too. Where'd you get this outfit?"

Diana jerked her thumb toward her office.

"No. You found them online?"

"In OtherWorld. And I didn't find them. You draw what you want, then send them the design and your measurements, and they make the pieces to order."

Ashley's mouth formed a perfect O as she looked down at her outfit, across to the door to Diana's office, and back again. "This is the same outfit . . . ?"

Diana nodded.

"It's much better in the flesh. You've got to show me how you do it."

Moments later they were sitting side by side in front of the computer. Diana scrolled through her inventory of OtherWorld places and transported Nadia to the unimaginatively named Main Street Mall. Sidewalks, trees, and storefronts, even a fire hydrant materialized around her avatar.

"Put it up over there." Ashley indicated the wall.

Diana toggled a switch and the screen went blank. Main Street Mall came up on the wall across from them. Ashley sat forward, staring at the massive image, her elbows propped on the desk. She whooped when Diana pressed the up key and Nadia rose into the sky. She skimmed low across store roofs, over a pergola, a town green, landscape materializing around her as she flew. Soared over a winding river and back.

Diana glanced over. Ashley was gripping her chair arms. It felt like 3-D without the 3-D glasses.

Diana brought Nadia down onto sidewalk. "You want to drive?"

"You bet."

They switched seats. Diana showed Ashley how to use the trackball and buttons to angle the view, and the keyboard's arrow keys to move Nadia and change direction. Ashley got the hang of it quickly. From behind, they watched Nadia saunter along, neatly avoiding colliding with a couple strolling hand in hand in the opposite direction.

"Those are . . . ?" Ashley asked.

"Not window dressing. There's a real live person somewhere in the world controlling each of them."

"This is way cool, love the way Nadia's hair is kind of springy, like a sea anemone. And that hip-swing thing she's got," Ashley said.

"Recognize it? It's your walk. I programmed it. And I sell it."

"You sell my walk? How come I don't get a cut?"

Ashley tapped the arrow key and Nadia continued, past a car dealership and a gun store.

"Okay, stop there," Diana said.

Ashley paused Nadia in front of a door that said HEADLESS BARBIE'S CLOTHING TO GO. Naked mannequins in the windows were displayed, as promised, without heads.

Ashley chortled. "How perfect is that?" She moved Nadia through the shop's door and inside. The store had pink walls and clothing racks on either side, a desk and a cash register in the front. Nadia was the only avatar there.

Diana took over the mouse and clicked on one of the clothing racks. A woman's voice said, "Can I help you."

"Custom order," Diana said.

A text box floated on the screen.

Customer?
Password?

Diana typed in Nadia's name and password.

Style?

Diana examined the invoice that had come with the new clothes and typed in the seven-digit style code she found. A

3-D image of her avatar's outfit—boots, jeans, jacket, cap, and sunglasses—popped up, revolving in space.

"You want it in a different color?" Diana asked Ashley. "It's easy to tweak." With a few clicks she'd turned the jacket orange and the boots bright blue.

"Ick. I liked it just the way it was," Ashley said.

Diana changed it back. "We just drag it over to the cash register." She clicked on the outfit and dragged it over. "And voilà. We're good to go."

She was about to click check out when Ashley put her hand out to stop her. "So, what else can you get here?"

Diana smiled. Ashley was so easily hooked. "Whatever your little heart desires." She offered Ashley the microphone. "And if you keep it simple, you can just say what you want."

Ashley thought a moment. Then said, "Long pink dress."

A floor-length, off-the-shoulder dress materialized and re-volved—a swirl of pale pink chiffon with a shimmering skirt—replaced a few moments later by a hot-pink strapless gown, replaced by a pink chintz number with muttonchop sleeves and tiny buttons going up the back to a ruffled high neck.

"That one's definitely you," Diana said. "*Little House on the Prairie.* Just enter your measurements, charge it to your credit card, and it's made to order."

"Leather jacket," Ashley said into the microphone.

Up came a brown World War I–style bomber's jacket, fol-lowed by a fitted black blazer, followed by a western-style jacket with serious fringe, followed by Diana's design.

"Order that one and I get ten percent," Diana said.

"Of what?"

"More than you can probably afford."

"I doubt that." Ashley set her chin on her hand as she watched leather jacket after leather jacket materialize and dematerialize. "I could definitely get into this."

WHILE ASHLEY CHANGED BACK INTO HER OWN CLOTHES, DIANA stayed in her office. It took just a minute to reorder the outfit. She planned to set the clothes aside for Ashley's next birthday. It was an expensive gift, but she'd never been able to adequately repay her sister for the way she'd been there for her when Daniel died.

As she waited for the receipt to print, she picked up the walking stick from the umbrella stand beside her desk. Bleached bone white, the long, smooth, slender piece of driftwood had belonged to Daniel.

She ran her hand along its surface. Her breath caught as pine resin—more a feeling than an actual smell—seemed to enter through the palm of her hand, swirl through her chest, and climb up the back of her neck and into her sinuses. Her eyes stung.

She shook herself out of it, put the walking stick back in the umbrella stand, slipped on her earpiece, and called Jake back.

"Diana?" Jake answered. "It's about time. Are you *trying* to get us fired?"

"They were headed for the exit long before I opened my big mouth."

"You don't know that."

"I sure as hell do. I know when I'm being played."

"Played? What are you talking about?"

"This makes at least the third time a client has circled the wagons the instant we get a lead on the hackers. All we're doing is damage control, plugging holes. I want to put the hole makers out of business."

"News bulletin: Gamelan provides a service. We do what our clients want us to do."

"Is that how you see it, Jake? They tell us what to do and we salute and march? Daniel would have—"

He cut her off. "Would you stop with Daniel already? The truth is, neither of us has any idea what Daniel would or wouldn't have done. Let's just stick with what's going on here and now."

"Here and now, we're supposed to have some kind of expertise that our customers are paying for."

"*Paying for.* Exactly. We're in business to make money. And it wouldn't hurt if we focused a bit more attention on the bottom line."

"What's that supposed to mean?" Diana said. If they were having a cash-flow problem, it was news to her. Jake did their accounting and Diana drew enough to live on. With what they were charging and the way the business had grown, there should have been plenty for her and Jake and more after that.

"We're doing fine," Jake said. "But it's a very small world out there and we can't afford to piss off clients. So could you at least discuss your next outburst with me before you go off half-cocked again? We're supposed to be partners."

Partners? More like the remaining two legs of a three-legged stool. Still, she couldn't disagree—she should have talked with him before the meeting.

"It's just that I . . . I get impatient," she said. "It's frustrating going after hackers and then getting stopped when we've barely slowed them down."

"Diana, these guys are just pulling the same kind of crap we were up to two years ago. Without them, we've got no work."

"So you're saying we shouldn't try to track them down? Gee, maybe we should put them on the payroll."

"I'm saying that even if you track them down, it won't fix the problem. You think there's just one group of hackers out there and they're targeting our clients?"

"Of course not. That's ridiculous. But still, it makes me furious. I want to know who they are. This time, and the time before that, and the time before that. We could lose our reputation just as fast as we gained it if it gets out that our clients are being shaken down."

"You don't know that's what's happening."

"You're right. But I'm sure as hell going to find out."

There was a pause on the other end. "What are you up to?"

"I set a little trap."

Jake groaned. She told him that she'd been banking on the hackers not realizing that they'd been detected and coming back to the same laptop, looking for more. "Before MedLogic wiped the laptop, I planted another data file on it. Only this time it wasn't just data. It had a program embedded in it—a digital LoJack that goes off when the file is opened."

"But they wiped the laptop."

"Not soon enough."

Jake chuckled. "God, I am so glad you weren't out there trying to bust us a few years ago." He added, "So what do we know about them?" Diana noted the shift from "you" to "we."

She clicked on the message that had come in and opened the attachment. She began scrolling through the lines of code that had come back from the hackers. Some of it she understood; most of it she didn't. "Want to see?"

"And who's paying for my time? We've got no client."

"That never stopped us before."

"Before was different."

"As you keep reminding me. You wouldn't have thought twice about doing this in the old days."

"Diana, I was perfectly happy with the way things were in the old days. You're the one who wanted to go straight."

She scrolled through the information that had come back. "Linux operating system. A half-dozen IP addresses. I've never heard of this e-mail server software they seem to be running."

She waited. Then sighed heavily. "I sure do wish I could figure out what this is telling me."

Jake laughed.

She added, "You know you want to see this. Come on, admit it."

"All right, all right."

Diana resisted the urge to pump her fist in the air. She attached the file to a blank message and uploaded it to the drafts folder of their shared e-mail account.

"Okay, it's in the dead drop," she said. She could hear clicking on Jake's end. "Find it?"

Jake grunted a yes. More clicks. She could hear Jake's intake of breath. "Holy . . . cool, very cool." Then silence. Combing through the file would be like sorting spaghetti, finding meaningful strands among the junk.

"You're good," he said. "Damned good."

Good at what? Diana wondered—at out-geeking a geek or at emotional blackmail? "I had the best teachers," she said.

"Let me look through this and see what I can figure out. We may not know who they are, but I should be able to get us in through their back door."

CHAPTER SIX

DIANA PUSHED AWAY FROM HER DESK. TALKING TO JAKE ALWAYS reminded her of Daniel. Again she drew Daniel's driftwood walking stick from the stand by her desk and cradled it in her arms, letting the tang of pine surround her. God, she missed him. Missed his touch. The sound of his voice. His face. That edge-of-a-cliff feeling of being around him, not knowing what he was going to do next.

She remembered the first moment she'd laid eyes on him. She'd been a junior at UMass Dartmouth with a work-study job in the office of the dean of students. Her boss was the dean's administrative assistant, Margaret Brown, a woman who reminded Diana of a lemon with all the juice squeezed out.

Diana had been alone in the office, answering the phones, when Jake—she'd met him at a frat party a year earlier—dropped by. With him was a guy in a biker jacket and torn Levi's. He was hot, with dark and heavy-lidded eyes, and so tall that he'd had to stoop coming through the door to the office. His hair was long and wild. He hadn't yet gone punk and shaved the sides of his head.

The three of them had gone out drinking that night, and ended up on the edge of a granite quarry in Quincy, about twenty miles from school. They'd sat smoking a joint, their legs dangling over a stone ledge, moonlight shining silver on the still black water that filled the pit before them. Daniel and Jake had stripped off their clothing and dived in.

"Come on!" Daniel shouted when he surfaced, splashing his arms in the water, the drops sparkling, ripples shimmering all around him. Even as stoned as Diana was, there was no way she could do it.

They'd returned to that quarry many times, but it wasn't until months later, in the middle of one of New England's hottest summers, that she'd gotten wasted enough to strip off her clothes and reckless enough to dive off the ledge. By then, she and Daniel were lovers.

It was Daniel who'd installed a program on Margaret Brown's computer so that it sounded like an old-fashioned typewriter every time she hit a key, and ratcheted and dinged when the return key was pressed. A built-in time delay guaranteed that the program didn't kick in until the middle of a day Diana called in sick so she wouldn't be suspected.

Diana's artistic talent had been recruited to forge Miss Brown's signature on a requisition for a massage table and portable Jacuzzi to be delivered to President McCafferty's office.

Then, a few months before the end of that year, there'd been an uproar when college administrators noticed that a bunch of the student names on transcripts had been altered. Elvis Pretzel and Wile E. Coyote were not students at the college. Diana's name had been changed to Mary Jane Watson, Spider-Man's girlfriend.

No one took Miss Brown seriously when she voiced her suspicion that Diana and her oddball friends had something to do with it.

Diana began her senior year but she never graduated. That October her mother was diagnosed with cancer. Ashley was still in high school and their father was long gone. So Diana had cleaned out her dorm room and loaded boxes into a borrowed Dodge van and headed home. She hadn't known whether to pack her books or throw them away. A brutal regimen of chemo and radiation therapy lay ahead, and Diana had no inkling of just how tough and resilient her mother would turn out to be.

The van's driver's seat was so high above the road and so close to the front bumper that Diana felt unnerved behind the wheel. On the drive home, sometime after midnight on Route 24, somewhere in the middle of Bridgewater thirty miles south of home, she'd started to feel as if the car was driving itself.

Her heart surged, and there was a sharp pain in her chest. She felt smothered, as if the air in the car had no oxygen. She gripped the wheel, trying to keep the van steady and gasping for breath. It was all she could do to keep the steering wheel from veering right and, as she could see clearly in her mind's eye, the van careening into the woods.

Was this a heart attack? It couldn't be. She wasn't allowed to be sick. Her mother needed her. Ashley needed her.

Finally she managed to pull the car over into the breakdown lane and stop. She clawed at the window and cranked it open. The air rushing in didn't help. Instead, impenetrable darkness seemed to fold in around her.

For what felt like hours, she sat hunched over the steering wheel, gasping and sweating, unable to move, unable to get out of the car and find the cell phone she'd stupidly packed in a satchel and thrown in the trunk.

Had that been her first panic attack? Probably. But when she was in therapy later, she remembered some earlier moments, like tremors foreshadowing an earthquake. There was the time when she was fifteen supposedly watching Ashley swimming at Wollaston Beach. She'd turned her attention away as a couple of cute boys from her high school sauntered by, and when she looked back, she could no longer see Ashley's head bobbing in the waves. That moment was frozen in time, but she had no memory of throwing herself into the water, of swimming out to where she'd last seen her sister, only to hear Ashley calling to her from the shore and waving Popsicles that by then were dripping down her arms.

The panic attacks had increased through her mother's illness. After her mother's recovery, they'd abated so completely that at times Diana was convinced that she'd only imagined them. After Daniel's death, they'd returned full force.

Her house, and in particular her office, where she now sat, had become her refuge. As long as she stayed inside and took her medication, she was safe from ambush. Just in case, she had Daniel's driftwood to calm her. She slid it back into the stand by her desk. Along with his ashes, it was the only thing of his that she had left.

Diana returned to the living room. Ashley had done what she'd threatened: picked up all the stray bits of garbage, straightened piles, and carried away dirty dishes. Only the UPS box remained in the middle of the floor. The minute Diana picked it up she realized it was empty. Inside there was only tissue paper, a whiff of licorice, and a note.

> Just *borrowing* them for tonight.
> Promise.
> xx oo

Diana lifted the shade and looked out the window. Ashley was standing by her car talking on her cell phone. Squeezing the phone between chin and shoulder, she unlocked the hatchback and dropped the pile of clothing into the car. Then she stood there, hip thrown out. As Diana watched, Ashley ran her fingers through her hair, shot a few heated words into the phone, and snapped it shut. Then gave the world at large the finger. A few moments later, she drove off.

Sure, Ashley would return the new outfit. Just like she'd returned the snakeskin miniskirt Diana had picked up at a secondhand store when she was living with Daniel in New Hampshire. By the time Diana discovered it in Ashley's closet, Ashley had "forgotten" that it wasn't hers.

Too late, Diana noticed that Ashley had left her laptop, half hidden behind the base of the coatrack. At least that guaranteed she would be back sooner rather than later.

Diana returned to her desk. There was a new message from her in-world friend PWNED. This one was marked with a little red flag.

PWNED: nu doc—2G2B tru

She had no idea what the person behind PWNED—a term that computer gamers used to mean beaten—looked like, but the avatar was a sexy platinum blonde who moved with the grace of a gazelle and liked to end her messages with *God is just an abbreviation for goddess.* From asides PWNED had dropped, Diana gathered that she lived near Boston. Her QuackPatrol blog was infamous for outing so-called doctors and health-care gurus who preyed on the desperate.

Diana opened the attachment. *Results within 7 days*, it began. Apparently Dr. Grande in Sedona, Arizona, assessed patients

through a telephone consult and a questionnaire. His revolu-
tionary regimen to cure autism involved a weeklong liquid
diet combined with six weeks of chelation therapy. Certainly
sounded too good to be true.

Diana shot back a response.

Let's nail him.

She spent the next hour researching chelation therapy. There
were boatloads of patient "testimonials" but no hard science.
She checked Dr. Grande's financial ties and found that all of
his clinics were owned by a corporation with headquarters in
Ukraine.

When she finished up, she e-mailed PWNED a summary of
what she'd discovered. A message came back less than a minute
later.

PWNED: ^5

Diana high-fived the monitor back. She realized, as she
glanced at the time in the corner of her screen, that it had been
over two hours since she last checked her security systems. That
was progress in her quest to hold paranoia at bay.

Video from the camera anchored over her front door showed
nothing more than a cardinal perched on her white picket fence.
Her firewall had only logged the usual pinging from drones in
the outside world.

She remembered the messages from GROB. She scrolled
down to find them. The first one that had come hours earlier
began:

GROB: Got time to talk?

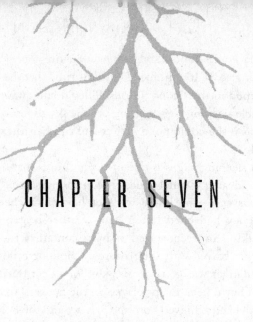

CHAPTER SEVEN

IANA WAS MORTIFIED THAT JUST READING GROB'S MESSAGE SET her tingling. He'd first contacted her months earlier in response to a question she'd posted in a forum for people suffering post-traumatic stress disorder. He'd had problems of his own to deal with, though he'd never told her what they were and she'd never told him hers.

The last time they'd "talked," she'd shared with him the little forays she'd made—walks into her own backyard and several times around the block—and her determination to return to the real world. He'd written her back:

> Small victories here, too. Today I drove to the bank and got out of the car instead of using the drive-up window. Lived to tell. World expands each day. When you are ready to take the plunge, we'll sit on a beach. Drink a toast. Tell ghost stories and scare each other to death. (Ha Ha!) Build a bonfire and sleep out under the stars.

Diana could almost smell the wood fire, burned down to smoldering coals. It reminded her of the time that she and Daniel had camped in the Grand Tetons. They'd lain twined together in a double sleeping bag, looking up, the sky so close that Diana had felt as if she could poke Jupiter and run her fingers through the Milky Way.

That sleeping bag was one of many things that she'd simply left behind after Daniel died, fifteen months, one week, and three days ago—she knew without having to check the calendar. They had been living in a weather-beaten farmhouse and working in a converted railway container tucked into a ramshackle barn. With their nearest neighbor miles away, the greatest danger was getting mistaken for a deer during hunting season. They'd been major players in the hackers' underground, and Daniel had achieved both the privacy and the notoriety he'd craved.

To earn the money they needed to support their spartan lifestyle and insatiable lust for the latest technology, they sold copies of Data Sucker, a program Daniel had written that infiltrated computers through the Windows operating system. Always the entrepreneur, Jake had then suggested that Daniel write another software that they called A-Sucker, which protected computers against Data Sucker. Turned out there was an even bigger market for that.

Diana remembered the day she'd had her epiphany. Daniel had been sitting at his computer, intent on a game he was into, his face aglow with colors radiating off the screen. With the sides of his scalp shaved bare like some shock troop commando, and his worktable mounded with coils of cable, jury-rigged circuit boards, hopped-up laptops, and surveillance equipment, he looked every inch his pseudonym, SOK0S. Sow Chaos.

"Daniel," she'd said.

He was using a headset, but still Diana could hear the apocalyptic drumbeat and gunfire. She waved to snag his attention. When he looked over she mimed taking off the headset. He took it down, letting it rest around his neck.

"You see this headline?" she asked. "'Death in a Medical Mix-up.' Charles River Hospital."

He rolled his eyes. "All we did was look around and bring down their database," he said, his gaze returning to his computer screen.

"We didn't just bring it down. Listen. 'Hackers wreak mayhem resulting in the death of at least one patient—'"

"Bogus. That is so not our fault." Daniel clicked the mouse. His screen lit up and Diana could hear the rat-a-tat of machine-gun fire.

"We destroyed their databases," Diana said. "They had to reconstruct medical orders from scratch. Apparently they got one of them wrong."

"Not our fault," Daniel said, his fingers dancing on the keyboard.

"But it was a foreseeable consequence of something we did."

"A lightning strike could have had the same results." He put the game on pause and turned to face her. "People like that deserve what they get. They stockpile a mountain of private information and then do a lousy job protecting it."

"Then once again, mission accomplished," she said, flashing him two thumbs up. "We'll get you a banner saying so. And I'm sure the woman who died thanks you too. She was fifty-two years old."

"All right already." Daniel looked longingly back at his screen.

"Daniel, she wasn't fragged in some combat sim. She had a name and a family, and they did everything that they thought

they were supposed to do"—Diana heard her voice catch, surprised by the rogue emotion that sideswiped her—"but she died
anyway, needlessly, meaninglessly, because we thought it would
be a great idea to trash their system."

He winced. She knew he hated raw emotion. Well, that was
just too damned bad.

"Remember when my mother had cancer? She turned fifty-
two between rounds of chemo. She could barely swallow a bite
of chocolate cake. I can't even imagine what it would have been
like for us if an accidental overdose had killed her."

Daniel groaned and got up from his chair. He put his arms
around her from behind and started to read over her shoulder.
"You know as well as I do," he said after a minute, "these guys
were an accident waiting to happen. Their backup systems were
for shit and not secured. If not us, then something much more
destructive would have bitten them. All we did was wipe out
some data. The chaos that followed? All of their own making."

She looked up at him. "Right. We expose weaknesses and
then wash our hands of what happens next."

"So what's your point? You knew what you were getting
into."

She held his gaze. "I thought I knew. But this time we've
gone too far. Even if you don't, I feel responsible for this woman's death. Daniel, I'm telling you just as clearly as I can, I can't
keep doing this."

He stood there, towering over her. "What are you saying?"

"I'm done. And I can't let you and Jake keep doing this
either."

"You think you're *letting us* do this?"

Her heart pounded but for once she didn't apologize her way
out of it. "I'm saying I've had enough."

Diana had been completely stunned when, a few weeks

later, Daniel had been the one to suggest that they sell the farm, move back to the Boston area, and open a security consulting company as a trio of rehabilitated black hats.

They'd settled on the name Gamelan. It was sufficiently obscure and she liked the way it sounded. It even made a kind of sense. Gamelan was a Balinese music ensemble of percussion instruments. Drums, gongs, xylophones, bells. The music sounded odd and discordant, like the way the three of them worked together.

Daniel was the one who'd suggested they celebrate the impending transition by climbing the Eiger. But only two of them had come back alive, and instead of a dissonant trio, Gamelan Security turned into a fractious duo. Numbed by loss, Diana had been reluctantly dragged along by a determined Jake.

The Klaxon alarm startled Diana back to the present. Her palms turned sweaty and the back of her neck felt like someone laid an ice pack across it. She wasn't expecting a delivery, and besides it was too late for that.

She silenced the alarm. Couldn't be Ashley—she was supposed to be meeting Aaron downtown. Had to be a false alarm, the calm voice in her head reasoned, but she could barely hear it over the alarm that kept right on screaming inside her head.

She checked the surveillance feeds. It was already dark out, and the lights around the house had automatically turned on. None of the cameras showed anything amiss. She toggled the sun icon to a moon, and the images changed to velvety black.

There! In the feed from the camera alongside the house, she saw a bright green mottled shape moving across the screen. It disappeared from view and was picked up in the security camera angled behind the house. It could have been a person on all fours. Low to the ground. But it would have to be a small adult or a child.

Diana watched as the shape meandered back to the side of the house. It was more likely a raccoon or a large dog with a longish tail. She wanted it to go away, and then finally it did, passing back through the electronic security perimeter and off the screens.

Diana pushed away from the monitors, feeling as if she'd been picked up and shaken. Even though she knew it was insane, she toured the house, checking that every window and door was latched.

She ended up in the kitchen. Rational analysis kept her bogeymen at bay, but just the unexpected jolt could stir up that still-potent residue of grief and trauma. She'd been on such an even keel that she'd gone a week without a single remote session with Dr. Lightfoot. She knew what her shrink's advice would be: Try to stay in the present. And along with that: Remember, you can't control what you can't control.

Diana checked that the back door was secure. Recognized the acrid smell of burned coffee. She'd left an empty pot on the warmer. Again. She shut off the machine and turned on the exhaust fan.

She opened the refrigerator. She hadn't eaten since breakfast. Her therapist had repeatedly warned her not to miss meals. Low blood sugar left her shaky and even more emotionally vulnerable.

She opened the package of American cheese Ashley had brought her and ate three slices. She was working on a Granny Smith apple when the phone rang. She lifted it off the wall. Ashley's cell-phone number glowed on the readout.

She checked the time. A few minutes to six.

"Hey, hon, you at Copley yet?" she asked.

"Getting there. What are you up to?" Ashley said. Diana

could hear the sounds of a city in the background. Traffic. A horn honking. Voices.

"I took a nice long walk on the beach."

"Really?" Ashley said. Then laughed. "Sure you did. But you had . . . me going . . . for a minute there." She huffed. It sounded as if she was walking.

"Sooooo?" Diana asked.

"So I dumped him . . . Aaron and me . . . we're history." There was the sound of a siren and laughter, not Ashley's. "I did it."

"Really? That's so great. How do you feel?"

"Sore. Wet," Ashley said.

"What?"

"I told him that I just wasn't that into him. The relationship wasn't going anywhere and I'd had it with his weirdnesses. So he just sits there, drawing circles on the bar with his swizzle stick. He goes, 'You sure?'

"I'm like, yeah. Completely. You okay with that?

"And before I know it, he grabs the leg of my bar stool and yanks. And just like that, I'm sitting on the floor, my drink is all over me, and Mr. Wonderful is staring down at me. The place goes dead silent. Longest ten seconds of my life. Finally, a waiter comes running over. Aaron is still there, shell-shocked, like he can't believe what just happened either. Then he grabs his coat and heads for the door. On top of that, he leaves me to pay the bill. Again."

"What a prince."

"You know what? It was worth it. Wish you could've seen his face." Ashley hooted. "Looked like someone had popped his . . . Wow, you should see this crowd. Diana. It's like—" For a few moments her voice was smothered by competing voices.

"So, other than sore and wet, how do you feel?" Diana asked.

"Strong. Tough."

"I'm so proud of you," Diana said. She was. For once, Ashley had broken up with a guy without having his replacement waiting in the wings. And now she was on her way to meeting new people. Alone, without a man on her arm.

"I knew you'd be impressed," Ashley said. A pause. "Uh-oh."

"Uh-oh what?"

"I thought . . . never mind. False alarm. Listen, I gotta go. Looks like this is about to happen. Call you tomorrow?"

"Hang on! You know you left your computer at my house?"

"I did? Shit. I thought I left it in my car. I'll come by for it Saturday or Sunday morning. Not too early."

That went without saying. On a weekend, "morning" usually started around noon for Ashley.

Diana could hear a man's voice shouting. "Synchronize! It's six o'clock . . . NOW!" Then applause.

"Diana," Ashley said, her voice a whisper. "Do you think I did the right thing? About Aaron, I mean."

"Of course I do!" But a burst of static cut across her reply. "Ashley? Are you there?" But all she heard was silence.

Diana stared at the dead phone. "You idiot. Of course you did the right thing." She threw the phone back into its dock.

Later, when she tried to get back to GROB, there was no response. Fair enough. She'd ignored him, now she deserved the same treatment.

CHAPTER EIGHT

Saturday morning, first thing, Diana checked the Spontaneous Combustion Web site. It said the video from the improv was *Coming soon!*

After a bowl of instant oatmeal, she got to work. For a second time, she opened the information that had come back from MedLogic's hackers. These were people, she reminded herself, individuals with friends and family, not disembodied evil entities. But who were they? Where were they? Though she didn't have the sophisticated knowledge and tools that Jake did, she could do some basic investigating.

First she traced the connections as the message had hopped from server to server on its way from the hackers' system to hers. Next to the start of the list were four numbers—that would be the IP address of the server that was providing the hackers their Internet access. She ran a DNS search and got the site name: Volganet.net. Entering that URL in her browser brought back a blank screen with an error message.

Volganet. The name made it sound as if they were somewhere in what had once been the Soviet bloc. That she could check.

She opened up Telnet and queried Volganet's time server. Back came:

```
Sat Apr 24 09:35:44 2010\n\0
```

09:35? That was Eastern Standard Time. Volganet was operating in her own time zone. Interesting for what it ruled out, but to narrow down the location further she'd have to sift through the lines and lines of information that had come back and use what she found to break into the hackers' system.

She was desperate to know if these were the same people who'd preyed on Gamelan's other clients. If it got out that their clients were being singled out, that would be the end of Gamelan Security. The end of everything she'd worked to build. The end of the one thing she had left.

She'd crush them before she'd let that happen.

While Diana was mulling over that cheery thought, envisioning appropriate payback, a message popped up.

```
GROB: RU there?
```

Her stomach turned over. She liked him, she really did— and that scared the hell out of her. Her hand hovered over the keyboard as she was still trying to decide how to respond when INTRUDER ALERT flashed in the corner of the computer screen. Diana silenced the alarm, but not before it sent her heart racing.

She checked the front video monitor. A man in a parka and a knitted cap was coming toward the front door. Slung over his shoulder was a canvas bag. He pulled out from it a rolled-up flyer, stuffed it into the handle of her screen door, and continued on to the next house.

Her phobia was exhausting and she was goddamned sick and tired of feeling wrung out, five or six times a day. Diana grabbed Daniel's walking stick and went to the door. Dr. Light-foot had recommended that she acclimate herself to the outside world again, building slowly, a little each day. So at least once each morning, she pushed herself out of the house.

The first time she'd tried it, a few months earlier, she'd made it as far as the front steps. Breathless, her heart hammering like a crazed bird trying to get out of her chest, she'd turned tail and burst back into the house, slammed the door, the urge to hide driving her body into a protective crouch.

Now her goal was to breach her own electronic fence once a day. She put her hand on the doorknob and counted down from ten. When she got to zero she took a deep inhale and pulled the door open, pushed open the storm door, and stepped outside. The skim of sweat on her forehead and at the back of her neck turned cold, but she welcomed the sensation, and the smell of smoke from someone's fireplace and the feel of dew as she touched the railing.

Next door, in the driveway of a big Victorian that the new owners had painted mauve, pale yellow, and gray green, her neighbor had the back door of her car open and was loading her toddler into a car seat. The woman had a long solemn face and dark hair, early Cher. She glanced over and waved. Diana waved back. The woman got in the driver's seat, started the car, and drove off.

The scent of exhaust lingered as Diana gazed at the empty spot in her neighbor's driveway, then at the closed door of her own garage. One day she'd actually get in her own car. Take a drive. Maybe even have the courage to introduce herself to her neighbor.

For now, just taking a walk in her own backyard was challenge enough.

Diana took a deep breath. She left the porch and stepped into the driveway. Crossing her arms to fend off the chill from outside and in, she began to walk the perimeter of her property. *Focus on what's outside not inside,* Dr. Lightfoot had suggested. The lawn was patchy and stringy, pale purple crocuses that had probably been planted by her mother decades ago were pushing their way up in front of bushes alongside the house. The quince bush was budding, and farther on, the tiny yellow blossoms on the witch hazel were already starting to open.

When she reached the back of the yard, she took a step beyond her own property line. She knew she'd breached the invisible electronic fence and the Klaxon would be going off in her office, alerting no one. She turned and looked at her house. All the window shades were drawn. The dark green paint around the windows was beginning to peel.

She beat back the urge to sprint back to safety. Instead, she reached into her pocket and pried open the lid of the container with her thumb, tipped it until she felt a pill in her palm. Tiny and white, it was no bigger than the birth-control pills she'd once taken daily. Just rolling a pill between her thumb and forefinger calmed her.

She slipped the pill back into the container, picked up a small stone from the ground, and completed her circuit. Back at the door, she placed the stone alongside others she'd lined up in the grass by the door, each marking another step forward, another time she'd breached the boundaries of her property and made it back alive.

She was squatting, counting stones—there were over fifty of them—when she noticed a dark limousine coming up her street. It reminded her of the limo she and her girlfriends had rented to carry them, dateless, to their senior prom. And the lecture the driver had given them about the hundred-dollar deposit he wouldn't return to their parents if any of them threw up. But a morning limousine wouldn't be picking up girls for a dance. More likely the passengers would be mourners on their way to a funeral.

It slowed to a crawl in front of her house. Diana ducked inside and locked the door behind her. She lifted the shade of one of the front windows and watched, shivering, as the car paused in front of her house, and then accelerated and continued on its way.

CHAPTER NINE

BY THE TIME DIANA RETURNED TO HER OFFICE, GROB HAD GIVEN up waiting. The chat window was closed.

She checked Spontaneous Combustion's Web site again—they'd posted a video of "Up in the Sky." First she scanned the file to make sure it was safe. Video downloads were a favorite way to distribute malware, malicious little programs that installed themselves. When she determined it was safe, she ran the video.

It opened with a man wearing a black baseball cap with the word DIRECTOR printed over the brim. He bellowed through a bullhorn, "Okay, agents. Listen up!"

The herky-jerky footage felt as if it had been taken with a handheld camera by someone being jostled by the crowd. The time stamp at the bottom of the video read yesterday, 6:03 P.M. That had been about the time Ashley called to say that Aaron was toast.

The man held up his cell phone. The camera pulled back to show a crowd of about a hundred people, clustered around him on the broad steps in front of the trio of granite arches at the entrance to the Boston Public Library. Almost everyone in the crowd had on sunglasses.

The camera panned from the library to the expanse of Copley Square across the street, a spacious area with brick walkways flanked by a fountain on one side and Trinity Church on the adjacent side. The facade of the church glowed an unearthly pink in the setting sun. The camera continued around to the facade of a hotel, and finally back to the crowd gathered on the library steps.

There! Diana thought she'd caught a glimpse of Ashley. But it was too quick to be sure.

The screen dissolved to black, and after some titles it returned to a close-up of the man with the bullhorn.

"Yo, thanks for coming out," he said. "Make sure Casey here has all your cell-phone numbers." The woman beside him, who had long blond hair and was wearing bright green-and-yellow-striped tights, waved a clipboard. "Up the volume on your ringers full blast. Then spread out across the street in the square. Mill about."

He continued giving directions as the camera pulled back to show the crowd, cutting to close-ups of individuals. None of them were Ashley. Jazzy percussion played through speeded-up footage of the crowd dispersing, people crossing the street to Copley Square and mingling with pedestrians in the plaza.

Then the screen went black and the word SHOWTIME! came up in white block letters. A wide shot of Copley Square took over the screen, followed by a close-up of a cell phone lighting up and the sound of cell phones going off. The ring tones weren't synchronized, so all Diana could make out were competing piano arpeggios and the *whooshes* of speeding bullets that rose to the top of the cacophony.

The camera closed in on one woman in the square. She had her dark hair pulled back in a thick ponytail. She held her cell phone aloft and pivoted to face the hotel across St. James Street. The camera drew back to show scores of other similarly frozen, sunglass wearers facing the hotel, cell phones raised. A crush of Superman-themed cell-phone rings filled the sound track.

Snippets of video showing the reactions of pedestrians were spliced together. Some just kept going. Others stopped and stared, then turned to look across to the hotel. A cop on the corner pushed back his cap brim and watched, his mouth open. A man hoisted a toddler onto his shoulder and the woman with him, pushing a stroller, raised a camera and took a picture.

Diana whooped. It was perfect.

For a brief moment, Diana thought she saw Ashley. The red hat, which would have stood out in morning sun, seemed nearly black in twilight. But the camera panned away before she could be sure.

Focus shifted to the facade of the hotel. A spotlight shone on a window near the top floor. The view zoomed in as the window raised and a figure leaned out. It was a man in bright blue with a red Superman *S* in a yellow field on the front. He raised his arm—not a wave but a stiff-armed salute.

That's when Diana realized that it was a mannequin in a Superman costume. The curl over his forehead would have done Christopher Reeve proud.

From behind, the figure was pushed out the window, headfirst. Its shoulders and ankles seemed to be attached to a wire. Then Superman was sailing through the sky across Copley Square, his red cape streaming.

Diana didn't spot Ashley again as the camera pulled back and scanned the watchers who were pivoting in unison. Super-Dummy slid at a leisurely pace across the square, got snagged by the spire that topped a tourist information kiosk, and then continued on. It crash-landed, headfirst, against a band of ironwork that bordered the top of a four-story office building on the opposite side of Boylston. A cheer rose as the dummy was hauled onto the roof by unseen figures.

Then a massive, three-story-tall crimson banner unfurled from that building's roof. In white letters, it said P2H4, followed by Spontaneous Combustion's URL.

P2H4—Diana Googled it—turned out to be the chemical notation for a highly combustible form of phosphorus.

CHAPTER TEN

Sunday morning Ashley still didn't come by to get her computer. She hadn't called either, which wasn't unusual but was still annoying as hell. She'd probably met someone and gotten involved in her own drama. Diana called and left a message. She sent her an e-mail which generated an automated out-of-the-office reply.

Diana tried to keep busy. She did some more research for PWNED on chelation scams. Worked on the proposal for a hot new client, Vault Security, who Jake was convinced would launch them to an entirely new level. Jake talked about their business like it was some kind of computer game, and they were advancing to the castle where they'd free the princess. The thought brought Diana back to Ashley. Where the hell was she and why wasn't she returning Diana's messages?

The possibility that something had happened to her was too terrifying to contemplate. Ashley had been her rock. She'd been there at the airport to meet Diana and Jake's flight back from Switzerland. She'd stayed for a week in the isolated farm-house while Diana sleepwalked through the motions of every-day life. When Ashley finally left, Diana had climbed into the four-poster bed she'd shared with Daniel and buried herself in a mound of his T-shirts and flannel and fleece tops, his pajama bottoms, all clothing that she'd dug out of the laundry bin. Bur-rowed her head under the pillow and slept.

She'd lost track of time, one day blending into the next. Ignoring the phone, rising only to go to the bathroom or nuke one of the frozen dinners Ashley had stocked in her fridge. Whenever she'd been jerked awake by another falling-off-the-mountain nightmare, she willed herself back to unconsciousness by envisioning the soft lap of a forest where she could lie half buried in pine needles, sensing Daniel's breathing, pulsing pres-ence all around her.

Day after day had turned into week after week. Then Diana had felt a touch on her shoulder. She'd tried to burrow deeper, barricade herself.

"Diana?" Ashley's voice tugged at her.

"Leave me alone, please, just go away." The words were only in her head; even the will to speak had fled.

A cool hand snaked under the mound of clothes and found her. She tried to break free, but she was held in a firm grip.

"Come on. Time to come out."

Diana tried to hold on to the pillow, then to the covers, but Ashley pulled them off. As cool air claimed her, Diana blinked and winced away the bright morning sun that slanted in through the window.

"Sweetie, you can't keep on like this." Ashley was crouched beside the bed, her face inches from Diana's. Beyond her, Diana could see Jake hovering in the open doorway.

"See this?" Ashley held the newspaper in front of her. Its

white background was blinding. "It's the middle of February. Twenty-five degrees out. The sun is shining. In a month the snow bells will be blooming, for goodness' sake. It's time to get up. Get out. It's been too long for you to still be like this."

Ashley and Jake had hauled Diana out of bed, wrenching her from the nest she'd built. Diana tried to climb back in but Jake scooped up the clothing and ripped away the bedding, leaving only a bare mattress.

"There's nothing for you there," Ashley said.

Diana backed up and tripped over Daniel's driftwood walking stick. She bent over and picked it up. It was solid and surprisingly light in her hand, and she cried out as her head seemed to fill with Daniel's presence.

The front door opened and closed. A few moments later, an older woman, a stranger with a soft, sympathetic face, stood in the bedroom doorway.

"Thanks for coming," Ashley said to her.

Later, after a long shower, Diana had sat at her kitchen table. A pot of beef stew burbled on the stove. Ashley sat on one side of her. Dr. Lightfoot, who would become her therapist, sat on the other side.

"I know," Dr. Lightfoot had said, warmth in her kind eyes, "you needed to bury him . . ."

Diana felt her insides wrench. ". . . and I couldn't. I can't . . ." She tried and failed to hold back a sob.

"It's hard. I know, it doesn't seem fair," Dr. Lightfoot said. She touched the back of Diana's hand.

"Maybe he survived," Diana said. "Because I still feel him. It feels just like he's still here."

"Diana," Dr. Lightfoot said, "accepting death and letting go is the first step. Until you do that, you won't be able to move on."

Following Dr. Lightfoot's good advice, over the months that followed Diana had tried to move on physically, even though the emotional journey would turn out to take much longer. She got rid of Daniel's clothing and gave away his books. She moved out of the farmhouse and back into the house where she'd grown up. Still, her heart refused to accept that Daniel was gone. Every time she touched Daniel's walking stick, it seemed to bring him back to her.

"That stick does not smell," Ashley had said. "And it's not even pine."

"It's not a literal smell," Diana had tried to explain. To say it was Daniel's essence sounded crazy. "It's more of a feeling. It's Daniel."

"It's you," Ashley had said. "And maybe his ghost in your own head. Your phantom limb."

That spring, around the time when Ashley had correctly predicted that the snow bells would be blooming in Diana's backyard, hikers near the spot where Daniel disappeared found remains, picked over by scavengers, and an orange ski jacket. Jake traveled to Switzerland to bring Daniel back, but all he'd returned with were his ashes in a brass urn. When Diana had held it in her hands, she felt absolutely nothing.

"See?" Ashley had said. "He's really and truly gone."

It was at that point that she'd surrendered.

In Switzerland, Jake had obtained documents that enabled Daniel to be declared legally dead. He'd convinced Diana to invest the life insurance settlement—all of the one million dollars—in the business that they'd been planning to start when they returned from Switzerland. She knew that helping her was Jake's way of dealing with the guilt he felt about Daniel—after all, Jake had been the one anchoring the rope.

The *ding* on her computer brought Diana back to the present. A chat window had opened.

GROB: U there?

This time, the interruption was welcome. A moment later he added:

GROB: I want to show you something. Meet me? 1329, 4655.

She stared at the coordinates, as if between the numbers or within the pattern she'd glean meaning. Was it safe? She'd learned the hard way about transporting to untested coordinates. Parts of OtherWorld were infested with willfully antisocial players who got pleasure from annoying everyone else. She'd once arrived at what she thought was a business meeting with a new client and found herself trapped in a combat sim. A cylindrical cage had dropped over her avatar. An avatar troll had appeared, knocked the cage over, and started rolling it down a hill and into a lake with Nadia trapped inside.

Diana had known it wasn't real, just "cartoon characters," as Ashley put it, but she'd been thoroughly freaked. Her heart had flipped into high gear and she couldn't catch her breath as Nadia's health meter plummeted and her body grew increasingly transparent.

It was an experience Diana had no desire to repeat, even though after "death" Nadia had simply transported home, where her "life" resumed as if it had never been terminated.

GROB: Come on. I won't bite.

She could hear Ashley's words: *Sweetie, don't you think it's time you let someone in?* Diana copied the new coordinates into OtherWorld's atlas. No, the area was not damage enabled. No complaints had been logged. She clicked and brought up a map showing the area surrounding those coordinates. A single yellow dot indicated that an avatar was already there. Just one. GROB was waiting for her.

Diana slipped on her headphones and transported Nadia. A bell sounded, and sand-colored dunes materialized around her. She touched an arrow key and Nadia started to walk up the gentle slope toward the other avatar, her legs sinking knee-deep into virtual sand with each step.

GROB was facing away from her. He wore a light gray cowboy hat, jeans, and black high-tops with white soles. His dark wavy hair came down to his shoulders. As she came up behind him, she could see the view he was taking in. Waves breaking and water extending to the horizon.

He turned, raised an arm, and waved. Beneath the brim of his Stetson, his mirrored sunglasses reflected back Nadia's image. That must have been a bear to program. He was handsome as hell, square-jawed and muscular. Diana wondered if this avatar bore even a passing resemblance to the person behind it.

Diana typed wave/ and Nadia raised her arm.

A voice balloon appeared over GROB's head. "You came." The voice that came through her earpiece sounded synthesized.

Diana angled the view, taking in the deserted beach dotted with coconut palms. "Wow. Where are we?"

"Ever been to Hawaii?"

"Never."

"We're on the Big Island. And over there?" GROB turned and pointed.

Diana angled the view 180 degrees. Behind them was the outline of a mountain range, not jagged like the Alps but gently rising and soft, as if its peaks had been sketched with pastel chalk.

"That big one?" GROB said. "That's Mauna Kea. Its name

means 'white mountain.' It's got permafrost and snow all year-round. Just an hour-and-a-half drive from this beach. But we can get there much faster. Take my hand."

GROB held out his hand to Nadia. Diana's hand spasmed into a fist. He wanted her to link Nadia to him. That gave him control over where they went.

Nadia is not me, Diana reminded herself. Avatars were impervious. They couldn't get mangled by outside forces. All she had to do was shut down OtherWorld if things got hairy, and when she brought it up again Nadia would be home again, no worse for the wear.

Diana forced her hand open and typed in the command link/. Nadia's hand grasped GROB's. When he rose up into the air, she flew beside him, soaring out over the ocean and then back over the beach and on toward the mountain range.

Diana felt breathless. She made Nadia point to a pair of nearby peaks, one twice the size of its neighbor, each with gently sloping cone-shaped sides and a dimpled depression at the tip. She loved mountains, and here were peaks as distinctive and yet so different from the imperious majesty of the Eiger or the Grand Tetons. She felt stirring in her an urge she'd nearly forgotten—she wanted to go there.

"Cinder cones," GROB said. "Wouldn't it be cool to walk out to the rim of that big one on a moonless night, to stay there until sunrise watching the stars? Too bad you can't do it. Native Hawaiians consider the place sacred."

They flew back to the beach and their two avatars walked hand in hand, side by side along the water's edge, their virtual feet leaving behind a trail of prints that washed away as each new wave lapped the shore. Diana told him about some of the places she'd hiked. Death Valley, in December, one of the most spectacular and spiritual spots in the universe. New Hampshire's

White Mountains in May—that had been three years ago—when a snowstorm nearly buried their tent in snow. But icefall climbing, she told him, was the most magical of all.

Surfing was more his thing, he said. That and nature. He told her about camping at a remote nature preserve in Costa Rica accessible only by boat. There, where the jungle ended at a white sand beach, the howling of monkeys and a symphony of birds woke him each morning.

They talked on and on. She told him about her sister "Susannah," a name she invented on the spot for Ashley. It felt good to admit, out loud, how worried she was. Ashley's absence was gnawing at her.

GROB told her about his brother, Tom, a recovered alcoholic who couldn't hold a job. GROB was the only anchor in his brother's chaotic life.

"I'm sorry. That must be hard for you," Diana said. "My sister's annoying. But truly, she's totally there for me. Except when there's a man in the picture or when she's convinced that she's deathly ill."

GROB laughed. "Hypochondriac?"

"And then some. We couldn't be more different. Her favorite color was pink; mine was red." Diana told him about the pictures in their family photo album from a typical Halloween—her blond sister posing in a leotard, pink tutu, and feather boa; dark-haired Diana, two years older and all knees and elbows, wearing a red cape she'd made out of one of their mother's old cocktail dresses, red tights, a leotard, construction-paper horns on her head, and a garden pitchfork clasped in her hand.

"Believe it or not, when I was little I was fearless," she said. "I jumped off our garage roof one time on a dare. Sprained my ankle. A month later I did it again, this time without a scratch.

Then I started charging kids in the neighborhood to watch. Earned enough to buy myself a Game Boy. Ash . . . uh, Susannah stood sentry and whistled if my mother was on her way out to investigate."

"Sounds like you two were quite a pair."

"Oil and water."

"Siblings," he said. "Definition: two people who run in opposite directions and end up crashing into each other."

Diana laughed. GROB sat on the beach. Nadia sat beside him. She unlinked Nadia's hand from GROB's, and the two avatars just sat there in a long silence that neither of them rushed to fill.

Finally, Diana said, "Thanks for telling me about yourself. And for sharing this special place."

"Special," he said, "and sad."

"Sad?"

"Yes . . . no."

"I'm sorry. Do you want to talk about it?"

"Maybe one day. But not here. If we ever meet . . . in the real world. I hope we do."

Diana stared out at the virtual ocean, wondering if she'd ever sit on the sand on a real beach and gaze out at the horizon separating sea from sky. In the real world, waves were irregular and unpredictable, not like these waves that unfurled as regularly as wallpaper patterns. Predictability. That was this virtual world's greatest strength and greatest weakness.

Suddenly little eddies seemed to be forming in the sand in front of them. The swirling patterns grew, and grew, until the entire beach heaved and boiled.

"Oh, shit," said GROB.

Instinctively Diana grabbed her chair arms and pushed back.

A downward whirling vortex grew in the sand, and up from its depths shot an avatar clad head to toe in gleaming battle armor.

"This is what you wanted to show me?" Diana managed to say.

"Hell, no!" In an instant, GROB was standing over Nadia, planted between her and the armored avatar that hovered over them. It raised its arm and an avalanche of blue phalluses fell from the sky and seemed to bounce off a barrier, like an invisible bubble surrounding her and GROB.

Flying phalluses. Soon there'd be tumbling toasters. It was completely ridiculous—Diana realized that. But still she felt assaulted, and when she tried to move Nadia and found she couldn't, she started to panic. She smashed down on the mouse, clicking over and over as she grew short of breath. She should never have come here.

"Take it easy," GROB said. "They can't hurt you,"

It took three tries before Diana typed /home correctly into the transporter, but Nadia simply disappeared and reappeared right where she was. She typed in random coordinates. Once again, Nadia faded and came back. Diana clicked all over the screen, trying in vain to get a menu to come up so she could get out of there.

Two more armored avatars circled overhead

"Assholes!" GROB said. "I hate this. Jesus, don't these people have anything better to do?"

More blue phalluses rained down around them, bouncing off the invisible barrier that she assumed GROB had created. Diana reared back each time one of the freakish objects splashed into the water or crashed into the sand and exploded.

Her hand shaking, Diana reached for her computer's power switch. It was the only way she could think of to make it stop.

She could barely hear GROB's voice over the sound effects. "I'm sorry . . . never should have . . . let's get . . ." GROB extended his hand toward Nadia. "Let's go now!"

Diana recoiled, standing and knocking over her desk chair. Was there anywhere safe? She had to turn the computer off. Press the power switch and hold it down until the system surrendered.

"Come on!" GROB moved closer to Nadia, his hand overlapping hers. For the moment, at least, the explosions had stopped. "I can get us out of here. Trust me."

Could she trust anyone? Her breath came in gasps as she steadied herself against the desk and stared at the monitor.

"Give me your hand!" GROB said.

It felt as if the sound still echoed as the empty voice balloon over GROB's head faded and disappeared.

She reached for the keyboard and watched her fingers as they typed link/, almost as if someone else were in control of them. Why would that work when nothing else she'd typed had made a difference? But Nadia's hand connected with GROB's, and instantly new surroundings materialized around them—the ocean and beach littered with phalluses became an old-fashioned town green with a pergola and trees.

With a click Diana had Nadia release GROB's hand and she could breathe again.

"I'm sorry," GROB said. "I'm so sorry. Did that freak you out? I thought it was safe to go there, but OtherWorld has become infested with griefers."

"I know," Diana said, wiping a skim of sweat from her upper lip. "I've run into them before."

"I shouldn't have taken you there. Are you okay? I'm really, really sorry."

"I'm okay," Diana said, even though she wasn't. "I have to go."

There was a pause. "Okay, okay. I understand. Can I see you again?"

Diana didn't answer. She could still feel lingering shock waves from the explosions.

"We might be safer in the real world," GROB said with a laugh.

"If only," Diana said. She watched the clock in the corner of her screen pulsing, pulsing, like a tiny beating heart until the minute was updated. "I really have to go." She clicked in the transporter window.

"Wait! Listen, if your sister doesn't show up soon, I might be able to help. I have connections."

That stopped her. "You don't think she's going to show up?"

"Me? You sounded worried that she wouldn't."

Diana had to admit, she was worried. "What kind of connections?"

"Access. I can check hospitals. Jails. Passenger lists of transatlantic flights. Reservations at fancy restaurants. Parking tickets. All I need is your sister's real name, DOB, stuff like that, and I'm on it."

REAL name? Alarms went off in Diana's head. Suddenly she was acutely aware that GROB's voice was synthesized. "I . . ." She managed a weak, "I'll let you know."

Before he could respond, she transported Nadia home.

Diana sat at her desk, still shaking, feeling as if someone had reached out in a dark alley, clamped his icy grip around her bare shoulder, slammed her against a wall, and pinned her there. She knew the griefers weren't his fault. And his assumption that she'd used a fake name for her sister was just common sense.

The guy was just trying to help. But Ashley had said she'd be back to get her computer during the weekend, and the weekend wasn't yet over.

She pulled over Daniel's walking stick and cradled it in her arms. Eyes closed, she concentrated on her breathing. In, out. In, out. Moving the inhalations deeper and deeper, feeling as if healing pine resin, Daniel's essence, were flowing off the walking stick and coating her throat, being drawn deep into her lungs and opening the tiniest alveoli. Her breathing slowed.

Being with GROB, or whatever his name was, scraped up memories, not to mention sensations that Diana thought had been smothered. The good news was that she could still feel.

CHAPTER ELEVEN

B Y MONDAY MORNING, DIANA WAS ACUTELY AWARE THAT THE
weekend was over. It was barely ten and her in-box was full
of messages from Jake that she'd left unanswered but not even
a text message from Ashley. Diana was still shaken by her ad-
venture with GROB in OtherWorld, and far too distracted to
work. Her morning pill was barely calming the gremlins in
the pit of her stomach. Ashley should have been at work, and
it seemed unfathomable that she hadn't bothered to come by
and pick up her laptop. Equally unfathomable that she hadn't
answered her e-mail.

Diana called Ashley's office extension at International Palm
Court Hotels headquarters. The line rang five times before
the call went to voice mail. Diana pressed zero. An operator
picked up.

"Hello, I'm looking for Ashley Highsmith," Diana told her.
"I tried her office, but there's no answer."

The operator put her on hold to strains of Vivaldi, then

came back and gave her what Diana knew was Ashley's cell-phone number. "Or I can leave a message for you," the operator offered.

"So you haven't seen her today?" Diana asked.

"I'm sorry. Who were you looking for?"

Earth to operator. It was all Diana could do not to shout. "Ashley Highsmith? Your event planner?" She took a breath. "She's doing such a great job, helping us plan for our big annual meeting there. So calm and competent. I had a question. It was a little complicated to leave as a message, so I was hoping you could tell me if she's there and if you could find out when she can get back to me?"

"Of course. Highsmith, Ashley," said the ever-polite voice. "I'll put you through to her extension."

"I already—" Diana started. Too late. She'd been trans-ferred. This time she let it go to voice mail.

"Hey, Ash, it's me. Again. How'd it go at Copley? Curious minds need to know. Please—" Diana heard the offhand tone in her voice turn brittle. She gave in to it. "I know you're a big girl and I shouldn't worry. But I can't help myself. Humor me and give me a call."

She hung up the phone. Her hand was trembling. She tried to identify the feeling that was giving her hand the shakes. Giving things names, she'd found, often made them easier to control. Not fear. Not anger. Anxiety. Not unwarranted, but still, there were a million explanations for why her sister hadn't called. If she'd merely overslept, she'd be furious with Diana for calling the hotel and drawing attention to her lapse.

As she imagined Ashley yelling at her to "get a life and stay out of mine!" her anxiety abated a notch. But not so much that it stopped her from opening the Spontaneous Combustion video on her computer and watching it, yet again, hoping to catch a glimpse of Ashley that she'd missed.

Systematically, Diana inspected the three-minute clip. There was Ashley, raising her cell phone skyward. Then the camera cut to close-ups of other participants, of pedestrians, of the hotel window and Superman's flight. It wasn't until near the end of the footage that the camera once again panned over the empty spot where Ashley had been standing. Diana ran the video forward and back in slo-mo, zoomed in and out, but she couldn't find any additional glimpses of Ashley.

According to the time stamps, the short clip represented thirty minutes of elapsed time. It looked like a montage of footage spliced together from at least four different cameras. So that meant at least two hours of footage had to have been taken, most of which hadn't made it into the final cut.

Diana found the Spontaneous Combustion Web site and shot off an e-mail, asking if there was any way she could see the raw footage from the various cameras filming at Copley. She explained why. Then she left the same message on their office phone. While she was at it, she found Spontaneous Combustion's Facebook page and posted an entry asking anyone who'd been to the event and seen a woman wearing a red newsboy cap to please, please, please get in touch with her.

There was nothing more she could do. None of this was getting her any closer to finding her sister. Meanwhile, more messages had stacked up in her queue. On top was another from Jake.

He began with "How's the Vault proposal going?"

"It's going," she typed back.

This was the third time he'd asked. Jake, a person who rarely resorted to all caps, had written in a previous message that Vault

Security was a VERY BIG DEAL. Vault had been contracted by the federal government to process medical insurance for everyone from government employees to elected officials to judges to federal prison inmates. SERIOUSLY DEEP POCKETS, Jake had added.

If hackers were targeting their clients, Diana foresaw SERIOUSLY DEEP RISK.

After Vault's head of IT approached them, Jake had flown to their corporate headquarters in Bethesda. He'd been given access to a ton of information about the company and about the computer system that they'd recently adopted with supposedly state-of-the-art security.

But Vault hadn't been bitten by a high-tech breach. Their head of billing—correction, their *former* head of billing—had left his laptop in a briefcase on a Metrorail train. He said it wasn't until after he got home that he realized he'd lost the computer, and not until the following day when he got back to work that he realized it had a flash drive attached with nearly 4GB of customer billing records. He couldn't explain why he'd felt the need to make himself a copy of the records. In any event, the data that should never have left the building contained tens of thousands of names, Social Security numbers, insurance ID numbers, and medical records. All the data was encrypted, but elsewhere on the laptop were the decryption algorithms.

Though no one had said as much, Jake suspected that the laptop also held access codes and passwords that could be used to open detailed medical histories, test results, and more, all of it intensely private information, some of it belonging to very public individuals.

The project was, of course, shrouded in secrecy. There was no way to know who'd ended up with the laptop, but if it was someone who knew how to exploit what was there, Vault wanted to be the first to find that out. Gamelan's reputation for discretion and insider knowledge of the computer netherworld was their wedge, their competitive advantage. Wearing a gray hat, they could be the underground eyes and ears of a legitimate company.

Diana opened the proposal she'd been working on. It was nearly finished. She'd taken special pains, referring frequently to the specifics of Vault's business and inserting statistics that would impress upon their management team how thorough, knowledgeable, and trustworthy Gamelan was. She wasn't about to take this client for granted.

A new text message popped up.

JAKE: You there? Call me.

Automatically she reached for the phone. Stopped. What if Ashley were trying to call her? She didn't want to tie up the line and she didn't own a cell phone—didn't need it since she never left home. Or . . . Then she remembered. Months ago, Jake had sent her a prepaid cell phone so she could make untraceable calls to various 800 numbers that hackers were using to hijack bank accounts.

She found the phone at the back of her top desk drawer. Flipped it open. Of course it was dead. She scrounged in the back of the drawer and found the charger. Plugging it in, she started to punch in Jake's number. Five digits in she changed her mind. Instead she started a message back to him.

Not now. Distracted. My sist

She stopped. Her concerns would only cement Jake's opinion that Ashley was an airhead. Texting his way through his one date with her had been his way of dealing with terminal boredom.

She deleted the words and wrote:

I'm here. Busy. Expecting a call. Working on Vault proposal. 30 min.

Work was usually good therapy—most of the time it occupied the mind and anesthetized the gut. But today she had to force herself to focus on finalizing their proposal. As she reread and edited, she had to admit it sounded pretty impressive. She'd hire them.

Satisfied, she opened the e-mail account that she shared with Jake, attached the proposal to a message, and saved it to their drafts folder. Then she shot Jake a text message telling him she'd left it for him.

Soon after, she found herself pacing through the house. She peered out between slats of the living-room blinds. Flinched as a minivan drove past. A Volvo station wagon was parked across the street. There was no sign of a gold Mini Cooper.

She turned back and surveyed the room. She'd done a sterling job of destroying what little order Ashley had restored. She did a quick tour of the room, collecting the discarded T-shirts and socks, a sweatshirt and a pair of sweatpants, and one sneaker. Where was the other one?

She checked behind the chairs and sofa, stacking books and newspapers as she went. There was the white toe of the sneaker, poking out from under the side of the couch. She reached down and pulled it free. A silver lipstick tube rolled out. Diana picked it up and stood. Not hers. It had been aeons since she used lipstick except virtually on Nadia.

She opened the tube and twirled the base. Touched her finger to the smooth stub of hot pink that remained. As she did so, a snap of licorice filled her head and she felt Ashley's presence so strongly that she had to sit down.

Ashley was the only person Diana knew who actually loved Good & Plenty candies. For her seventh birthday party, Ashley had wanted only pink and white balloons, pink paper plates, pink plastic forks, and candy to match. She'd been delighted when most of her friends left their candy-filled party cups untouched. Their mother, in a rare burst of domesticity, had baked white cupcakes and iced them with pink frosting.

Diana wondered—maybe Ashley had called their mother.

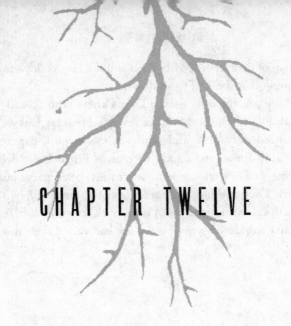

CHAPTER TWELVE

"WHAT'S WRONG?" HER MOTHER SAID THE MINUTE SHE HEARD Diana's voice on the phone.

"Why should there be something wrong?"

"Because you never call me. I call you. Your sister calls me. That's the way things work in this family."

"So has she?"

"Why is it always a contest?"

Diana took a breath. "Let's start over. Hi, Ma. How are you?"

For the last five years, her mother had lived in Jensen Beach, Florida, in a condo surrounded by golf courses. "Men golf," she'd explained to Diana, forever hopeful that she'd find a better partner than Diana's father, who'd disappeared from their lives long before he'd taken off with the woman whom Diana and Ashley referred to as Tiffany because that was her favorite place to shop. She had not long after been replaced by Tiffany II.

"Sorry. Do I sound cranky? I can't complain. A few creaky joints. I always thought that was a figure of speech but it turns out they do creak. And click. It's unnerving. I mean, I make a fist and the knuckles . . . make this sound. And my back. Doctor tells me to walk more. Says it's normal for my age. Do you think he's just telling me that because there's nothing for it? Like I say, can't complain."

Her mother snorted a laugh. "Guess I *can*. Ha ha! In fact, I'm really good at complaining. But actually, on the whole and considering everything, I'm good. Hey, I beat the Big C. What else can He throw at me? Carpe diem, that's what I say. Carpe diem every single goddamn day. How about you, sweetie pie?"

Her mother actually paused. Diana waited until she was certain her mother wasn't going to answer the question herself.

"I'm good."

"Good? Just good? That's nice. I guess. You getting out of the—"

"Some."

"Good. I'm glad you're getting out. And if you're not, take a vitamin D supplement. You don't want osteoporosis to get you when you're my age. My friend Barbara just broke her radius getting up out of a beach chair."

"It's too cold here to go to the beach."

There was a moment of silence. "You know, all I want is for you to be happy. Your sister tells me—"

"So she did call?"

"Last week. She was supposed to call this morning. Monday morning she usually calls."

Monday morning Ashley usually answered her messages and showed up at work, too.

"Has something happened to your sister?" her mother asked.

"Because all weekend I felt like something was off. I thought it was me. Then today she doesn't call and you do. Dee Dee, is something up?"

Diana cringed at the nickname she'd so outgrown. "Nothing's up with me, and I don't think anything's up with Ashley, but I haven't actually talked to her either."

"Since?"

"Friday."

"Ah." A longish pause. "Did you check her apartment?"

"She's not answering her phone."

"Because she's not there? Or . . ."

The silence that followed felt laden with accusation, and an image of Ashley, lying on her kitchen floor, paralyzed and unable to reach the phone, floated into Diana's head.

"If I don't hear from her soon, I'll get someone to check," Diana said.

"When you find her, would you tell her to call me?"

"I will, as soon as I hear." Diana's voice sounded tiny and deflated.

"I'm sure she'll turn up, hon, she always does. Try not to worry too much," her mother said. Two years ago, Diana would have been the one trying to reassure her mother.

"Good advice."

"I'm full of good advice. Don't you know that?"

"Thanks, Ma. I'll tell her to call. Bye—"

"Shh!" Her mother cut her off. From the day she had been diagnosed with cancer, Diana's mother insisted that they never end a conversation with any version of "good-bye."

"Sorry. I meant talk to you soon," Diana said.

"Knock wood."

By midday, Diana had worked her way through most of the items on her to-do list plus three loads of laundry and a weekend's worth of dishes. She'd also polished off the pint of rum raisin ice cream. Ashley still hadn't called, and as far as Diana could tell, she hadn't shown up at work either.

If Diana had been a normal person, she'd have driven over to Ashley's apartment. She got as far as her garage, where she pulled the old shower curtain off the car, a three-year-old, gunmetal-gray Hummer. Daniel's car. He'd hacked the city's telephone network to ensure that he'd be a radio station's 198th caller to win it. It still looked like your average muscle car, but Daniel had had it tricked out with hydraulic lifts that could raise the truck bed and added custom, oversize wheels and tires. The special hubcaps were like black rubber starfish, each chrome tentacle outlined in black. She had no memory of backing it into the garage for the last time, though she must have been the one to do it.

Diana touched the hood, then jerked away as if the thing had thrown off a spark. Just thinking about driving made her nauseous. She would do it one day. Really she would when it became absolutely necessary. But not until she'd exhausted all other avenues.

Maybe one of Ashley's friends knew something. Diana went back inside and started writing a list of friends she'd heard Ashley mention. The list was pathetic, all first names or, even worse, nicknames. She had no idea how to reach any of them. They'd all be in Ashley's BlackBerry, which was presumably wherever Ashley was. That's when she remembered. Ashley's laptop. It was still sitting on the floor beneath the coatrack.

She carried Ashley's computer into her office, booted it up, and waited until the icons materialized. If Ashley was like most people, she'd have backed up her address book on her laptop. Sure enough, there was the BlackBerry icon. Diana opened it and navigated through the menus until she found Ashley's contacts. She made a list of about twenty-five names she thought sounded familiar, then started writing an e-mail message.

In the subject line she typed:

Desperately seeking Ashley Highsmith!

That ought to get their attention. The rest of the message she wrote with a light touch, saying she had needed to talk to Ashley, and if anyone had seen her around in the last few days, please let her know.

She blasted the message to the entire list. Seconds later, she heard *ding, ding, ding* as responses piled into her queue. A glance told her they were error messages for invalid addresses plus a pair of "Out of the Office" automated replies. She watched the message queue but nothing new popped up.

Move on, she told herself. Next, track down other tenants in her building.

That was easier still. She used a reverse-address search to find people whose address was the Wharf View condo complex, where Ashley had lived for the last two years. With a dozen names and phone numbers, she reached for the prepaid cell phone, now fully charged. There was no answer at the first number. Second, third, fourth tenant, no answer either.

On the fifth try, the line had barely rung once when someone picked up. "Hello?" A woman's voice.

"Uh . . ." Diana had no idea what to say, how to explain without sounding crazy.

"Who's there?" the woman demanded, her voice was frail

and quavering. A hang-up call would probably freak her out completely.

"I'm sorry to bother you," Diana started. "You don't know me but my sister lives at Wharf View, and you live at Wharf View, and . . . I know this might sound a little bit bizarre, but I'm just trying to find out if she's okay."

"Who are you? And how did you get my number?"

"I"—Diana was about to say "Googled you" but stopped herself. Instead she said, "I found your name in the phone book." Before the woman could think about how unlikely that was, Diana rushed on. "I'm sorry. Did I catch you at a bad time? I'm not selling anything. Really I'm not. It's just that I need someone to—" Her voice broke and a sob escaped. There was silence on the line as she covered the mouthpiece, getting herself back under control.

"Oh dear, is your sister in some kind of trouble?"

The overwhelming relief that Diana felt at this tiny bit of sympathy gave her back her voice. "I . . . I honestly don't know."

There was a little gasp on the other end of the line.

Uh-oh. She didn't want this lovely woman going into a panic—one of them in that mode was plenty. "She's a little flaky, you know? And it's probably nothing, but . . ."

"But you're worried. Of course you are. Younger or older?"

"Pardon me?"

"Your sister."

"Younger."

"Mmmm." The sound was pregnant with meaning. "Which apartment is she in?"

"Eighty-eight N."

"River view."

"Do you have a nice view, too?"

The woman sniffed. "Parking lot."

Diana's pulse quickened. "You can see the parking lot? Maybe you can see her car. She drives a gold Mini Cooper."

"Oh dear. I'm afraid all cars look pretty much the same to me. Though I do remember when it was easy to tell them apart. Cadillacs had fins. Buicks had those funny little holes in the side. And Thunderbirds—"

"You'd be able to tell this car, Mrs.—" Diana paused.

"Fiddler."

"Mrs. Fiddler. Her car is teeny, and it looks like a miniature bus. Oh, and the body is gold but the roof is black."

"Goodness. Let me see." There was a grunt, like Mrs. Fiddler was getting herself up out of a chair. "I'm looking out the window right now."

Diana crossed her fingers as she waited, though she didn't know whether to hope that the car was there or not.

"The lot's pretty empty. Weekday, you know," Mrs. Fiddler said. "So many people work. But I don't see a car that looks like a little bus. Nothing gold with a black roof. That would stand out, even from up here. Of course I can't see all the cars."

"You can't?"

"There's underground parking too. But I can take a walk down there and look around. I can even pay a visit to your sister's apartment, if you like."

"Mrs. Fiddler, I'd be so grateful if you would."

"You said 88N? I'll call you back—"

"I don't mind waiting," Diana said, afraid that if she lost the connection she might never get Mrs. Fiddler back.

"It might take a while."

"Take your time."

Diana heard the phone being set down and, a little while

later, what sounded like a door closing. While she waited she checked for new messages and then started a game of solitaire.

Finally, after three rounds: "Hello?" That same quavery voice. "You didn't tell me your name."

"I'm Diana. Diana Highsmith."

"Your sister's Ashley Highsmith?"

"Yes, yes! Did you find her?"

"I'm sorry. I didn't find a car like that. And I knocked on your sister's door but no one answered."

Don't panic, Diana told herself. No car and no one answering to a knock on the door were exactly what she would have expected midmorning on a Monday.

"One thing, though," Mrs. Fiddler went on. "The mailman left some mail for her on the table in the lobby."

Diana knew that the mailboxes were small—oversize items typically got left on the table for tenants. "Magazines?"

"*Vogue.* And also what looked like bills and a bank statement." She hesitated. "I hope it was okay to snoop. I hate people who do."

Diana swallowed. "Did you look in her mailbox?"

"From what I could see, it looked pretty full. And another thing. There were a couple of menus in her door. You know how they stick them in the doorjambs? I get those too, and I think these came Saturday." Mrs. Fiddler sounded as devastated as Diana felt.

Menus left stuck in the door? Mail overflowing onto the table? It didn't sound as if Ashley had gone into or out of her apartment building in days. The queen of hearts, the last card she'd turned over in solitaire, stared placidly back at her.

"Hello? Are you still there?" Mrs. Fiddler said.

"Thank you so much," Diana said, trying to sound calm. "If

you notice anything else, could you give me a call?" She gave Mrs. Fiddler her phone number and disconnected the call.

What in the hell was she supposed to do next? Damn Ashley. It was so inconsiderate of her to take off like that. And so typical . . . But when Diana tried to remember other instances when Ashley had disappeared without a word, she could come up with none.

Ding! A message popped into her queue.

RE: Desperately seeking Ashley Highsmith!

Surely here were the answers she'd been aching for.

Ding! Ding! Two more replies to her e-mail asking about Ashley popped in.

Diana whipped through the responses, but excitement quickly faded. No one had seen or heard from Ashley. Not since Friday.

Diana pushed herself away from the computer. She needed to think. What was she missing? Maybe Ashley's supposedly soon-to-be former boyfriend hadn't given up. Maybe pulling the bar stool out from under her and leaving her to pay the tab wasn't enough. Maybe—a possibility Diana could barely contemplate—he'd followed her and turned violent.

Aaron. At least Diana remembered the jerk's first name. Should have thought of him earlier. She went back to Ashley's contacts list and checked that she hadn't missed him. She hadn't. Diana knew that Ashley had at least two e-mail addresses, and she wouldn't be using her corporate account to communicate with Aaron.

She opened a browser window on Ashley's laptop and clicked to drop down the list of most frequent Web sites visited. Near

the top was GMAIL. She picked it and the welcome screen appeared. AHIGH88 was in the user name box and a series of dots
in the password field on the opening screen. *Yes!* Diana pressed
enter and she was in.

181 unread messages

Ashley was addicted to her e-mail. She would have been
incapable of going even a single day without checking it. Three
days? Couldn't happen.

CHAPTER THIRTEEN

S-M-I-T-H." DIANA FINISHED SPELLING HER SISTER'S NAME TO the operator at St. Elizabeth's Hospital.

"Sorry, we have no one here by that name," the answer came back.

Diana hung up the phone and checked off the last of a dozen hospitals within a twenty-mile radius where she'd called. There was nothing left to do but contact the police.

She dialed 911. Her call was routed to an officer with a gravelly voice.

"I want to report"—her voice caught—"a missing person. My sister. Ashley Highsmith."

"And you are—?" His Boston accent turned "are" into "ah."

"Diana. Her sister." Haltingly she managed to explain the situation to the officer.

"So you last saw your sister downtown at—"

"I wasn't there. She was. I saw her in video footage that was on the Internet. And she called me from Copley Square at six."

"Okay. Friday. That's—"

"Three days ago. I wasn't worried at first. I mean, I know she's a grown-up. She lives alone. Owns her own condo. Has a great job. But she's supposed to be at work and she's not in her office. They don't know where she is."

"Was she—?"

"Sure, at times she's a little flaky but she wouldn't just disappear like that." Diana knew she probably sounded hysterical but she couldn't stop herself. "And she left her laptop at my house and she hasn't come back for it. And she's not at work or"—she cleared her throat and tightened her fingers around the phone— "I don't know where she is. None of her friends know where she is. It's been three days without a word." Finally she took a breath.

The officer made conciliatory noises. Then: "Could you come down here and file a report? Bring a photograph of your sister?"

Briefly Diana envisioned herself at the wheel of the Hummer. Crashing.

"Wouldn't it be faster if I e-mailed you a picture?"

"That works too. But there are forms, and questions—"

Diana rushed on. "I asked one of her neighbors to look for her car. It wasn't in the parking lot. And she said there are flyers stuck in her door. Flyers that came days ago. Days ago!" She choked up and her vision blurred.

"You have keys to her apartment?" the officer asked.

Diana gulped. "Yes."

"But you haven't gone there and checked for her?"

"I . . ." Panic welled up in her. "I can't find the key."

There was a long pause. "And you can't come in person and file a report?"

Diana wiped a skim of cold sweat from her forehead. "I'm laid up with a stomach virus."

There was longer silence on the other end of the line.

Finally Diana said, "Listen, I can't come. I just can't. What difference does it make why? This isn't about me. My sister is missing. Something's wrong. I know it." She hiccuped a sob, snagged a tissue, and blew her nose.

"Tell you what," the officer said. "We'll send a patrol car over to your sister's place. Check things out. Talk to the neighbors. Ascertain whether there's anything to be concerned about."

If she could, she would have reached through the phone and hugged the guy. "Thank you. Thank you so much."

"I'll call you as soon as we know something. But depending on what we find, you may have to come in."

Diana couldn't come up with a reply to that.

DIANA PACED HER HOUSE WHILE SHE WAITED FOR THE POLICE TO call back. She straightened. Washed the dishes that were in the sink. Finally she sat down at her computer and scrolled through header after header of Ashley's unread e-mail messages.

There she found the most recent message that Ashley had actually opened. It was from APRITCHARD, it was dated Friday at 4:33 P.M.—just before Ashley would have left to meet Aaron at the bar. Diana opened it.

C U @BOUCHEE—LVG WORK NOW

That would be the jerk himself. Aaron, looked like his last name was Pritchard.

He's been weirding me out, Ashley had said. *Checking up like he's some kind of control freak.*

Diana looked up Mr. Control Freak on Google. Back came links to a bunch of social and business networking Web sites. She clicked on the Facebook link. There were three Aaron Pritchards on Facebook. One in Bend, Oregon. The second one had a photo of what looked like an eight-year-old boy. The third one had to be him. His public profile pegged him as an investment banker. Single. Interested in dating. The photo was of a handsome guy with a well-tended beard. He was shirtless, on his back, bench-pressing what looked like fifty-pound dumbbells. *Ick.*

She'd send him a message, but what to say? She wanted to find out what he knew, not scare him away. She typed:

> Hi, Aaron –
> I'm Diana, Ashley's sister. A friend of mine just came into some money and Ash said you'd be a good person for her to talk to. She wants to make the right decision. Needs to decide soon.

She ended with the number of her prepaid cell phone and hit send. She set the cell phone down on the desk. Beside it, her landline sat mute.

She checked the time. Did *We'll send a patrol car over* mean right this very second? Even if it did, fifteen minutes was too soon to hear back. She hoped that an officer was at least on the way over to Ashley's apartment.

Diana turned her attention back to Ashley's e-mail. She sifted through the unread messages. There were Facebook and LinkedIn updates. A party invitation. A reply to a back-and-forth about a friend's wedding shower that Ashley was helping to organize. Lots of ads and travel offers.

Diana stopped when she got to a message dated Sunday with

the subject line "Everything okay?" Opened it. It was from Janine Gagne, a friend Diana vaguely remembered Ashley mentioning.

> Guess you must have forgotten all about me. Sunday brunch at the Centre Street Cafe, your fave??? Hope he's cute.
> :-(

Diana stared out into space. Even if there was a new man in her life, Ashley would never have stood up a friend.

Were the police at Ashley's apartment yet? Were they talking to the super? Diana imagined them trying Ashley's door and finding it unlocked. As they opened the door, the menus that Mrs. Fiddler had said were stuck in the jamb fluttered to the ground . . .

AN HOUR LATER, DIANA WAS HOLDING ASHLEY'S LIPSTICK AND staring at the phone, willing it to ring when her intruder alarm went off. She bashed the button that silenced the Klaxon. Echoey silence followed. She felt a stone drop into her belly when she saw, in the front video monitors, a police cruiser parked in front of the house. A uniformed officer was striding up her walk. The doorbell rang.

Why come and not telephone? Diana pushed away the obvious answer. As she made her way to the door, she felt as if she were moving through sludge.

The doorbell rang again.

Hands shaking, she fumbled opening the dead bolts, pinched her finger removing the security bar, and finally punched the security pass code. She pulled the door open.

The officer filled the doorway—not so much with bulk as with uniformed presence. Before she could say anything, he said, "Diana Highsmith?"

Diana recognized the gravelly voice. "You're the officer I talked to on the phone?"

He nodded. "Officer Wayne Gruder. Your sister doesn't appear to be in her apartment."

Appear to be? Was that good news or bad?

"But her mailbox has been emptied," he added.

Only Ashley had the key to her mailbox. Diana's hand flew to her throat. "Thank God, she's back!"

From the way his sharp eyes probed her reaction, she knew there was more than just an all clear. "So why the hell hasn't she returned my calls?"

He suppressed a smile, then his look turned somber again. "The thing is, she's not answering her door. I knocked. Rang the bell three or four times. I haven't got probable cause to bust down the door."

"Maybe she came and rushed out again?" Diana said.

"That's possible," Officer Gruder said, giving her a long level look.

A chill passed through her. "You think she could be there? Inside? And won't . . . or can't answer the door?"

"I have no way of knowing. But you seemed so concerned. And you said you have a key."

"I do. Of course I do. And that would be the wise thing to do, wouldn't it?" Her voice sounded robotic. "Go over and let myself in and just see what's up."

"Seems wise. " He seemed infinitely patient. Diana couldn't help thinking it sounded as if he were talking to a child. "But if it was my sister, I'd want to check to be sure. In person. It's a reasonable thing to do."

He stood to one side, as if he were waiting for her to come with him.

Diana took a step back, even though she knew she had to go. She had no choice. She looked past him to the police cruiser parked at the curb.

"Ma'am? Are you all right?"

All she had to do was get from here to there. Beyond her electronic fence, but just a few steps beyond, barely farther than she pushed herself every day. This was the moment that she'd been training for. First she needed to find the key to Ashley's apartment.

"Just give me a minute," she said.

She forced herself to slow down, to move deliberately and breathe evenly as she walked into her bedroom. She found her wallet in the top drawer of her bureau and stuffed it into her pants pocket. Scooped her key ring from a bowl. Checked that the key to Ashley's apartment was still on it.

Stay in control.

Then she continued into her office. From there, she armed all the doors and punched in the code that would activate the inside security system. Thirty seconds. That was how long she had to get out and lock the front door.

"Quite a setup." The voice came from behind her.

Raw panic surged through her and she spun around. Officer Gruder had followed her into her office. Diana clapped her hand over her mouth and the scream she hadn't realized she was making stopped.

Gruder's eyes widened and his hands flew up in a gesture of surrender. He stumbled, tripping over his own feet in his haste to back out of the room and down the hall toward the front of the house.

Diana sat in her desk chair, gasping for breath.

"Sorry if I startled you," he called.

Sorry? What the hell was the matter with him, violating her space? Had she invited him in? Surely it wasn't standard procedure to follow a citizen, deep into her home.

"I'm going outside. I'll wait for you by the car," he added.

She steadied herself against the desk. She had to stop overreacting to every unexpected thing that happened. She couldn't afford for this police officer to dismiss her as a nutcase.

"That sound okay?" Gruder's voice came from farther away.

"Okay," she managed to call out, her voice hoarse. "I'll be right there. I just have to . . ." She remembered the alarm. It would go off any second. She raced to the keypad. What the hell was the code to cancel? Her mind had gone blank.

When the eight-digit code finally came to her, her fingers felt like fat sausages. Twice she keyed it in wrong and had to start over. Again she tried. Just as she was about to press in the final number, a deafening Klaxon started, blaring from speakers both inside and outside the house.

Moments later, her phone rang. She grabbed it. "Ashley?" She had to hold her hand over her ear to block out the clanging. "Ashley?"

"Twenty-three Linden Place?" said a woman's voice.

"Yes?" Diana shouted.

"This is Metro Security. Verifying an alarm."

Of course. This was what they were supposed to do. "It's a false alarm. Can you turn the damned thing off?"

"I need your name and verbal password?"

"What?"

"The name on the account?"

Diana gulped for air. "Diana Highsmith."

"Password?"

She cupped her hand over the receiver. "Daniel."

"Thank you. Verified."

An instant later, the alarm fell silent.

"Thank God," Diana whispered.

She hung up the phone and lifted the shade to look out the front window. Officer Gruder was out front by the patrol car, waiting for her as promised, apparently unfazed by the alarm. She slipped the pill bottle from her pocket, took out a pill, and rolled it between her fingers. But that didn't help. She still felt jumpy, on the verge of a meltdown.

Another whole pill would knock her out. She broke the pill and swallowed half of it dry. *Automatic pilot,* she told herself. *Don't think, just do.*

She set the alarm again. At the last moment, she remembered to grab Ashley's laptop.

CHAPTER FOURTEEN

THIS TIME SHE WAS OUT OF THE HOUSE WITH TIME TO SPARE. THE cruiser was parked not more than twenty feet away from her front door. She'd ridden in a car a million times. It would be like riding a bike, she told herself. You climbed on and it came back to you.

But as she started down the front walk the distance seemed to lengthen. She stumbled and fell, and in an instant Gruder was out of the car, coming toward her. He put his arm around her and helped her up.

"You sure you can do this?" he asked, studying her closely.

She nodded. She had to.

Gruder walked her to the cruiser, supporting her like she was old and infirm. The sight of the mesh barrier between the front and backseat forced her into reverse. She scrabbled back, feeling the same panic she'd felt when that cage had dropped over Nadia.

"Whoa," Gruder said. "Take it easy. I know, it looks like jail in there. Freaks a lot of people out. Would you rather follow me in your own car?"

"I . . ." A car, a black limousine with dark tinted windows, accelerated past, followed by a battered red pickup truck, its muffler pipe dragging. Diana swallowed. "I don't think I can."

"How about this?" Gruder opened the front passenger door. "You ride up front with me."

She leaned down and peered in. Static crackled from an oversize console installed roughly where a car radio would be. This she could manage.

Diana sat. Reassuring smells of coffee and vinyl enveloped her.

Gruder leaned down. "Okay?"

She managed to nod and swung her legs into the car.

Gently he pressed the door of the cruiser shut. Was that pine? The scent that she so associated with Daniel unnerved her, but just for a moment. Then she noticed the green cardboard pine tree silhouette swinging from the rearview mirror. Car freshener.

Gruder got in the driver's side. The car beeped when he inserted the key. He slid her a sideways look. "Seat belt."

She'd forgotten about seat belts. Daniel had always loved that New Hampshire held out, the last state with no seat-belt law—"live free or die" was their motto. She buckled up.

The car started to pull away from the curb. "So, have you always been like this?"

Diana couldn't hold back a bleat of hysterical laughter. "Like what? Afraid of my own shadow?"

Gruber shrugged. "My sister-in-law gets panic attacks. That's what it is, isn't it?"

Diana nodded. "And no, I haven't always been like this."

Diana had grown up pushing past boundaries, not cowering behind them. She'd crossed streets before her mother gave her permission. Ridden her bike to places much farther away than her mother would ever have allowed her to go. She'd been eager to learn to drive, and even before she got her license she'd snuck the car and driven to Cape Cod to hear Sandra Day O'Connor speak at Barnstable High School's graduation.

She'd been so together, or so she'd thought, and determined to become a political activist. Then her mother got sick and she'd come apart. Daniel had glued her back.

As the cruiser rode through the center of town, Diana tried to anchor her attention on what she saw, streets both familiar and not. The movie theater was shuttered. The corner coffee shop had a new name. The storefront that years earlier had been a children's bookstore was still empty. They continued along residential streets, past a blur of houses and small apartment buildings.

Gruder turned, following a sign to the town's boat basin at the mouth of the Neponset River. At the end of the road was the entrance to Wharf View, the massive two-tower complex where Ashley lived. Gruder turned in.

"What kind of car does your sister drive?" Gruder asked.

She told him.

"That should be easy to spot. You look right, I'll look left."

He started driving slowly through the outdoor parking, up one aisle and down the next. Most of the spaces were empty. It was easy to see that Ashley's car wasn't there.

"Her neighbor said there's underground parking too," Diana told him.

Gruder found the entrance and drove down the access ramp, taking them from sunlight into shadow. Diana tried not to flinch as beams passed overhead so close it looked as if they'd whack the cruiser's roof. She pasted her attention on the occasional parked vehicle that seemed to slide past.

No gold Mini Coopers.

They emerged aboveground. Diana realized she'd been holding her breath. She let herself exhale as Gruder pulled the cruiser into the otherwise empty visitors' parking opposite the front entrance to the complex. They both got out.

A fierce wind sliced off the river. Diana shivered and pushed through it, carrying Ashley's laptop up the brick path toward the building entrance. Video cameras were mounted over the glass double doors. She counted up eight stories to the floor where Ashley lived. A figure stood looking out of one of the windows.

Diana broke into a trot, and Gruder caught up with her and strode past, holding open one of the doors. She stepped through, into the familiar lobby. Philodendron cascaded down a backlit wall of glass brick. A blast of warm air greeted her and she felt immediately calmer.

She started toward the elevators and paused at a bank of mailboxes. They were brass, each with a little window in it. She found 88N and peered into the dark interior. Gruder unhooked a flashlight from his belt and shined the light through the slits in the metal door, confirming Diana's first impression. Empty. Most of the mailboxes surrounding Ashley's looked like they had mail. Ashley had to have come back and picked up her mail, Diana assured herself.

"Elevator's here," Gruder called to her. He was holding the elevator door open for her.

Diana took a quick look through the mail scattered across a long, narrow hall table beneath the mailboxes. Nothing there was for Ashley Highsmith.

Feeling relieved, she started toward the elevator. But when she got there, she hesitated. The compartment was so small.

"You want to take the stairs?" Gruder asked. "We can do that. It's seven flights up."

Would climbing the stairs be any easier? Diana pushed herself forward and stepped into the elevator. Gruder followed. She took a step nearer to him as the doors slid shut with a sigh. If he minded her hanging on to his sleeve, he didn't say.

The elevator rose slowly, dinging as it bypassed each floor. The doors slid open on the eighth floor and she followed Gruder out. The hallway, with its fancy gold sconces and white-on-white wallpaper, was comfortingly familiar. At the same time, a warm floaty feeling bloomed from her chest, across her shoulders, and wafted up the back of her neck—the extra medication she'd taken was kicking in.

She followed Gruder down the hall. It seemed shorter than she remembered it. He stopped in front of Ashley's door.

"No restaurant menus," Diana murmured. Elation pierced the haze of medication and she pushed past Gruder. "Ashley?" She knocked. Pressed the bell. "Ashley, are you in there?"

She could feel Gruder standing there, watching her as she banged on the door.

"Ashley Highsmith! You answer the door this minute!" Diana felt her face grow warm. She sounded exactly like their mother.

At the opposite end of the hall, a door opened and a man stuck his head out. He had on a loose-necked undershirt and his hair was tousled. He seemed about to yell at them when he registered Gruder, there in his police uniform. Before the man could disappear, Gruder went over to him.

Diana watched them, listening at the same time for any movement behind Ashley's locked door.

Gruder spoke to the man. She couldn't hear what he said, but the man just shook his head and yawned in response. Gruder asked another question. This time the man pointed toward Ashley's door. Diana's heart leaped. Gruder took out his pad and took a few notes.

A few moments later, the man went back inside his apartment and Gruder returned, looking perplexed.

"Did he see her?" Diana asked. "Did he see Ashley?"

"No. But he says a man was out in the hall an hour ago."

"What was he doing here?"

Gruder took a step back. "Our friend didn't stick around to find out. He was just throwing out his trash."

"Young? Old?"

"Not old." Gruder referred to his notes. "Average height. Dark hair. Jacket zipped with the collar covering the lower part of his face. He had the impression that the man was well built."

Immediately Diana thought of Aaron, pressing his fifty-pound weights. "Well, did he talk to him? What did he say? Wouldn't the cameras out front have caught him? Can you find out?" *Can you do it now?* Diana could hear the desperation in her voice.

"Why don't we check her apartment, first," Gruder said, tilting his head toward Ashley's door.

She knew that was eminently reasonable, but she wanted to grab Ashley's neighbor and shake him until she knew what he knew. Instead, she took out her keys. Ashley's had a dot of hot-pink nail polish on its round head. She tried to jam the key into the lock but she couldn't make it go.

"Here, let me," Gruder said. He rotated the key and it slipped in. Smoothly he turned it and opened the door.

Diana pushed past his outstretched arm and burst into the

apartment. She set Ashley's laptop on the carpet just inside the threshold. Light streaming in through living-room windows seemed to bounce off the white Berber carpeting.

"Ash?"

She almost fell over the pair of red cowboy boots lying in the front hall as she raced into the spotless living room, past the pink-and-green chintz overstuffed sofa and chairs and a glass coffee table with a drift of mail on it, into the dining area with its plate rail lined with delicate Wedgwood and Royal Doulton, and around through a galley kitchen that Diana knew Ashley rarely used other than to warm leftovers.

She circled back to the cowboy boots in the entry hall. Diana picked up one of them. The toe and ankle were stained with whitish splashes. Looked like remnants of the drink Ashley had told her she'd ended up wearing when Aaron pulled the bar stool out from under her.

"Ashley had these boots on when she went to Copley Square on Friday." She set the boot on the coffee table and began to pick through the mound of mail. Bank statement. Credit-card bill. A big envelope from Staywell Bodyscan that said *Here's the material you requested* on the front. Flyers from a local pizza place and a Chinese restaurant were there too.

"I guess she's back after all," Diana said. "But I don't under-stand—" She hiccuped, her voice breaking. It was so inconsid-erate, so typically inconsiderate of her sister. She'd come back, long enough to change shoes and pick up her mail. Now where the hell was she?

"You want to check the rest of the apartment, just to be sure?" Gruder jerked his head toward the hallway with doors to a bedroom and bath, both closed. "Or do you want me to?"

Diana rose to her feet. She walked past Gruder to the closed bathroom door. She knocked on it. "Ashley! You in there?" She didn't expect an answer and didn't get one. She knocked again, then pushed the door open a crack.

The bathroom had barely space enough to turn around, and the world's smallest bathtub. There, from a mirror over the sink, her own face gazed back at her.

It had been months since she'd seen her own reflection. Her skin was pale, and her hair—oh God, her hair—she reached up and touched it. Shapeless curls nearly to her shoulders looked like a dull cloud of frizz around her face. She pushed her hair back from her face. She didn't remember having cheekbones, yet there they were. The dark smudges she'd always had under her dark eyes were more pronounced, making her eyes look as if they'd sunk into her skull.

Diana ran warm water in the sink and splashed her face. On the bathroom wall over the hand towel hung the Hypochondriac's Calendar—a Christmas gift she'd given her sister. On today's date, Ashley could have had "such a pain in my neck." Tomorrow: "Bowlegs."

Diana opened the medicine cabinet. A phalanx of vitamins and minerals and herbal supplements stood on its narrow shelves, sorted alphabetically. Vitamins from A to E, biloba tablets, folic acid, gingko, iron pills . . .

"Find anything?" Gruder asked.

"She'd never have left home for an extended period without her arsenal of pills and supplements," Diana said, holding the medicine cabinet open.

Finally she checked the bedroom, not bothering to knock. Ashley's queen-size bed was neatly made up with a white down comforter and a pile of lace-covered pillows. Along one full wall were shelves and clear Lucite drawers with meticulously folded clothing layered inside. The door to the walk-in closet stood open. Diana stepped inside.

Some clothing lay in a little heap on the closet floor. Diana lifted a crumpled T-shirt and shook it out. The fractured word HACKER was printed across the chest. Diana buried her head in the cotton and inhaled—picking up mostly the scent of store-bought newness and just a whiff of Ashley's licorice.

When she looked up, Gruder stood in the doorway looking in at her. She met his gaze. "This and those cowboy boots out in the front hall are what she had on. She borrowed this outfit from me on Friday."

Gruder's gaze traveled across the rods along the three inside walls of the closet where Ashley's clothes hung, sorted in orderly precision by color and season.

"My clothes she leaves jumbled up in a heap," Diana said. "Hers get princess treatment."

"So she came home, changed, and took off again?" Gruder asked.

"Seems like it."

Diana carried the jeans and T-shirt that Ashley had borrowed from her into the living room. There, she carefully folded them. She picked up the red boots and laid them on top.

She found the leather jacket hanging in the coat closet by the front door. She slipped it on and slid her hands into the pockets. In one she found the sunglasses she'd lent Ashley. In the other, a slip of paper. She pulled it out. It was a cash register receipt from Bouchée on Newbury Street. Friday. 5:45 P.M. A cosmopolitan—Ashley's favorite—a white Russian, and an order of frites. Nearly thirty dollars before tip. The price for cutting Aaron loose?

Diana shoved the receipt back into the pocket. The only piece of the outfit that was missing was the red cap.

Gruder opened the apartment door and held it for her. "Happens all the time," he said. "As far as missing persons go, fortunately for us false alarms are more common than not."

False alarm—was that what this had been? Maybe. And maybe Ashley was back and on her way into work. But it wasn't like Ashley to disappear for days. Not like her to be late for work. Not like her to forget to call Mom on Monday.

Diana glanced over at the coffee table—and not like her to leave mail scattered all over the table.

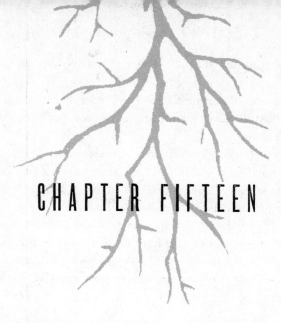

CHAPTER FIFTEEN

Reluctantly Diana gathered up the clothes Ashley had borrowed and left the apartment. She locked the door, then hung there for a few moments, wondering who had been the last person to lock that door.

Gruder was halfway down the hall. He looked back. "What?" he said.

"I'm just thinking, it's too bad there's no surveillance cameras out here." Then she remembered. "But there are surveillance cameras outside. I saw them. Maybe one of them caught her—"

"If she came in that way." He continued down the hall to the elevator and pressed the call button. The doors opened immediately.

"There might be cameras in the underground parking too," she said.

The elevator doors had closed before Diana realized that she'd stepped inside without hesitating.

Gruder pressed the lobby button and the elevator started down.

Diana said, "She must have come back between the time that I talked to her neighbor and when you got here the first time. That's just—"

"A forty-five-minute window," Gruder said.

"It's not like days. It wouldn't take long to fast-forward through the surveillance video," Diana said. "And maybe it'll show the person her neighbor saw in the hall."

The elevator doors opened on the first floor and Diana stepped out. "He had on a jacket. He must have come from outside."

"Okay, okay," Gruder said. "As soon as I get a minute, I'll get in touch with the management company and see about getting access."

It was midafternoon by the time Diana was back in her office fortress. The avatar outfit was neatly folded on the floor by her desk. New messages were stacked up on her screen, including several from Jake. There were automated "Out of the Office" messages from Ashley's office e-mail—replies to the messages Diana had sent earlier in the day. There were more e-mails from Ashley's friends, all telling her that they hadn't heard from Ashley, only increasing a miasma of unease that had settled over Diana. She was not at all convinced that Ashley was fine.

The message-waiting light blinked on the prepaid cell she'd left on the desk. She grabbed it. The only person with that number was Ashley's creepy investment banker, if that's what he really was.

She listened to his message. "Hello, Diana? This is Aaron.

Ashley's friend. Actually, I'm glad you called. I'm worried about your sister." Well, that made two of them. "Please, call me back." Mr. Don't-Call-Me-I'll-Call-You left his phone number.

She called back immediately.

"Do you know where she is?" Aaron asked, taking the question right out of Diana's mouth. "Is she all right?"

"Why do you want to know?" Diana found herself snapping back.

"We had a . . . a misunderstanding. I've been trying to reach her ever since."

"Since when?"

"Friday. We had drinks and I was an asshole. Afterward, I . . . I wanted to apologize. I followed her but couldn't catch up. I didn't want to make a scene, so I left. Besides, she was already talking with some guy."

"At Copley Square?"

"I was across Boylston."

Diana's hand tightened on the phone. Was it the same man Ashley's neighbor had seen? Or had Aaron crossed the street himself and accosted Ashley? "What did he look like?"

"I don't know, maybe five ten. He was wearing sunglasses."

They all had on sunglasses, she wanted to shout back at him.

"And a Red Sox cap," he added.

Also not helpful. Boston was a baseball-mad town.

Her landline rang. Caller ID told her it was Jake.

"Listen, I'll tell her you want to apologize," Diana said. "But I can't say what she'll do. She's not good at following orders, particularly not from me."

"Or me. Turns out that's what I like about her," Aaron said, and grunted a laugh. "Go figure."

Maybe the guy wasn't a complete and total jerk, after all. The phone rang again.

"Sorry, I've got to take this call," Diana said. "But I'll let her know you're trying to reach her."

"Hold on a sec. What about your friend?"

"My what?" Her phone rang a third time. "Oh—yeah. The one with the money to invest. I'll have her call you." Without waiting for Aaron's response, Diana disconnected.

"I thought you'd fallen off the grid," Jake said when she picked up.

"I did. Briefly. It's Ashley. I thought she'd disappeared. I even called the police." She told him about going to Ashley's apartment with the police.

"So, she's back?"

"Looks like she came back and changed. But she hasn't returned my phone messages and she isn't answering e-mail."

"If she came home in a rush—"

"I'm sure you're right. When I actually talk to her, then I'll be completely convinced and completely furious." Meanwhile *worried to death* was a more apt description.

Jake didn't say anything.

"You think I'm overreacting," she said.

"No, not at all. Your reaction is completely understandable."

Understandable? She knew what that meant.

"She's probably busy at work," he added.

"Then why hasn't she called me?"

"Diana, your sister's a grown woman. She doesn't have to answer to you—"

"Or to anyone else, for that matter. Believe me, I'm well aware. It's just that . . . I don't know what I'd do if . . ." Diana couldn't bear to even finish the thought. "I don't know what I'd have done without her and you too, Jake. I know I don't say so, but I appreciate your sticking with me." She brushed away a tear.

Jake cleared his throat. After an uncomfortable pause, he rushed on. "You did a great job on the Vault proposal. Very impressive." Diana remembered how hard it had always been for Jake to accept gratitude of any kind.

He continued, "I made a few changes and left it for you. Go ahead and send it. And I invoiced MedLogic. For the hours we worked, plus a little extra for the insult—"

"And time wasted," Diana added. It seemed like weeks rather than just a few days ago that MedLogic had cut them loose.

"I analyzed that log that came back from their hackers. They're using a server named Volganet."

"I saw that."

"It's somewhere in Eastern Europe. Probably Russia."

"Russia? But . . ." Diana remembered Volganet hadn't been set to Eastern European time. "You sure about that?"

"One of their ports was vulnerable and I got in."

Jake had been able to penetrate further than she had. Maybe the hackers had adjusted their system clock to mislead outsiders.

"Did you get a chance to check out the stolen data file?"

"I'm working on decrypting it," Jake said.

She almost blurted out, *Decrypting it?* The file she'd opened had most certainly not been encrypted.

CHAPTER SIXTEEN

AFTER JAKE'S CALL, IT TOOK JUST A MOMENT FOR DIANA TO FIND the copy of the stolen file that she'd saved to her hard drive. She opened it. The first line began:

WXIDyktaADIUe+PywKwS3KdKlahCteEKxi

Diana stared at it in stunned silence. That pure gobbledygook was definitely encrypted data. Unless she'd gone completely around the bend, it had looked nothing like that when she'd opened that same file on Saturday.

What the hell was going on? She checked her firewall settings. They were all up-to-date and set for maximum protection. She opened the firewall log and began to scroll down. After scanning the hundreds of events when an outside computer had tried to connect to hers over the last forty-eight hours, she found nothing beyond the usual chaotic noise of the Internet.

She opened the stolen data file one more time. Could she

have imagined that it was now encrypted? It made no sense. But there it was. She'd never have mistaken these random letters and characters for what she'd seen earlier.

Then she remembered, she'd made a copy of the file when she attached it to an empty e-mail message and left it in their shared e-mail account. She opened the mail program and clicked on DRAFTS.

There it was—no addressee, no subject line, just an empty message with a file attached. She opened the file.

All she needed to see was the first line.

D3S1358. D7S820.

She pulled her fingers away from the keyboard as if they'd been singed. She hadn't imagined anything. The original file had contained regular old text, exactly what she remembered seeing before—data that meant something to someone, not a complicated code that had to be transformed into meaningful information with a decryption key.

But how? Data didn't spontaneously transform itself. Someone had to have broken into her computer and encrypted the other data file. Diana plugged a flash drive into her computer and saved a copy of the unencrypted data file and its encrypted doppelgänger. For extra insurance, she forwarded copies of the files in an e-mail to Ashley. "Do not delete" she put as the subject line.

Seconds later, an e-mail came back. It was from Ashley. Then Diana read the subject line.

RE: DO NOT DELETE

Finally! Diana clicked it open.

Sorry, I'm out of the office at an offsite meeting until Monday. If you need to reach me, call me on my cell.

If Ashley had come back and gone to work, the first thing she'd have done was turn off that automated reply. It was the kind of thing she was meticulous about . . . just like she was meticulous about her belongings.

Diana remembered Ashley's clothing neatly folded in Lucite drawers and hanging by color and season in her closet, her spices lined up from allspice to vanilla. The only notes of disarray had been the boots in the front hall, the jeans and T-shirt crumpled on the closet floor, and the mail heaped on the coffee table.

A wave of nausea rose up inside her. Had Ashley really returned home? Or had someone unfamiliar with her personality quirks tried to make it look as if she had?

Diana ran into the bathroom and dry-heaved over the toilet. She gagged and tried to vomit. But she'd eaten nothing since the ice cream hours earlier. She sank down to her knees and convulsed again and again.

Finally, she slammed down the toilet lid and pushed herself back against the wall. She dropped her head between her knees. *Just stop,* she told herself. *Relax. Breathe.* She slowed her breathing, deepened the intakes and exhales. When she was ready, she sat up and pressed her spine against the cool tile wall.

She had to convince the police that something was wrong.

Diana stood. Steadying herself against the sink, she soaked a washcloth in cold water and put it over her face. Wiped the back of her neck and the insides of her arms. Then, very deliberately, she wrung out the cloth and folded it, matching the corners neatly the way she imagined Ashley would have before hanging it on the towel rack.

On her way to the phone, she checked every door and window to be sure they were locked.

Back in her office, she called Officer Gruder. She explained, as calmly as she could. "Someone tried to make it look as if she returned home. But they don't know her the way I do."

"You're basing this on a pile of unopened mail and some clothes left on the floor?" When he put it that way it did sound flimsy.

Still . . . "I know my sister."

"And I know missing persons. There's just not enough evidence to—"

She cut him off. "There's a man named Aaron Pritchard. He was there, at Copley Square, when she disappeared. He's a former boyfriend. Says he saw her talking to a man, and maybe he did. But I think it's also possible that he might have talked to her himself."

Silence on Gruder's end. Maybe now she'd gotten his attention. "I have his phone number," she said. As she recited it, she could hear clicking like he was typing.

"Did you look at the surveillance video from her building?" she asked.

There was a pause. "We're working on getting permission to access the building's security systems."

Since when did police need permission to view surveillance video? Had he even tried to get it?

He went on. "I'll check out Mr. Pritchard. And of course please call me if anything else"—*that you neglected to mention,* she heard the unstated accusation—"turns up on your end."

"And you'll let me know when you've looked at the surveillance—" Before she could finish, he'd hung up.

Diana smashed down the phone. To hell with him. She knew

what she knew. Something had happened to Ashley, and it probably started Friday night at Copley Square. Hundreds of people had been there. At least four video cameras had been capturing the action. One of them had to have seen the mystery man whom Aaron claimed he saw talking to Ashley. Surely she'd have had a response by now to her request to see the original footage.

She scrolled down through her stack of unread e-mail messages.

There it was, a message from P2H4.

RE: VIDEO CAMS

She read on.

> Got your message. Sorry to hear about your sister. Whatever we can do to help. We had 6 cameras going. Come over and have a look. Call first. We're in and out.
> - Jess

At the end were an address and a phone number.

Diana mapped the address. It was downtown, just opposite Copley Square—probably an office in the same building from which they'd hauled Superman onto the roof.

Come over and have a look. The person from Spontaneous Combustion might as well have told her: *Fly to the moon.*

Diana called the number. Jess wasn't there, but someone named Eddie was. He'd be there until six, and someone would be there all day tomorrow from ten on. She was welcome to come by. They had an editing suite where she could examine the footage.

"Is there any chance you could post it so I can look at it online?" Diana asked.

Sorry, was the answer. "We don't have the permissions we'd need. Besides, these files are huge. There's an hour plus on each cam."

Surely she'd find traces of Ashley in six hours of digital video. "I'll be there," she heard herself say. "Thanks."

She hung up and printed off the message and the map. It was already five. She'd have to move if she was going to get there before they locked up. But how?

She could take a cab. She gagged at the thought of getting into a taxi with a driver who was a stranger to her. She'd have to drive herself. The car keys were still in the olive-drab canvas backpack she used to carry everywhere, back in the day when she actually went places without thinking twice.

She could practically hear Daniel's voice: *Lean on me.* She pulled his walking stick from her umbrella stand. Grabbed the cell phone and charger and dropped them into the backpack. Checked her video monitors. Outside it was quiet. A cardinal was perched on the fence again.

Trying not to think, just do, a minute later she'd armed the doors and reset the security alarms. She pulled open the kitchen door and stepped into her garage. There she leaned on Daniel's walking stick, and the smell of pine overwhelmed the odors of gas, mold, and skunky pheromone that rose from the garage floor.

Hands trembling, she keyed in the security code. Checked twice that the door was secure.

She could do this, she told herself, hugging the walking stick to her chest as she turned to face the Hummer. It had been backed into the garage. She pressed the button on the key ring and heard the reassuring click as the doors unlocked. She pulled open the door, stepped up onto the shiny chrome bar and into the driver's seat.

Dropping her backpack and the walking stick on the floor, she slipped the key into the ignition and anchored both hands on the leather-clad steering wheel. A few feet in front of her was the closed garage door. She shut her eyes and took deep breaths, counting down from ten.

When she opened her eyes, she saw the Dunkin' Donuts cup sitting in the drink holder. The program from Daniel's memorial service was lying on the floor. Diana remembered the line from the poem Jake had read, his voice choking. *May the road rise to meet you.*

She forced herself to focus, to turn the key. The engine whinnied until she released the pressure. The engine light was on and the needle on the gas gauge had jumped to half full. She pumped the gas pedal and tried the key again. On the third try, the engine caught, roared to life, and kept right on roaring. Diana coughed as fumes filled the closed garage. It took her a moment to realize she had her foot jammed down on the gas pedal. She pulled it off.

She pushed the remote to raise the garage door and jumped as the mechanism clanked and then whirred. The door's hinges gave a loud creak. Diana's heart pounded as the door tilted open and a sliver of light grew at ground level. She gripped the steering wheel to keep her arms and shoulders steady. Slowly the door rose in front of her.

All she had to do now was shift into drive and accelerate out of there. Once the car was in the clear, the garage door would lower automatically.

She stared at the needle pointing to park. Moved her hand to the gearshift, her hand clawed, knuckles white.

A shadow fell over her. She jerked her head up. A car was coming up the driveway at her. Shiny. Black. Diana screamed, and as if answering her cry, the car screeched to a halt just a few feet from the Hummer's front bumper.

Diana screamed again and bashed the remote over and over until the garage door started to descend, cutting her off from the intruder. Then she yanked the keys from the ignition, threw herself from the car, and stumbled to the door, keying in the security code and falling into the house without looking back.

She slammed the door behind her, threw the dead bolt, and raced into her office. In the echoing silence, the doorbell rang, but Diana barely heard it. The security camera in the front of the house showed an empty driveway. The black car that she knew had to still be there appeared to have vanished, and that same damned cardinal was perched on the front fence.

On top of that, not one of her alarms had gone off.

CHAPTER SEVENTEEN

DIANA CRAWLED UNDER HER DESK AND SAT THERE, HUGGING HER knees to her chest. In her mind's eye she could still see the black car. Why didn't her security camera see it too? Why hadn't it triggered her security alarm? And how come each time she'd looked out through the front camera, the same damned bird was perched outside?

Diana shivered. All she could think was her security systems had been sabotaged, her electronic fence disarmed, and live video feed had been replaced by an innocuous video loop that replayed over and over. How paranoid was that?

The pile of avatar clothing was on the floor near the desk. She reached out and pulled the leather jacket toward her. The faintest whiff of Ashley's licorice scent wafted up to her.

Home was no longer safe. Her griefer-infested virtual world wasn't either. Where to go? And how the hell was she going to find the courage to get herself there?

She draped the leather jacket over her shoulders and raised

the collar so it framed her face the way Nadia's jacket collar did. She pulled the sunglasses from the pocket and put them on. Through the tinted lenses, the room around her took on new clarity and depth. Her stomach settled and her hands grew steadier, as if some of Nadia's courage were seeping into her.

She crawled out from under the desk and stood. She laid the jacket over the back of a chair. Then she crept to the living room, lifted the shade, and peered out the front window. The black car was gone. The street was quiet. She checked the security alarm. The word ARMED glowed back at her. A lie.

She returned to her office. Nadia was waiting for her, suspended on the screen in OtherWorld, right where Diana had left her in the replica of Diana's office.

A bell sounded, then sounded again—two new messages.

> PWNED: U there? You gotta see this. 1293, 4681
> GROB: Hey. Got a minute. 1655, 196

She wasn't alone, she reminded herself. She had friends, friends in OtherWorld with alter egos in the real world.

Diana hovered the cursor. PWNED or GROB? She felt a connection to GROB, as if she'd known him much longer than she actually had. But PWNED had been one of the first to friend Diana in OtherWorld. And there was nothing complicated about their relationship.

Diana transported Nadia to the coordinates that PWNED had sent her. A meadow materialized and, in the distance, a futuristic landscape of crystalline structures. She brought up an area map. A mass of yellow dots, each an avatar, was clustered a short distance due west.

She turned Nadia and ran her in that direction, through an allée of cyprus trees, along a stone wall, and on to a massive stone gateway. Stepping Nadia through the gateway, she emerged at the topmost rim of an amphitheater that seemed to have been hollowed out from the side of a hill.

PWNED came up the steps toward her. Tall and lithe, the avatar wore black, crotch-high boots, a microskirt, and a crop top. A diamond twinkled from her navel and her platinum hair was wrapped in a Princess Leia breakfast Danish over one ear.

An empty voice balloon appeared over PWNED's head. "I wanted you to see what you helped create." Her voice was soft and breathy.

A banner across the stage read FIGHT BACK. LIES KILL. A speaker was standing on the stage, addressing a crowd of avatars seated around him.

"Is this amazing or what?" PWNED continued. "And it's just the tip of—"

Diana interrupted. "I need help. Can I . . . I need somewhere to stay. I'll explain later, but I need to get somewhere safe. Right now." She tried to swallow but she couldn't.

"Real-world help?"

"The realest. You're near Boston?"

"I'm in it. Can you drive?"

Diana realized she still had the keys to the Hummer clutched in her hand. "I'm going to have to."

PWNED didn't ask another question. She just gave her address and offered to get on the phone and guide Diana there.

By the time Diana had transported Nadia home, she was sweating and having trouble breathing. Meanwhile, on the computer screen in her virtual office, Nadia stood cool and serene, game for whatever awaited them. If only Diana could absorb her avatar's strength and nonchalance.

Diana held the leather jacket out in front of her, considering. It was beautifully made, the black leather soft and supple, the lining a soft, pale gray silk. She draped the T-shirt over the back of the chair and spread the jeans out on the seat. She set the red leather boots upright, side by side on the floor. Ready to roll.

"Okay, I'll navigate. You drive," Diana told Nadia. The avatar didn't even crack a smile.

AN HOUR LATER, DIANA STOOD IN THE BATHROOM. THE SPRAY bottle with the mixture of hydrogen peroxide and water that she'd used to lighten her hair sat on the counter. The wastebasket was half filled with a mass of her own hair that she'd snipped off with a nail scissor. She ran her fingers through the short uneven curls she'd left intact. Her hair would never be straight and spiky like Nadia's, but at least now it was . . . just to be sure, she yanked out a single strand of hair . . . blond verging on platinum. If only she hadn't trashed every single mirror in her house.

She put on Nadia's clothes. This time, before she tried to leave, she made a list:

> *Get directions*
> *Send Ashley cell-phone number*
> *Shut down computers*
> *Disconnect systems*

And so on, through getting out of the house. She envisioned Nadia performing each step with cool, methodical precision. Then she began.

PWNED's address in the South End was just blocks from downtown. She found directions on MapQuest, printed them out, checked her messages one last time, and shut down her computers. She unplugged her server and disconnected the routers and modems that gave her redundant connections to the outside world. Before she unplugged her landline, she used it to call Ashley's office and home numbers and leave the number of the prepaid cell phone that she'd be taking with her.

As she finished each task, she ticked it off. There were just three more things she needed to take with her—the car keys, directions, and her laptop. Her backpack and Daniel's walking stick were still in the car.

Ready to go, she hesitated, touching her throat. There was one more thing she needed—a necklace that Daniel had given her. She found it in her bedroom in the little jewelry box she'd gotten for her eighth birthday—a pair of gold *D*s, written in script, hanging from a black leather cord. She fastened it around her neck.

She returned to the kitchen and set the security alarm. Was a bona fide security company really tied to the alarm system, or was that as much of an illusion as the cardinal on the fence? It no longer mattered.

She locked the door to the garage behind her. Climbed back into the Hummer. Set the map and directions she'd printed out on the passenger seat. *Check, check, check.*

It had grown darker outside, and she could barely see where to insert the key in the ignition. She took off her sunglasses. The eyes staring back at her from the rearview mirror were bright and anxious.

Diana rummaged around in her backpack and found an eye pencil. She turned on the overhead light, angled the rearview mirror so she could see herself, and applied dark lines to her upper and lower lids, then smudged them. That white-blond hair would take some getting used to.

She turned off the light and deliberately pressed the remote to raise the garage door. The door slowly lifted. A car drove past on the street and Diana flinched. She was at the controls, she told herself, just like when she was at her computer, watching the world through a shield.

With a quick turn of the key, she started the Hummer, then adjusted the rearview mirror so she could see the empty passenger seat behind her as well as one of her own eyes. Nadia's eye. It winked at her. *We have ignition.*

She shifted into gear and released the brake. When she touched the gas, and touched it again, the car pulsed forward. Another touch and the Hummer shot out of the garage, across the sidewalk, and into twilight.

Behind her, the garage door clanked and whirred as it descended.

Just take it one step at a time. Again Daniel's calm voice urged her on.

She pulled out onto the street. Shadowy tree branches, silhouetted against a blue-black sky, passed overhead as she drove a block, then another to a red light. She glanced at the map on the passenger seat. Total distance: 8.7 miles. On a day with good traffic karma, it was about a thirty-minute drive.

When the light turned green, she accelerated, watching the needle inch up from ten miles an hour. She could feel the suppressed surge of the powerful engine. The Hummer always made her feel as if she were in a tank, as much of an alternate reality as the world of her computer.

Each time she accelerated, the car seemed to jerk and cough, as if clearing the moisture that had gotten into its systems—after all, it hadn't been driven in more than a year. As she retraced much of the route Officer Gruder had taken that morning, she focused on the road, trying to come down so easy on the brake so she wasn't thrown against the steering wheel.

In her mind's eye, she could see a map of the neighborhood where she was heading, Harrison Avenue in Boston's South End. As of a year ago, at any rate, the upper floors of industrial buildings there had been turned into warrens of artists' studios and galleries. She'd opted for a route through city streets, though the highway would have been faster. She wanted to take it easy her first time back on the road.

The sun was setting as she crawled up Dorchester Avenue, a storefront-lined street of long shadows that ran into Boston from the south-stick into an ice-cream bar. The street widened at major intersections, then narrowed again to a single lane each way in between.

A car behind her beeped. She'd have beeped herself. The needle on the speedometer hovered at twenty.

She accelerated to the thirty-mile-an-hour speed limit, still too slow for Boston drivers. She turned off the main street and wound through increasingly dense urban neighborhoods where the crush of cars and pedestrians made her feel more anonymous, invisible even.

The number 2497, the Harrison Avenue address that PWNED had given her, was hand-painted across a purely functional steel door to a five-story brick industrial building with oversize, multipaned windows. In front was metered parking, all of the spaces occupied.

Diana double-parked in front, waiting in a pool of light under a streetlight as traffic streamed past. She found her cell phone and called PWNED.

"Hello?" She recognized PWNED's soft, breathy voice.

"I'm out front," Diana said.

There was a whirring sound on the line. Then: "Can you see me? I'm up on the fourth floor."

Looking up through the windshield, against the dark sky, she saw a hand waving from an upper-floor window. "Yup, I see you."

"Look, there's a car pulling out on the other side of the street, two buildings down. Bang a U-ey."

Diana shifted into gear and signaled a left turn.

"Hurry," PWNED said, "before someone else grabs it. I'll meet you downstairs. The lobby's a bit basic. Don't freak out."

CHAPTER EIGHTEEN

WHEN THERE WAS A BREAK IN TRAFFIC, DIANA MADE A U-TURN and got over just in time to slip into the space that a van had just pulled out of. At least she still remembered how to parallel park.

She turned the car off, set the emergency brake, and sat there for a few moments, taking in the buildings that surrounded her, imagining that she was angling the view on her computer screen. She picked up Daniel's walking stick from the floor of the car, anchoring her senses on its familiar feel.

Get out of the car. She tapped her fingers on the stick, as if on a keyboard, typing the command /out.

Diana grabbed her backpack and laptop case and waited, watching her side mirror as cars came from behind and passed her. She opened the door and got out. Slammed it shut and clicked the remote before crossing the street and walking back up the block to the building entrance.

Up close, she could see shadows of graffiti beneath the gray paint on the steel door. A piece of cardboard had been slipped into the doorjamb where the latch would have engaged. Diana pushed and the heavy door swung open.

A naked lightbulb—the spiral-shaped energy-efficient kind—hung from the ceiling, casting a dull glow over a cramped interior. The walls looked battered, like someone had used them for target practice, and the floor was covered with small square ceramic tiles that had once been white. Diana breathed in. She smelled pine cleaner over urine.

Across the adjacent wall was a massive sliding door to what looked like a freight elevator. Opposite that was a door with a little window in it. She pulled that door a crack. Just beyond was a broad concrete stairway going up.

Clank. Diana whirled around. There was a hum and then a breeze inside the vestibule, as if someone had opened a window. The elevator was in motion.

Diana knew it had to be PWNED, doing what she said she'd do—coming down to meet her. But as the hum grew louder, Diana felt as if the space she was in was compressing.

She darted through the door and into the stairwell. It seemed to take forever for the door to drift shut. She watched through the little window.

The humming stopped. Another clank and a *scree* announced the elevator's arrival. A rectangle of light fell on the floor of the vestibule—the elevator's door had slid open.

There was that whirring sound again, and into the vestibule rolled a wheelchair. Sitting in it was the hunched-over figure of a woman. She was pitched forward as if straining to see, her clawed hand gripping the joystick on the arm of the chair.

Diana pulled the stairwell door open and stepped out.

"Nadia?" The woman propped herself up against her chair arm with one elbow and offered her other hand. "I'm Pam. Dr. Pamela David-Braverman if you want to get technical about it."

"You're a physician?" Diana asked, grasping Pam's cool, stiff hand.

"You bet." Pam's mouth opened in a generous smile. Despite braided white-white hair, Pam's smooth, unlined face suggested she was barely forty.

"I'm Diana. Diana Highsmith."

The elevator door began to close, but before it could do so, Pam backed her wheelchair into the opening. The door crashed into it and rebounded. Then a buzzer started to ring. Pam seemed unfazed.

"Your car is okay parked where it is for now—until the parking Nazis arrive in the morning. Then I've got a resident permit we can leave on the dash." As Pam talked, Diana could feel her sharp gaze picking her apart—as if she were being autopsied. Pam must have recognized the leather jacket and red boots as part of Nadia's getup. "Let's go up." Pam backed the wheelchair up a bit to make room for Diana to slide past.

When Diana hesitated, Pam said, "There was a guy inspecting this thing a few weeks ago. It might look like shit but it runs. Otherwise, it's five long dark flights up. I understand they've had a problem with homeless people sneaking in and harvesting lightbulbs. But hey, it's your call."

Pam backed the wheelchair up farther to make more room. Diana stepped into the elevator and pressed her shoulder against the wall as the door clanked shut.

Pam tipped her chair back so it balanced on its two oversize wheels. She raised the seat and pushed the button for the fourth floor.

"This new wheelchair has changed my life," Pam said as the seat lowered. With a groan the elevator started to ascend. "Stays charged for a week. Turns on a dime. Even climbs stairs." Pam reached for Diana's hand, and Diana knew her friend was chattering away to help Diana stay calm.

Finally the elevator stopped and they got out. One of the doors on the dark corridor stood open. Pam rolled toward it. The raucous sound of a bird singing leaked from inside.

"That's a clock," Pam said, tossing the words back over her shoulder. "My sister's idea of a Christmas present. She's into clocks. She also gave me one shaped like a hen that clucks on the hour and lays an egg. That one's still in the box."

"My sister's into dietary supplements," Diana said, following close behind. "And body lotions."

"Equally useful, I'm sure, but not nearly as charming."

The birdsong clock turned out to be hanging on one of the cavernous apartment's bare brick walls. The multipaned windows looked as if they'd been original to this turn-of-the-century manufacturing complex. Diana had read enough local history to know that it would have once been waterfront property before landfill extended Boston's shoreline.

Waist-high bookcases divided the space. Scanning them, Diana saw mostly medical texts and travel books, including a guide to trekking in Tibet and Bill Bryson's book on walking the Appalachian Trail. Tucked in also was a well-worn copy of *Heidi*.

Flowering plants—including African violets in a range of colors and shapes that Diana had never seen before—and framed photos lined the top shelves. One of the pictures was of a little dark-haired girl of about eight with huge eyes who smiled at the camera from a wheelchair. The two adults, a man and a woman standing beside her and beaming, were probably Pam's parents.

Against the back, windowless wall was a bed and about ten feet of built-in closet with a rod chest-high. Computers in a setup that rivaled Diana's own were arrayed in a front corner under a window. Pam's wheelchair, with its black-cushioned seat and leather armrests, was the ideal desk chair.

Once inside, Pam rode smoothly, despite the uneven pine-plank floors. The chair must have had shock absorbers, maybe even a gyroscope to keep it so perfectly balanced.

Sitting on a cushy white couch accented with hot-pink and deep purple silk throw pillows and drinking a cup of dark, smoky oolong tea that Pam prepared for her, Diana told Pam about Ashley's disappearance and apparent reappearance. Pam listened, absorbing each revelation as if she were listening to the weather report.

"And you don't think your sister came home at all," Pam said. "Someone else left the clothes and picked up the mail to make it look as if she did."

It sounded preposterous. "I've left her a gazillion messages. On her home phone. On her cell. At work. She's got the number of the cell phone I've got with me." Diana slipped it from her pocket to make sure she hadn't missed a call. "If she's back, why hasn't she called me?"

"And you think someone tampered with your security systems?" Pam paused to consider this, as if it were a completely rational possibility. Diana felt herself relax another notch. "Seems like there ought to be a connection. Think back. Did anything unusual happen before your sister disappeared?"

"Ashley broke up with the guy she was seeing. That's pretty unusual. For Ashley. And he wasn't too thrilled." Diana told Pam about the scene Aaron had made in the bar. How he'd followed her to Copley Square to apologize, then backed off.

"You think he might be the person your sister's neighbor saw in the hall?"

"He could be."

"And you know for sure that your sister was at Copley Square three days ago?"

"She called me from there. And there's video footage, posted online, that shows her at the improv event."

Diana went over to Pam's computer. The forum in the amphitheater on OtherWorld was still going on. Pam had left PWNED sitting on the stage, watching the speakers.

"May I?" Diana asked, her hand poised over the mouse.

Pam nodded.

Diana opened a new browser window and typed in the Spontaneous Combustion address. She clicked the "Up in the Sky" video they'd posted. As the opening music played, Pam rolled her wheelchair over.

"This was Friday," Diana said. She fast-forwarded to the clear shot of Ashley. "And that's my sister, Ashley. There are just a couple more glimpses of her." She fast-forwarded to the next one, and then to the next.

"That's it?"

"That's all I could find in the montage they posted. But of course there's got to be more footage. Lots more." She told Pam about the different video cameras that had filmed the event. "I called, and they offered to let me examine the rest of the footage. But I've got to get over there to do it."

"So what are we waiting for?" Pam said. "We can go right now."

"They're closed," Diana said. It was nearly seven o'clock already. But Pam called anyway, hitting the speakerphone button so Diana could hear.

The phone rang three times. Then: "We're here from 10 A.M. until 6 P.M.," a recorded voice informed them.

Pam stabbed at the phone and disconnected the call. "First thing tomorrow we head over there."

OVER DINNER—A MEZE PLATTER AND KABOBS THAT PAM BROUGHT back to the apartment from a Middle Eastern restaurant around the corner—Diana reconsidered Pam's question: Had anything unusual happened before Ashley disappeared?

She explained to Pam the kind of work she and Jake did, resolving security issues for clients in health care. "The same day Ashley disappeared, another client blew up in our faces. As soon as we'd found the breach, before we could track down the hackers, they called us off. It's the third time that's happened. I was furious."

"Can you tell what these hackers were after?"

"I can show you one of the files they took. It didn't mean a thing to me."

Diana connected her laptop to Pam's wireless network and got into her e-mail account. She opened the data file she'd left in the drafts folder and turned her laptop so Pam could see.

All it took was a glance. "That's a DNA profile," Pam said. She scrolled through it. "A unique individual, somebody some-where. If we knew what we were looking at, we could find out all sorts of things about him."

"Him?"

"Him." Pam pointed to a line of data. "But that's just the beginning. An expert could analyze the genetic code and tell us something about this man's ethnic background. Certain genes make a person susceptible to specific viruses and immune to others. Or deadly allergic. Or—"

"But what good is it? I mean, why would someone want to steal this stuff?"

Pam propped herself up, straightening her spine and shifting in the chair. It occurred to Diana how uncomfortable it could get, sitting in the same chair all day long.

"Assuming they could link the profile to a person, like through a Social Security number, I can think of lots of information in a DNA profile that someone wouldn't want others to know—and that you certainly wouldn't want your insurance company or your employer to get wind of. Just suppose, for example, that you have the gene for ALS. Or you've got a chromosomal abnormality that's been linked to violent behavior? Or sexual perversion? I can easily imagine—"

Pam was interrupted by what sounded like a dog barking. It was coming from her computer. "My network watchdog," she said.

She rolled over to her computer, clicked the mouse, and the sound stopped. "It just stopped a message from going out." Frown lines deepened on her forehead as she stared at new information that had popped up. She turned to Diana. "Looks like it blocked an outgoing message that originated on your computer."

"But I didn't send anything."

"Well, your computer sure as hell did. Or at least it tried to. Must have been when you connected to the Internet." She swiveled the screen so Diana could see.

OUTBOUND LEVEL 1 BREACH INTERCEPTED.

Below that was a message addressed to USER003 on Volganet. All it contained was:

42.33765016859684−71.07173681259155

"I have no idea what those numbers mean," Pam said. "Do you?"

"They're geocodes," Diana said. She pulled up the Web site WhereUAre.com and pasted the numbers into a search box. "Shit," she said, the back of her neck prickling as a map of the South End came up with a virtual pushpin on Harrison Avenue in the precise location of Pam's apartment building.

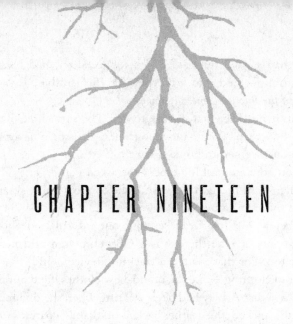

CHAPTER NINETEEN

THE GOOD NEWS IS . . . THAT MESSAGE NEVER MADE IT OUT," PAM said. Diana found that only marginally reassuring.

It didn't take long for Pam to find the program that had launched it. She examined the code. "This is awfully clever. Simple but effective." She looked over at Diana. "But how'd it get here?"

"*When* did it get here?"

"I can tell you that. Hold on," Pam said. A few clicks later, Pam pointed to the screen. "Just under a year ago."

"No way." Diana had owned the laptop for about that long—since Gamelan started. For that entire time it had been broadcasting her whereabouts to Volganet? She dropped into a chair. With all the fancy security systems that Jake had set up for her, how was that possible?

Diana watched as Pam deleted the program. *We have no privacy.* She remembered Daniel's rant about how the Internet, which had started out as a haven for freedom, had been co-opted, transformed into a playpen for Big Brother. *Every time you're on the Internet somebody knows where you are.*

Pam handed the laptop back to her. The tiny circle over the top of the screen, a built-in video camera that she'd never bothered about, seemed to blink at her.

"You got any masking tape?" she asked Pam.

When Pam brought her a roll, she tore off a tiny scrap and stuck it over the camera lens.

If her laptop had been sending out information about its whereabouts, maybe there was a GPS chip transmitting from the car too. For that matter, a tracking device could have been sewn into clothing—like the brand-new clothes she'd purchased online and that Ashley had been wearing when she disappeared.

Diana picked the leather jacket off Pam's coatrack where she'd hung it and turned it over in her hands. She wondered how small and well camouflaged a GPS emitter could be. She examined the metal fittings on the jacket. Could it resemble a snap or be embedded in a buckle?

She ran her fingers up inside the lining and rolled the collar and cuffs between her fingers, feeling for any kind of anomaly. Then she examined the jeans and T-shirt that she still had on. Then the red boots that she'd shucked when she came into the apartment.

She pulled out her cell phone. Didn't they come with embedded GPS locators? She'd have to take that risk. It was the only way that Ashley could reach her, and she couldn't turn it off—not until she was sure Ashley was safe.

THAT NIGHT, DIANA TRIED TO FALL ASLEEP ON A BLOWUP MATTRESS on Pam's floor. It was comfortable enough and she was warm under a down comforter, but her insides were tied up in knots. She timed her morning tranquillity pill so it would be at full strength for the trip to Copley Square. It was only ten blocks away, but just looking out the window to the street below gave Diana the jitters. Even with Daniel's walking stick, she'd never make it on foot. Driving the Hummer into the congested downtown and finding a parking spot near Spontaneous Combustion's office—how likely was that?

She needn't have worried. Pam offered to drive.

They rode down in the elevator together. Pam went outside, her wheelchair easily navigating the steps down to the sidewalk and off the curb. Pam's silver van was parked in a handicapped spot in front of the building. She used a remote to open the van's door. A platform slid out and Pam rolled onto it and waited for it to rise. When it was level with the van, she rolled inside and positioned her chair where the driver's seat had been removed.

The passenger door slid open and Diana got in, holding Daniel's walking stick. She sat back, barely aware of the door sliding shut, of Pam whirring up and back, positioning the wheelchair and locking it in behind the steering wheel. The van was so much like the one Diana had been driving home from college when she had her first full-blown panic attack. So high off the ground, the windshield so close to the car in front of them. That first time, she'd been ambushed. This time she saw it coming.

Pam started the van and, using one of the hand controls attached to the steering wheel to accelerate, pulled out into traffic. Diana grasped the door. Her heart sped and the walls of the van threatened to fold in on her, but a part of her seemed to remain on the outside, watching and monitoring her response, observing pedestrians darting across the streets or making their way up and down the sidewalks. That detachment—it was her pill doing its work.

"Take your time. Control it," Pam said as she crossed over the highway and into downtown Boston.

Diana looked over at her, startled. She understood.

Pam rolled down the windows on both sides of the van and cold air filled the interior. "Just breathe."

Diana sat back. The vise that gripped her slowly loosened.

Minutes later, Pam parked the van in a handicapped spot alongside Trinity Church, its steps and arched front now in deep morning shadow, its central tower and two side towers looming overhead.

Only about a dozen pedestrians were in Copley Square. Like a holographic image, Diana envisioned Ashley standing there in the middle of the plaza, barely fifty feet from where they'd parked, wearing the same clothes Diana had on now and offering a cell-phone salute to the Fairmont Copley.

Across the street was the pillared front of the library where the improv participants had assembled. Behind her was the Copley Plaza Hotel, where Superman had been launched from a top-floor window.

"Spontaneous Combustion is in that building over there," Pam said, pointing past the plaza, across Boylston. Diana recognized the building with the decorative ironwork at the roofline. "You ready?"

Pam waited until Diana nodded before rolling up the windows and opening the van doors. Holding Daniel's walking stick, Diana got out. She raised her jacket collar and folded her arms. With Pam rolling along beside her, Diana walked to the spot in the center of the plaza where Ashley had stood. *She was right here.* Diana looked around, envisioning what it had been like with the plaza crowded with pedestrians. She looked across the street and imagined a glowering Aaron Pritchard, standing at the light watching her. But then what happened?

THE OFFICES OF SPONTANEOUS COMBUSTION WERE ACROSS THE street, on the top floor of a building tucked between a CVS and a Starbucks. Eddie, who'd talked to her on the phone, set up Diana and Pam in a small, windowless video editing room. The walls were painted black, and three computer monitors were set on a shelf over a worktable with a single keyboard and mouse and banks of control panels. Eddie showed them the basics of how to work the system and left them to it.

There were six video files. The first one started with Eddie, standing on the library steps, wearing a director's cap and addressing the crowd through a bullhorn. The camera stayed with him. Diana slowed to half speed whenever the camera zoomed out to take in any of the crowd.

A few minutes in, Diana thought she spotted Ashley. She paused the video and backed up. Sure enough, there she was, standing at the back of the crowd listening to the director's instructions.

Diana replayed the video, more slowly. The camera caught Ashley throwing a look behind her, then stepping into the crowd and getting swallowed up. Diana backed up again and froze the screen on Ashley's face as she looked over her shoulder and in the direction of the camera. She zoomed in.

"A little blurry, but what do you make of that expression?" Pam asked.

"She looks—" Diana searched for the right word.

"Pissed off?"

"Exactly right. And I'm guessing she sees Aaron, the guy she'd just dumped." So where was the other man Aaron had claimed he'd seen Ashley talking to?

Diana grabbed a pencil from the table and a piece of paper from the trash. On the blank back, she drew a crude map of Copley Square and the surrounding area. She jotted an *A* at the approximate spot on the plaza where Ashley stood, and the 6:03:25 time stamp from the video.

Diana pushed play and the view shifted back to the director, and stayed with him except for cutting away once to capture the brief drama of Superman getting snagged on the spire, and once again lingering on the unfurling banner at the end.

The first camera's video contained only one Ashley sighting. Diana prayed the others would yield better results.

The video from the second camera had been taken from the roof of the building they were now in. The angles were all long shots across Copley. Individual people looked small and insignificant. It was slow going, backing up and inching ahead, zooming in to examine the crowd. There might have been another Ashley sighting. And another. Both were near where she'd been spotted earlier. Diana penciled in more *A*s and time stamps on her map.

Footage from the third camera yielded nothing new. The fourth camera focused on bystander reactions. Diana spotted the red hat again. Ashley had her back to the camera, her arm raised. Diana jotted an additional *A* on her map with a new time. As the camera meandered through the crowd, its operator seemed particularly enamored of a young woman whose abundant cleavage overflowed her low-cut top as she raised her arm in a cell-phone salute to the hotel.

A fifth camera also caught the proceedings from sidewalk

level. This one had caught Ashley crossing the street, from the library to Copley, and later in mid-pivot as Superman crossed overhead.

The sixth video file was much smaller than the others. It had in it only five minutes of footage, shot from Spontaneous Combustion's office window. It began at 6:53 A.M. the next morning and showed a gray, deserted Copley Square with a single pedestrian moving slowly across it. Traffic was sparse, and the headlights of about half of the cars were turned on.

Diana sat back. By then Ashley had vanished, gone off the grid as Jake would have put it.

"Hey!" Pam said. She was pointing to a figure sitting at the edge of the fountain.

Diana blinked, unsure of what she was seeing. She froze the video and zoomed in. Wrapped in a blanket beside the fountain alongside Copley Church sat what looked like a homeless woman with a wheeled cart stuffed with clothing. On her head, she wore a newsboy-style cap.

CHAPTER TWENTY

SURE LOOKS LIKE THE HAT YOUR SISTER HAD ON," PAM SAID WHEN Diana had enlarged the frame even more.

Diana stared closely at the image. The hat seemed to be the right shape, and it might have been red, but really it was just a blur. The woman wearing it was definitely not Ashley.

"Even if it is, it doesn't get us anywhere," Diana said. "Better to focus on what we know."

She flattened the hand-drawn map on which she'd noted the times and places they'd spotted Ashley. "She starts out here." She poked the map at the first *A* at 6:03:25 on the library's front steps. "Then she's here and here." She moved her finger to the *A* still on the steps at 6:11:02 and on to the one in the middle of Dartmouth Street at 6:16:23.

Diana went on, tracing all eleven points in time and space. "So, the last time we see her for sure is at 6:23:05," she said. "Three minutes later, poof."

"People don't just disappear."

"Right. So, what happened between 6:23 and 6:26? With six video cams going, one of them must have picked up something." As she said that, Diana felt the prickle of excitement. There had to be clues buried somewhere in all that footage. There just had to be.

Diana used all of the monitors to bring up videos from all six cams. She froze each at 6:23:05, the time of the last Ashley sighting. Each of the cameras had a different view, and in one of them, Ashley was standing in the square, facing away from the camera, her cell phone raised.

Diana started the videos, synchronized to the same time and all running at the same slow speed. Ashley stood in a frozen salute. The camera cut away from her to show a woman pushing a double stroller, stopping to look. Simultaneously, another camera was capturing a cop looking baffled. Another focused on Super Dummy appearing in the hotel window. It started its descent. In the panoramic video shot from the office window, almost every pedestrian in Copley Square was frozen, attentions riveted as Super Dummy flew overhead.

"There!" Diana pointed to a pair of figures walking out of the square, the only two in motion. She froze the video.

From overhead, it was impossible to see their faces, and the man's body shielded the other figure from view. It was hard to make out details, but it looked like a man wearing a baseball cap with his arm around someone smaller.

Diana started the video again in slow motion and they watched as the couple neared the sidewalk.

"Noooo!" Diana howled when the camera cut away for a close-up of the dummy, impaled on the needle-nose spire of the information kiosk. The glitch was the perfect cover.

It felt like forever until the dummy was tugged free and at last there was finally another long shot across Copley Square.

But by then, the man and his companion were gone. Time stamp: 6:26:15.

"Where the hell did they go?" Pam whispered.

By then it was afternoon and Eddie needed the video editing suite back. After extracting a promise that Diana and Pam wouldn't make copies or post clips from the videos, he gave them a DVD with the footage from all six cameras. If only Diana could combine all the snippets of information into a single stream and project Ashley's likely trajectory out of there.

But how? The answer didn't come to her until she was rushing to keep up with Pam's wheelchair as it sped back across the plaza's brickwork to her van. First she had to find a version of Copley Square in OtherWorld that was rendered approximately to scale.

As soon as they got back to Pam's apartment, Diana logged onto OtherWorld and began to look for a reasonably accurate version of that area of downtown Boston. Meanwhile Pam loaded the digital video files from the improv event onto her server.

Diana entered the coordinates of a virtual Copley Square that had drawn the most visitors and had the fewest complaints about griefers. The new location rezzed around Nadia. Diana angled the view—it included all the landmarks she needed, from Trinity Church to the Copley Plaza Hotel to the Boston Public Library. Even the subway station just past the library on Boylston was there. But was it to scale?

She angled the view up, pulling higher and higher until she could see everything on a single screen. From that far away the image was reduced to a schematic. Nadia was the single yellow dot on a rectangle that was Copley Square.

Diana compared the shape and size of the virtual square to a Google map of the actual area. They were close enough for what she needed.

Pam rolled her wheelchair over and stopped beside Diana, holding the little handwritten map that Diana had put together of Ashley sightings.

"Okay. Move Nadia here"—Pam pointed to a spot in the virtual Copley Square that was about a hundred feet in front of the center entrance to Trinity Church where Ashley had stood, cell phone raised—"and set the time to 6:21:15."

Diana tapped at the arrow keys. She watched the yellow dot move to the location. Then she froze the image and set the clock to 6:21:15. She and Pam continued, placing Nadia in each of the places Ashley had spotted in the Virtual Copley Square. When they were done, Diana had marked five locations and five times.

"Okay, let's see what we've got," she said. "Connect the dots."

Diana ran the clock, and Nadia's yellow dot moved from spot to spot as the seconds ticked. First the yellow dot appeared in the middle of Copley. A dashed line crept out to what would have been about fifty feet away. The second dot appeared, followed by another dashed line that continued as far as the sidewalk where a third dot appeared. At 6:25:05 the line stopped.

"And less than a minute later, she's vanished," Pam said.

"Let's project her trajectory. How far could she have gotten?" Diana drew a circle around the final point on the sidewalk where they'd seen Ashley. "And if she started to run—" She drew a second wider circle around the first. She groaned when she saw how much territory that took in. Ashley could have gotten as far as the entrance to the T, or gone into the library.

"Let's assume for the moment that she didn't tear ass out of there," Pam said. "And she sure as hell didn't levitate. So her most likely path would have been to continue this way . . ." She traced her finger across what would have been sidewalk to the curb. She tapped the spot. "So what was going on over here?"

On her laptop screen, she brought up the video footage that had been taken from the office window. She froze it on a 6:21 view and pointed to the row of vehicles pulled up at the curb near that exact spot. There were two light-colored vans, one behind the other, then a police cruiser, behind that a light-colored compact car, and behind that a much larger black sedan.

She fast-forwarded to 6:26, when Ashley vanished. The same vehicles were still parked there.

"Can you come in closer on that black one," Diana said.

"You're not going to try and read those plates," Pam said as she zoomed in. "There's no technology in the world that will do that."

"I know, I know. But"—Diana pointed to the black sedan—"back up, just a little bit. Good, good. Now zoom in even closer right here and run it very slow."

Images blurred as Pam ran the video back, then forward at about half speed. Two figures crept toward the black car. The rear door opened. One person got in and the other crouched by the open door. Because of the camera angle and distance, it was impossible to make out much detail.

"We're just assuming your sister is in the backseat," Pam said. "But you really can't see squat."

"What about that?" Diana said, pointing to a misshapen object lying on the sidewalk by the open car door.

Pam squinted at it, then rolled her eyes at Diana. "A shadow? A puddle?"

"It's my hat. I know it is."

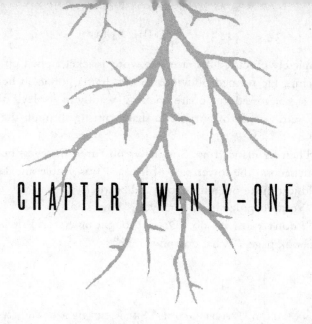

CHAPTER TWENTY-ONE

THE PRINTER UNDER THE TABLE CHURNED AS, DOT BY DOT, THE freeze-frame image of the person crouched beside the black car took shape. When it was finally finished, Diana pulled the image off and stared at the dark blur on the ground.

"I can't believe she'd get into a car with someone she didn't know." Diana pinned the printout to the bulletin board over Pam's desk and stood back. "Well, whoever he is, he didn't come out of nowhere. Where was he before this?"

Pam queued up videos from the four camcorders that had focused on crowd reaction and tiled the windows across her laptop screen. She ran them simultaneously at half speed, starting moments before Ashley disappeared.

The cameras moved through the crowd, showing individuals as they watched Superman's flight. But Diana was focusing past them.

"There!" she and Pam said simultaneously, spotting a figure in the background, on the move. The brim of a baseball cap completely obscured his face. He wore a jacket zipped up over his chin. He seemed oblivious to the drama going on behind him as he crossed the square, moving steadily in Ashley's direction with a sense of purpose, a shark cutting through the still crowd.

Then he glanced up. Sunglasses obscured his eyes, but for a split second the lower part of his face was visible and Diana could just make out a mustache and beard.

"You recognize him, don't you?" Pam said.

"I don't know if I do." Diana brought up Aaron Pritchard's Facebook page. "What do you think?"

DIANA CALLED OFFICER GRUDER. SHE PACED UP AND BACK AS SHE explained that she'd been combing through the Spontaneous Combustion video. She paused long enough to e-mail him stills—one of the man crouched alongside the black car and the other of the man moving through the crowd toward Ashley—and then went back to pacing as she waited while he opened the files.

"And you think your sister is inside that car, and this man—"

"His name is Aaron Pritchard. And he's—"

"You recognize him from these?" he said, his voice without affect.

Diana stared at the pictures. Neither one of them showed enough detail to identify anyone. "He told me he was there. And she'd just dumped him, humiliated him in a bar full of patrons. He grabbed her, then he tried to make it look like she'd come back to her apartment. Did you get the surveillance video from my sister's apartment building? Did you look at it? Did you—"

"I examined the surveillance video," Gruder said.

Diana stopped pacing.

"I can tell you this," he went on. "Your sister drove back to her apartment on Monday and she left about twenty minutes later, right before I got there."

Diana dropped into a chair, and the room receded around her. "You're sure?"

"We matched the plate numbers."

"And you saw her coming into the building and leaving?" she asked.

He didn't say anything for a moment. "Not exactly."

"What do you mean, not exactly?"

"There's a gap."

Diana stood up. "A what?"

Gruder cleared his throat. "A gap in the footage. A power surge knocked it off-line for about thirty minutes. But we see her car pulling in. And when the power comes back, the car is gone."

"How convenient," Diana said. "Do you have any idea how easy it is to alter surveillance video?"

"The outage affected several buildings in that area," he added.

"So all you really know is her car came back. But that doesn't mean she was in it."

"What else could it mean? And it's not just that. Her mail was picked up. She changed clothes. There's no evidence of a crime."

"And that's it? You're done?"

He didn't say anything.

"Well, I'm not." She hung up the phone.

Pam rolled over to the bookshelves and grabbed a bottle and two glasses. She steadied the bottle of bourbon between her legs, pulled out the cork, and poured an inch of rich brown liquid into one of the glasses. She handed it to Diana.

Diana knocked back the contents. It seared her throat, cauterizing a residue of self-pity.

Pam refilled Diana's glass and then filled her own. She sipped thoughtfully as Diana told her what she'd learned from Officer Gruder.

"So you're thinking that this man, whoever he was, has Ashley's car, drove it over to her apartment, and tried to make it look as if she came home?"

"I know it sounds improbable. But at least that would account for all the facts, and it explains why she hasn't called me or returned a single one of my goddamned messages." Diana choked up and her eyes misted over.

Pam laid a hand on Diana's arm. "We should eat something. Okay if I order a pizza? Salad too? Oil-and-vinegar dressing on the side? After dinner, we'll go over everything, step-by-step, one more time."

Diana nodded, swallowing the hard lump in her throat.

"Can you shut everything down for me?" Pam said, shifting her laptop to the table. She put the liquor bottle on the coffee table and rolled off toward the kitchen end of the loft.

Diana drank the bourbon in her glass and shuddered. One by one, she closed the video windows. There was nothing more to see.

"Pizza delivery in fifteen minutes," Pam called out.

Diana corked the bottle. Two shots on an empty stomach and she was already feeling it.

Her OtherWorld session remained open. Nadia still stood frozen in the middle of Copley Square. Steady as a rock. Diana flinched when a message popped up.

GROB: Hey? U OK? How's your sister?

She had no idea how to answer those two simple questions. Knowing it was pointless, she found her cell phone in her jacket pocket and, once again, called Ashley. By now she had her on speed dial.

The line rang once. Twice. Another message popped up in OtherWorld.

GROB: Let me know if I can help.

The phone stopped ringing in the middle of the third ring. There was silence on the line. Had she lost the signal? She took the phone from her ear and looked at the screen. Still connected.

Pam rolled over toward her, giving her a questioning look. She mouthed, "Your sister?"

Diana nodded and put the phone back to her ear and her hand over her other ear to block out sounds around her. For a moment, she thought she heard something—or was that just static? Then: "Mmmm. I . . ."

"Ashley?" Diana focused on the voice on the other end.

"He . . . uh . . ." Then: "Ooof." And labored breathing. "Shit."

"*Ashley!* Are you there? Are you okay?"

"This better be 'portant," Ashley said. She said something else, slurred and indecipherable. Then: "Whosis?"

"It's Diana," Diana practically shouted into the mouthpiece as relief coursed through her. "Your sister. Remember me? Where are you?"

No answer.

"Ashley?" Diana shouted. "Can you hear me?"

"Shhhhh."

"Do you know where you are?"

"Looks like . . ." There was a grunt, like Ashley was trying to lift her head and look around. ". . . home."

"Can you wiggle your fingers?" Diana asked.

She heard a *tap-tap,* like Ashley was tapping on the mouthpiece of the phone with a fingernail.

"I'll take that for a yes. Do you know how long you've been there?"

"So freakin' tired," Ashley said.

"How *long* have you been there?"

"Mmmm . . . Home."

"Right. You're in your apartment."

"Bing!"

"Do you know what day it is?"

"Bzzzz." Then a longish pause. Finally, a bunch of syllables that sounded like *"Saturday."*

"Honey, it's Tuesday."

"No. Uh-uh." Ashley cleared her throat. "No way in hell." Her voice was back. "Can't be. What happened?"

"You met that guy Aaron at a bar? You remember breaking up with him?"

"I did? I did."

"Yeah, you did, sweetie. Then you went to an improv event. Remember Superman streaking across the sky over Copley Square?" Diana wiped away a tear. She was so relieved.

"And Batman. 'N Lone Ranger."

"And probably Tinker Bell." Diana laughed, feeling giddy.

Ashley started to laugh too. "Ow, that hurts."

"And what happened after that?" Diana said. "That was four days ago."

"I . . ." Dead silence.

"Ash?"

A hiccup and a sniffle. Ashley was crying.

"I'm on my way over there right now. I'll be there as soon as I can. Twenty minutes, max. Do—not—go—anywhere. You got that?"

Ashley didn't respond.

"You're going to wait until I get there, right?"

Finally Ashley mumbled something and Diana disconnected the call.

Pam rolled over. Piled in her lap were Diana's jacket, her laptop, backpack, and the driftwood walking stick. "Let me know what happens. Here's my phone number." She indicated a Post-it note that she'd stuck to the laptop case. "Or just show up. Anytime. Day or night. And if there's anything I can do . . ."

"Thanks. I'll probably take you up on that."

"And I hope you don't mind, but I checked your computer. Made sure that there weren't more programs broadcasting your whereabouts. I found a key logger and trashed it too."

Key logger? That meant someone had been spying on her, capturing her every keystroke.

"There might be more, but I ran out of time. Someone's really been messing with you."

"Tell me about it," Diana said. She kissed Pam on the cheek, grabbed her things, and flew out of the apartment.

She's back. She's back. She's back. Diana repeated the words, trying to make herself believe it as she sprinted down the stairs, not bothering to wait for the elevator. She passed the pizza deliveryman on the way in. Opened the Hummer with the remote and jumped in. Started it up with a roar and peeled out onto the street.

Unleashed by bourbon and Xanax, Diana did everything she detested in other drivers. Tailgated and flashed her lights at cars poking along in front of her. Passed on the right. Revved her engine and leaned on the horn when the car in front of her failed to accelerate the instant a light turned green. Barreled through lights that had just turned red. Earned herself more than a few emphatic honks and expressive fingers.

Hey, bad behavior was rewarded—despite afternoon rush-hour traffic, she made what would normally have been a thirty-minute trip from the South End to the Wharf View apartments in under twenty.

Diana screeched to a halt in a visitors' space in front of Ashley's apartment building and got out of the Hummer. Between the old-fashioned street lamps, the high-beam spotlights mounted on the building, and a huge yellow moon that seemed to be rising right out of the Neponset River, the parking lot felt lit up like a stage set.

Parked right next to her was Ashley's Mini Cooper. The side window had been left open. Diana peered in. Ashley was damned lucky that no one else had noticed the huge white purse, sitting there on the backseat in broad view, asking to be appropriated. Diana reached in and grabbed it before hurrying into the building.

The wait for the elevator seemed longer than the drive over. On the ride up, Diana shifted Ashley's purse to her other shoulder. What was she carrying around in there? Cinder blocks? She peered inside. A copy of *Vogue* accounted for some of the weight. Also a quart-size container of hand sanitizer.

The elevator door opened and Diana trotted up the hall. She was about to knock on the apartment door when she realized that it was ajar.

CHAPTER TWENTY-TWO

APARTMENT DOOR LEFT OPEN? PURSE LEFT ON THE BACKSEAT OF her car? Diana burst into the apartment. A quick glance told her Ashley wasn't in the living room or kitchen.

She closed the door and attached the chain lock. Ran to the closed bedroom door and pushed it open. Inside, it was dark and smelled like steamed gym socks. She could just make out the bedcovers mounded over what looked like a body.

"Ashley?" she said, creeping closer.

Ashley's blond hair was all that was visible. Her BlackBerry was on the floor by the bed, still on, apparently where she'd dropped it. A pile of clothes was on the floor.

Thank God! Diana fell to her knees by the bed, overcome with relief. She'd been girding herself for another impossible loss.

She turned on the bedside lamp. Ashley winced. She was pale, with dark circles under her eyes. Diana slid her hand under the covers and pulled out Ashley's arm. She pressed her fingers against Ashley's wrist. The pulse was strong and steady.

"Ouch!" Ashley pulled her hand away.

"Sorry, hon," Diana said.

Ashley opened one eye. Then the other. She shrieked.

"What?" Diana said.

Ashley just pointed at Diana's head. It took a moment for Diana to realize what she was going on about.

"So? I'm a blonde."

"I guess. You cut it yourself?" Ashley's eyes widened farther still. "You're here? How . . . ?"

"Don't you remember? We talked on the phone. Fifteen minutes ago. I said I'd come over."

"You drove?"

"I can, you know," Diana said. "I even have a driver's license."

"Sure you do."

Diana ignored the sarcasm. "Are you okay? I've been so worried."

"My head." Ashley touched her forehead and grimaced. "Jesus, this feels like the mother of all hangovers."

The old Superman theme started playing.

"What the hell is that?" Ashley asked.

"It's a bird, it's a plane . . ." Diana said, offering Ashley her BlackBerry. "It's your phone."

Slowly, painfully Ashley raised herself on one elbow and stared at the cell phone, which was lighting up neon blue.

"Don't you remember?" Diana raised the cell phone the way the improv participants had saluted the hotel. "Copley Square?" She looked at the readout. "Lucky you. It's Mom."

"Don't answer it. I'll call her Monday."

"Ashley, that's next week. It's Tuesday already."

Deep furrows formed in Ashley's forehead as her eyebrows came together.

The phone rang again. Diana answered. "Hi, Ma."

"Diana?" A pause. "Did I call you? Because if I did, I didn't mean to."

"You called Ashley. I answered the phone. She's"—Ashley shook her head a little too vigorously and winced—"not feeling too well. She's hungover." Ashley rolled her eyes. "Or something."

"Or something?"

"She's fine. Really. She'll call you back, okay? Tomorrow?"

After a few more back-and-forths, Diana managed to get her mother off the phone. By then, Ashley was sitting up in bed.

"It's Tuesday?" she said. "How could that be? Where have I been?" Diana heard the distinct note of panic in her sister's voice.

She took Ashley's hand. It felt cool and dry. "I don't know. I've been trying to reach you. I was here yesterday and it looked as if you'd come back. Do you remember coming back to your apartment? Picking up your mail? Changing your clothes?"

Ashley shook her head and raised her hand to wipe away a tear that trickled down her cheek.

"Hey, don't cry." That's when Diana noticed the mottled bruise on the back of Ashley's hand. "What's this?"

"How'd I get that?" Ashley asked.

Diana ran her fingers gently over the tender spot, right where veins branched. "I don't know."

"I . . . I don't know either." Ashley shook her head and winced again.

Diana stood. She handed Ashley her purse. "I found this in the backseat of your car. You parked in one of the visitor spots in front of the building."

"I didn't. I never park there."

"Well, someone parked your car there." She set the purse

in Ashley's lap. Ashley just stared at it. "You want to check that everything's still there?"

Ashley pushed herself up and rummaged through the bag. Found her wallet and checked the billfold. Sifted through the magazines and file folders. She drew out an oversize mailing envelope.

Ashley looked baffled. She tore open the seal and pulled out some papers. The top page was a form labeled IN-PATIENT RELEASE.

"Can I see that?" Diana said. She recognized the mother-and-child logo of Neponset Hospital. It had been one of Gamelan's earliest clients.

Ashley handed her the sheaf of papers. The form on top began:

Patient Name: Ashley Highsmith

Ashley had been released from the hospital in this condition? What had the doctors been thinking? And why hadn't someone called her? She was Ashley's emergency contact.

Diana scanned the rest of the page. "According to this, you were checked in to the hospital on Friday night after eleven. Checked out yesterday morning."

Ashley's eyes widened. "Was I sick?" She rummaged in her purse again and came up with a compact. She opened it and looked in the mirror. "Am I sick?"

"You look fine," Diana said, even though Ashley looked far from it.

She examined the rest of the hospital documents, trying to penetrate the thicket of charges. "They gave you blood tests. A CT scan. Echocardiogram. Intravenous therapy."

Ashley stroked the bruise on the back of her hand. "So this—maybe it's from an IV?"

"Here's a doctor's card. You can probably call and find out." Diana showed her a business card stapled to one of the sheets of paper. "And look, this is an FAQ on trypanosomiasis."

"What?" Ashley's hand flew to her throat.

Diana read down. "It's a kind of sleeping sickness."

"Sleeping sickness? But how . . . ? Isn't that something people get in Africa?"

"You weren't in Africa."

"Duh." Ashley felt under her chin, like she was looking for swollen lymph nodes. Then she let her head fall back onto the pillow. "I may look okay but I feel terrible. Like my head is packed with wet wool."

"Apparently you had the nonlethal variety. This says you might be somewhat disoriented for a few days. Your sleep can be disrupted for up to two weeks. It's important not to get dehydrated." Diana went into the bathroom, filled a glass with water, and brought it back. She handed Ashley the glass. "How on earth did you manage to contract sleeping sickness?"

Ashley sat up and took a sip. "How? Well—" She set the glass down and sat up taller. "Maybe from a hotel guest? I ran a wedding at the hotel. Last weekend. The bride was from Nigeria or South Africa, I can't remember which. Or . . . on the plane? I read about how airplanes harbor all kinds of lethal stowaways. Rats with bubonic plague." That thought seemed to perk her up considerably. "Disease-infected spiders. All it takes is one, hiding in one of those blankets."

"There are no more blankets."

"There are in business class." Ashley finished off the water.

"Ashley, what's the last thing you remember?"

Ashley sank back against the pillows and squeezed her eyes shut. "I remember . . ." She opened her eyes. "Dumping Aaron." She smiled.

"He called to apologize."

The smile grew broader. "He did?"

"Do you remember Superman?"

Ashley's brow wrinkled. "Coming out of the hotel window. And a man came up to me."

"Ashley, this is important. Did you recognize him?"

Ashley looked confused. "His face was kind of covered."

"Do you think it could have been Aaron?"

"Aaron?" Ashley considered it. "No way. I'd have recognized him. This man, he acted like we were old friends. He thought I was—" She broke off the thought, her jaw dropping as realization kicked in. "He called me Nadia."

"Of course. You were registered as my avatar. Ashley, do you have any idea what happened next? I've looked at videos taken during the improv event and it looks as if you walked off with that guy who approached you. You might have gotten into a car with him."

"All I remember is being downtown. Superman's in the air. That guy's got his arm around me, which is kind of freaking me out. Then . . ." Ashley touched her upper arm. "Then . . . then nothing. It's like the movie just stops. Except for nightmares."

"What kind of nightmares?"

Ashley shuddered. "A long worm tracking slime up my arm. Headless talking Ken dolls."

"So you don't remember being in the hospital? Getting a CT scan? Getting released this morning? Driving your car back?"

"None of it." Ashley picked up the sheaf of hospital forms and shook them at Diana. "Four days, I was out of it. Sleeping sickness! Go figure."

A half page of paper fluttered to the bed. Diana picked it up. "You've got a script for Ambien here."

"More sleep. Just what I need." Ashley put her hand to her chest. Then her stomach. "Know what? I think I'm hungry. Starving, in fact. And what is that smell?" She sniffed her own armpit and made a face. "You think I can take a shower?"

"You feel up to it?"

Ashley swung her legs out of bed and Diana helped her stand.

"Whoa," Ashley said, holding on to Diana's shoulder.

"Want me to go in with you?"

Ashley gave her a horrified look. "Just give me a minute."

Ashley steadied herself. Finally she pushed Diana away and headed for the bathroom. Diana started after her but Ashley put up her hand. "I'm okay. Really, I'm okay." She left the room, crossed the hall, and shut the bathroom door behind her.

Diana put the hospital forms together and straightened the pile. She clipped the prescription to the top. Its letterhead read COMPASSIONATE CARE MEDICAL, P.C. with an address in Boston's Back Bay. The list of physicians included Dr. William Kennedy—the doctor whose business card they had. But the physician's signature scrawled at the bottom was not Dr. Kennedy's. Instead, it began with what looked like initial caps *P* and *D,* followed by *B* and an indecipherable wavy line with squiggles. Diana skimmed to the top of the page where the partners names were printed. The only name the signature even vaguely resembled was Pamela David-Braverman, MD, known to her friends in OtherWorld as PWNED.

CHAPTER TWENTY-THREE

WHILE ASHLEY SHOWERED, DIANA SPREAD OUT THE HOSPITAL forms on the bed. It would take more than paperwork to convince her that Ashley had spent four days in a hospital recovering from an exotic disease.

She pulled out the doctor's business card and dialed his number. The call was picked up without even a single ring.

"Compassionate Care Medical Associates," said a woman's recorded voice. "Our hours are weekdays from nine A.M. to five P.M. If this is an emergency . . ." Diana left a message, pretending to be Ashley and asking for the doctor to call. She left her cell-phone number and hung up.

She set the card aside, picked up the prescription form, and examined it. It was dated Monday, yesterday, probably written in the morning when Ashley had been supposedly released from the Neponset Hospital. Later in the day, Pam had been running her forum, its banner FIGHT BACK. LIES KILL. There was more than a little irony to that.

"The signature on the form wasn't all that legible, but the initials *P* and *B* were clear. She Googled Pamela David-Braverman, MD. Back came thousands of hits. She'd been an activist for handicap rights at NYU Medical School. There were news articles about demonstrations and petitions she'd organized to get the teaching hospital to adapt equipment to the needs of physically handicapped physicians. Her nickname had been "Hell on Wheels."

Diana found plenty of links between Pam and Cambridge City Hospital. Lots of mentions of her in connection with the Spaulding Rehab Center and the Fund for Science, Honesty, and Morality. She also found the home page for Compassionate Care Medical, P.C., with Pam's name listed along with Dr. William Kennedy and three other physicians.

If Diana had saved the access codes to Neponset's systems, she could easily have checked whether Pam was one of their attending physicians. But it was standard practice, part of Gamelan's contract with every client, to obliterate from their systems every bit of information and every copied file when a project ended. Overwriting the data from a completed project was time-consuming, but it was a ritual Diana had diligently followed from day one.

GROB had offered to help. Would his "special access" get her answers?

The pipes thunked as the shower turned off. It would be at least another fifteen minutes of blow-drying her hair and getting dressed before Ashley emerged. Diana opened a session in OtherWorld and activated Nadia. While she waited for her home office to rez, she checked to see if GROB was in-world.

He was.

She hesitated for a moment. She'd never invited another avatar, not even Jake's, to her virtual office. A few typed numbers and a click later, she'd sent GROB its coordinates.

She didn't have to wait long before a chime sounded. She clicked yes, he could come in, and GROB materialized. He took off his mirrored sunglasses to reveal dark, deep-set eyes. He did a 360 as the person controlling him checked out her office. The "room" felt much smaller with him and his broad-brimmed Stetson in it.

"Thanks for coming so quickly," she said.

"I'm afraid to ask." She recognized his synthesized voice. "Your sister? Is she okay?"

From the bathroom, over the hair dryer's buzz, Diana could hear Ashley singing, "I will survive!" and doing a shockingly decent Gloria Gaynor imitation.

"I found her. She's turned up, back in her apartment, incoherent at first. She's literally lost four days of her life. She had some paperwork that shows she was at Neponset Hospital for four days with trypanosomiasis. That's sleeping sickness."

GROB whistled. "Sleeping sickness?"

"Right. How likely is that? And the paperwork she came back with? It feels wrong. Like there's a hodgepodge of tests that I doubt they'd have ordered. Of course I'm no doctor, but you offered to help and I'm hoping you can check it out."

"Sure. Neponset Hospital?"

"I want to know. When she was admitted. When she was released. The names of the doctors who treated her. Anything that can be verified."

"Do you have the release form?"

"Right here."

"Good. That makes it easy. There should be a case number somewhere on the top of the first page. Can you find it?"

Diana read it off to him.

"I'll do a little digging and get back to you as soon as I can."

"Are we talking minutes? Hours?"

"Depends. But if I run into a problem I'll let you know." GROB held out his hand to Nadia.

She wanted to make her avatar take it but she stopped herself. Touching meant linking, and she couldn't risk losing control of Nadia. She wasn't taking any more chances.

"Thanks," she said.

His hand dropped to his side. "Friend?" The empty voice balloon over GROB's head seemed to evaporate slowly.

"Friend," she said. *Please, be a true friend.*

GROB hesitated a moment more, then vanished.

It would be a while before GROB got back to her. Anxious and edgy, Diana listened for reassuring sounds of life from the bathroom while she checked through the stack of messages from Jake. In one dated yesterday, Monday afternoon, after Diana had fled her apartment, he said he'd submitted the proposal to Vault Security and left her a copy of it in their shared e-mail. A few hours after that, he sent her an update saying that Vault had received the proposal. Then another update, later that evening: initial reactions were positive but the company's executives had a few follow-up questions. Was she available the next morning for a call?

The next two messages, sent late into the night on Monday, had wanted to know if she'd received the previous messages. Then a message sent this Tuesday morning. "Never mind" was in the subject line. He'd been able to address their concerns.

A final message had been sent an hour ago.

RE: FOUND VOLGANET

First Jake confirmed what she already suspected. Volganet was not in Eastern Europe. Their server's time clock had been altered to make it look as if they were. He'd used satellite tracking, triangulating on their signal, and determined that they were actually located not far from Boston.

His message went on:

F*ING tapeworms. Parasitic scum.

Two years ago, the three of them would have deserved precisely those sobriquets.

His message continued:

You were right. This is not the first time we've been hit by them. They've been onto us for weeks. Maybe more. I shut them out. Gave them a taste of their own. My bad.

Inside for weeks? How many? Had the creeps behind Volganet been targeting their clients? Were they responsible for infiltrating her security systems too? Jake said he'd shut them out, but was it really safe for her to go home? Was it any safer to go back to Pam's? She looked around Ashley's apartment and shivered. Was it safe anywhere?

Ten minutes later, a chime sounded, and she let GROB back into her virtual office.

"Your sister definitely was at Neponset Hospital." The electronic voice pronounced it Nep-on-set, like it was three words. "Admitted last Friday, released yesterday morning. You must be the Diana that your sister lists as next of kin."

Diana tried to catch her breath. He probably had her home address now too.

GROB went on. "There were two physicians connected to her case: Dr. William Kennedy." Diana didn't bother to copy the phone number he gave her. It was the same one that was on Dr. Kennedy's business card.

In the bathroom, the hair dryer switched off.

GROB continued, "And Dr. Pamela Braverman. Same number."

Diana winced.

"Diana, you can talk to one of her doctors," GROB said. "But I wouldn't advise you do that until you hear the whole story."

"What whole story?"

"I can't tell you . . . not here."

"Why not?"

Ashley emerged from the bathroom dressed in a white terrycloth bathrobe.

"Hang on," Diana said to GROB. She muted the sound and lowered her laptop screen.

Ashley sank down on the edge of the bed, her brush pulled halfway through her long hair. She returned Diana's gaze. "What? Have I got soap on my face?"

Diana reached over and wiped an imaginary soap bubble from her sister's forehead, noting as she did so that Ashley didn't feel feverish. "You still hungry?"

Ashley eyed the folded over laptop screen, then narrowed her eyes at Diana. "It's that GROB, isn't it?"

"I thought you couldn't remember anything."

"You think I don't notice things, but I do."

"I like your hair that color," Diana said. "Nice highlights."

"Nice try. I'll be in the kitchen when you decide to get real." Ashley heaved herself to her feet. She left behind a swirl of jasmine and ginger.

Diana raised the laptop screen again. GROB was still there. She unmuted the sound. "Why the hell can't you tell me now?"

"Because this Wi-Fi connection might not be secure. What

I can tell you is . . . that diagnosis? It's bogus. And there's more. I'm not even sure I understand everything I found out."

The room went fuzzy as Diana's throat constricted. She tried to swallow.

"Meet me," he said.

"When? Where? And how will I know who you are?"

But before she had an answer, GROB had vanished.

"How do you make rice?" Ashley called out to her from the kitchen.

A moment later, a text box appeared. It contained the words:

I'LL KNOW YOU. NOON TOMORROW.

Beside that were two numbers—a pair of real-world GPS coordinates.

Ashley cleared her throat. "Diana?"

Diana looked up and saw Ashley staring at her from the doorway and holding a glass measuring cup.

"Okay, now I know someone died," Ashley said.

"Don't be ridiculous."

"Are you going to tell me what's wrong?"

"Nothing is wrong."

"Now you're being ridiculous."

The last thing Diana wanted was for Ashley to worry, not until Diana knew what they should be worried about.

"Okay, okay. You're right. It's GROB. He wants me to meet him."

Ashley's face broke into a grin. "That's great. Oh, honey, that's really wonderful. Are you going?"

Diana forced a smile. "I'm going to try."

"When?"

"Tomorrow."

"Where?"

"I'm not sure." Diana brought up a map and entered the coordinates. "Somewhere in New Hampshire."

Ashley's look turned somber. "Diana, it's been a long time since you were out there. Are you sure you know enough about him? I mean, he's just someone you met online. He could be anyone."

"You're a fine one to talk, Miss Match Dot-Com."

"Diana." Ashley gave her a hard look.

"Ashley . . ." Diana stuck out her tongue. "Listen, you've been wanting me to get out. I'm getting out!"

"Promise me you'll stay out in the open where there are lots of other people."

"And if I get into trouble, I'll call. Promise."

Ashley shook her head and sighed. "So, where in New Hampshire?"

Diana turned the computer so Ashley could see a little flag that was midway between Concord and Manchester at a town called Mill Village.

Ashley sat beside her. "You ever been there?"

Diana shook her head.

"Me either. But it looks like that's about a ninety-minute drive. You up for that? Alone?"

Diana zoomed in and toggled to STREET VIEW. A black-and-white photo of a street lined with typical, mid-twentieth-century New England storefronts came up. Cars were parked at meters on the street.

She rotated the view. Down the street was a brick building from the fifties with plate-glass windows, probably once a department store, and the same vintage motel. She rotated the view some more. Across the street was a broad expanse of lawn, the town green with trees and benches and a bandstand, and beyond that a neat row of Victorian houses with gingerbread trim.

"Looks like a very darling village. Très New England," Ashley said. "Want me to come with?"

Diana shot her what she hoped was a withering look. "Don't you have to work?"

"Okay, okay. Just asking." She held up the glass measuring cup. "Rice?"

"One part rice to two parts water," Diana said. "Salt and a little butter."

Ashley flashed her a thumbs-up and returned to the kitchen.

Diana toggled back to the map and street view. Mill Village was set on the banks of a tributary of the Merrimack River, just south of where it widened into what looked like a lake.

She could hear GROB's synthesized voice in her head: . . . *that diagnosis? It's bogus.*

CHAPTER TWENTY-FOUR

T HAT NIGHT, DIANA TRIED TO FALL ASLEEP ON ASHLEY'S PULLOUT
couch. What could GROB have to tell her? That Ashley
hadn't been sick at all? Or that she had something more serious wrong with her, like HIV/AIDS or MS? Or—and now
Diana knew she was being paranoid—that she'd been exposed
to some highly contagious viral infection or deadly toxin that
would panic the public. And what did Pam, aka PWNED, have
to do with all of this? Diana's mind churned the possibilities.

She took a pill and finally fell asleep. But an hour later she
was awake again, bathed in anxiety. She'd been dreaming that
she had to pack her clothes and meet Ashley at the airport, only
she couldn't find her suitcases, then she couldn't find Ashley's
car. She fell back to sleep, only to wake up terrified by the kind
of mountain-climbing nightmare she hadn't had for months.

The next morning she felt more exhausted than she had
when she'd gone to bed. Before Ashley left for work, she insisted that Diana take her GPS tracker, loaded with the coordi-

nates of her destination. Ashley's parting shot had been "I can't get used to that hair," followed by "Call me. Because I'm calling the police if I don't hear from you by five o'clock—"

"Eight," Diana said.

"Six," Ashley said. "And not a minute longer. And if the police don't get on the stick fast enough, I'm coming up there to find you myself."

"YOU HAVE REACHED YOUR DESTINATION," ANNOUNCED THE RO-botic, British-accented female voice on Ashley's GPS. The screen told her it was 11:50 A.M. She was ten minutes early. The drive had been easy, any remaining rush-hour traffic having dissipated by midmorning. The sky had gone from clear to overcast.

WELCOME TO MILL VILLAGE announced a cheery sign. Diana was stopped in traffic bunched up at the one stoplight in the center of town. The borders of the Hummer's broad windshield framed her surroundings. There was the town green with storefronts surrounding it. The gazebo. The center of Mill Village was exactly like the town green in OtherWorld, where GROB had transported her after they'd been attacked on the beach.

She checked her rear- and sideview mirrors. GROB had to be here, somewhere. In a parked car. Inside one of the businesses lined up along the street. Walking on the town green. Was he dressed like his avatar, as she was like hers?

An elderly couple strolled by, the woman in a summery straw hat and white parka and the man in starched tan trousers and windbreaker. They stopped in front of Tweets, a pet store, and looked in at a person-size birdcage in which a bright green parrot hopped about. They both carried umbrellas, and Diana smiled to herself, imagining the bird checking them out: a pair of winter birds that had returned prematurely to New England.

A man strode down the sidewalk toward her, a knitted cap pulled down over his forehead and a plaid muffler around his face. GROB? Diana gripped the steering wheel and her heart lurched. She ducked down as he hurried past without even glancing at the Hummer. She watched, breathless, as he ducked into what looked like a luncheonette.

Diana sat forward and unstuck her T-shirt from her sweat-slicked back. She tried to swallow. She'd taken a pill before leaving Ashley's apartment. She didn't want to think about what she'd be feeling if she hadn't.

A car behind her tooted. The light had changed.

Diana continued slowly up the block, looking for a place to park. Finally she pulled into the lot of a motel. Its black sign with RITZ in bold white letters outlined in neon tubing welcomed cars to a deserted parking lot. The proprietor must have had a flare for irony because the place looked a whole lot more like the Bates Motel than the Ritz-Carlton. Diana didn't need anyone to cue the scary music.

"Turn around when possible." It took her a moment to realize that the GPS had picked that moment to put in its oar. It told her she'd overshot her destination, and that it was now 11:58.

She turned off the GPS and slipped it into her jacket pocket. Then she waited for a break in the traffic, pulled out, and drove back the way she'd come in. She found a parking spot in front of the luncheonette. Painted in yellow letters across the plate glass, it said THE SUNNY SIDE UP. As she watched, unseen hands pulled from the window a sign advertising *Full Breakfast* for $3.99 and replaced it with one advertising *Meatloaf Plate* for $6.99.

Now what? She was here, but where was GROB? He'd never find her behind the Hummer's dark tinted windows. She rolled down her window an inch. Chilly air seeped in. No matter what the calendar said, this late March felt wintry.

Across the street a woman wearing a short puffy jacket, a long skirt, and boots biked across the town green. Its empty gazebo was large enough to double as a bandstand. The structure was set, like a wedding-cake topper, on a little rise at the center of the grass with six footpaths radiating out from it. It offered a perfect vantage point, an unobstructed view of the storefronts and houses and, more important, GROB could see her.

Diana zipped her jacket and turned up its collar. In her rear-view mirror, her dark-rimmed eyes looked back at her, wide and frightened. She found the sunglasses in her jacket pocket and put them on. Ran her fingers through those blond curls. Ashley wasn't the only one who found her new hair jarring.

She pictured Nadia getting out of the Hummer. Crossing the street and walking decisively across the green, and stepping into the shadow of the gazebo. She could do it too. Diana grabbed Daniel's walking stick before opening the car door a crack. When there was a break in the traffic, she opened the door farther and stepped into the street.

Fighting the impulse to dive back into the car, she slammed the door, pressed the remote to lock it, and crossed the street. She could feel the vibrations traveling up her legs as her boot heels connected with the brick walk with each deliberate stride toward the gazebo. She climbed the steps and stood on the platform, as tall and straight as Nadia might have stood in Other-World, waiting for GROB to show himself.

She checked her watch. It was 12:05. Cars drove by. There were plenty of pedestrians, but no one was coming her way.

She sat down on a bench in the gazebo and picked up a newspaper that had been left there. She settled back and waited. Made a futile attempt to read the news.

12:11. Still no one had approached her.

A week ago she could never have contemplated doing what she was doing, sitting alone on the town green of a village that, until an hour ago, had been nothing more than a dot on the map. *To new beginnings.* That's what Daniel had said the night before their last climb.

The three of them had rented a one-room condo at the foot of the Eiger to use as their base camp. Over a dinner of spaghetti, warmed in a microwave oven, Daniel had raised a paper cup with an inch of brandy in a toast to their future.

"You guys sure you want to do this?" Diana had said, or words to that effect. "Leave behind your checkered past? No more free Hummers, you know."

Daniel had laughed, snorting brandy.

"And what will NASA do without our drawing attention to their security lapses?" Jake added.

Daniel drew a little hash mark in the air and poured another inch all around. "Here's to the time we turned that bank's Web pages upside down—"

Jake broke in, "And replaced their surveillance camera feeds."

That had been Daniel's brainstorm. He'd hacked in and replaced South Savings Bank's video surveillance feeds with a continuously looping five-minute Three Stooges clip. Before the bank could fix it, another hacker replaced the Stooges with continuous porn.

Jake and Daniel went on, passing their escapades back and forth like they were kicking a soccer ball downfield. Diana had prepared for just that moment. She pulled out a narrow scroll of paper on which she'd listed all the hacks she'd heard Jake and Daniel talk about and all the ones they'd pulled off since she joined up with them. She struck a match and offered it to Daniel. He lit the end of the paper.

"To starting over," Diana said as she dropped the burning paper into a garbage can and they watched for a few moments in silence. When just curls of ash were left, Daniel and Jake exchanged a look. They both grinned.

"This is gettin' on my noives," Daniel said.

"Shut up," Jake shot back.

Daniel poked a finger at Jake's chest. "You talking to me?"

"Nah. I'm talkin' to the fish."

It was another of their endlessly recycled Three Stooges routines, and Diana had heard it so many times that she could intone the reply at the same time as Daniel.

"Don't call me a fish!"

Daniel reached across and smacked Jake in the back of the head, and a minute later he and Jake were rolling around on the floor together like a couple of overgrown puppies.

When it was time to go, Jake had paused in the doorway, his hand up for Daniel and Diana to hold on to. "All for one!" he said. It was the start of yet another Three Stooges routine.

"One for all!" Diana said, joining her hand to theirs.

"Every man for himself!" The three of them chorused the punch line.

That had been a lifetime ago. A fat tear fell on the front of her jacket and she smeared it across the black leather.

12:25. Still, no one had approached her in the gazebo. The air turned a notch cooler, and she realized the sound she heard was light rain falling on the roof. Was there really some big secret about Ashley's medical condition? Or was it just a ploy to get Diana out there?

Diana fished the cell phone out of her pocket, turned it on, and called Ashley. The call went immediately to voice mail.

"It's me," Diana said. "I'm here and I haven't been kidnapped by the Ripper." She paused. She couldn't bear to deliver the pathetic news that she'd come all this way only to be stood up. "I should be heading home soon."

She was about to put the phone back when the message-waiting alert went off. Had to be Ashley, seeing the missed call. But when Diana went to retrieve the text message, she saw it was from a number she didn't recognize.

She nearly dropped the phone as she started to read.

Sorry. Car crapped out. Sunoco on 3A at 189. Meet me? GROB

She didn't know what to feel. Dread that there was still, at the very least, unsettling news about her sister? Relief that she hadn't placed her trust in a creep who was just out to make her look like a fool? Guilty excitement that he was waiting for her?

She pocketed the phone and used the newspaper to cover her head as she sprinted back to the car. She opened the door, tossed the walking stick into the back, climbed into the driver's seat, slammed the door shut, and jammed the key into the ignition.

"Hello, Diana." The familiar voice walloped her.

CHAPTER TWENTY-FIVE

S HIT, SHIT, SHIT!" SHE HELD ON TO THE STEERING WHEEL WITH both hands, waiting for her vision to clear, her heart to stop galloping.

She turned around. Jake was sitting in the backseat. He looked transformed since they'd last met in person, his head completely shaved, a reddish Vandyke beard and mustache on his face. If it hadn't been for the voice and the John Lennon glasses, she'd never have recognized him. He'd caught Daniel's walking stick and had it pointed at her like a javelin.

"What in the hell are you doing here?" she said, her voice shaking. It felt as if Jake had sucked the oxygen from the air in the closed car. She gasped for breath. That's when she saw the cell phone, sitting on the seat beside him.

Idiot! A pall of mortification settled over her. No wonder GROB had used a voice synthesizer. GROB was Jake.

"I'm sorry, I'm sorry." He put his hand on her shoulder. "Take it easy, please, don't freak out." In a single fluid move, he slid between the front bucket seats and into the front passenger seat.

Diana screamed and pressed herself against the door. She had to get out of there. She clawed for the handle, but before she could open the door there was a dull *thock*. Doors locking. Diana felt her blood thrumming in her ears. Her keys were no longer in the ignition.

"Take it easy, take it easy," Jake said. "I'm sorry for freaking you out."

"Let me out," she said. "Jake, please, let me out now. Whatever you have to say to me, you can say it out there." He didn't move.

"Help!" she screamed, banging at the window. "Help, help!" She screamed as loud as she could, but not a single person was near enough to hear, and the tinted glass made her invisible. She started to reach into the backseat for the walking stick.

"Stop!" Jake cupped his hand behind her head, twined his finger in her hair, and pulled it taut, immobilizing her. "Calm down. I was afraid you'd be like this."

"Ow!" she cried as he tightened his grip, and she felt the skin pulling at the corners of her eyes.

"I can explain." He brought his face close to hers and stared back at her. "Let me explain. Okay?"

Diana could smell coffee breath, aftershave, and the metallic scent of her own fear. She took a shuddering breath and managed a nod. Jake loosened his grip.

"Okay?" he said.

She nodded again. Slowly Jake let go. They sat in silence for a few moments, and Diana felt as if she were in a cage staring out at him. Her chest hurt as she took in air and exhaled.

"O-kay. Let's start over," he said. "I'm sorry I had to do it this way, but I need you to come with me. Diana, it's okay, really it is." He was talking to her like she was a child. "You can trust me."

"Trust"—Diana's voice was hoarse—"is something you earn. You trick me to get me to come here. Hide in the back-seat and then scare me half to death, and now I'm supposed to trust you?"

"I'm sorry. I had to wait in the Hummer because I wasn't sure it was you. You look . . . different from what I was expecting."

"I thought I was meeting . . . There's nothing wrong with my sister, is there?"

His silence confirmed it.

"You made me think she was deathly ill. My sister, the last person I can trust in this world. Except for you, of course. Don't you realize—?"

He returned her entreaty with a blank stare. Of course he didn't realize. Couldn't, really. Jake had never been able to fathom anyone's emotions but his own paltry array of them.

"Jake, why didn't you just ask me to meet you?"

"And you would have come?"

She thought about that. "Maybe not right away. But eventually I—"

"I couldn't wait for eventually."

"I don't understand."

"I can explain, but not here. Not now."

"Why not?"

"It's complicated. I wanted to show you this amazing place we've got set up."

"We?"

"You'll see. I promised I wouldn't tell you. But you know how you wanted to track down the hackers who've been after our clients? Well, now you're going to get your wish."

This was about Volganet? Were they part of Jake's post-

Daniel business model? Nadia set up the chumps and then Volganet fleeced them—with Jake collecting from both sides.

"So we have a silent partner?" she asked.

He gave her a narrow look, as if he was trying to glean what she knew. "I guess you could call it that." Uncertainty was something she'd rarely seen in Jake.

"And what if I don't want to go with you?"

"Diana, after what happened with your sister, I'd understand. But I think you'll change your mind, once you see everything. And if we get there and you decide you don't want to stay, I promise you can leave. Trust me."

"Trust you? I don't even know who you are anymore."

"Fair enough. But come with me and let me show you." He reached into his pocket, pulled out her keys. "Here. You can get out right now, or you can drive."

As Diana stared at the keys he offered to her, she realized that she really didn't have anywhere to go back to.

THE WIPERS SWEPT SLOWLY BACK AND FORTH, ACROSS THE WINDshield, and drizzle had turned to a steady rain by the time Diana drove past the town's final convenience store and the driveway to the last house abutting the road. Jake, who'd looked tense when she'd started the car and pulled back out into the street, had settled into his seat.

When they reached the highway entrance, he said, "Just stay with the road we're on."

The terrain was hilly and the road narrowed as it snaked through dense forest, a blur of trees surging past on either side. Jake leaned forward and peered through the windshield as the wipers stroked and cleared.

"We're almost there. Slow down," he said.

She remembered the map of this area and tried to imagine where "there" was—north, or maybe northwest of Mill Village, five or six miles. There'd been a lake or reservoir in this direction.

"Turn there," he said, pointing to a dirt road.

Diana slowed and turned onto it. It was impossible to go more than fifteen or twenty miles an hour on the rutted surface.

"It's a ways in," Jake said. "Just keep going."

In a thicket of brush and trees, Diana could make out what had once been a building foundation. The chimney and the remains of a brick wall seemed to be standing in a shroud of fog. Beyond that they passed a field and a small pond.

The car lurched and once again they were on paved road, skirting a perimeter of chain-link fencing that surrounded a multistory brick complex that looked like an old industrial mill. The first-floor windows were boarded over, but on the floors above, glass was all still intact.

The Hummer rocked in and out of potholes before Diana had to come to a halt at a sliding gate. Jake took his own cell phone from his jacket pocket, punched in a number, and a few moments later the gate clanked and slid open.

"Go ahead," he said, pointing ahead. "Not much further."

Diana hesitated.

"Change your mind?" Jake said. "Because I can get out right here and walk the rest of the way. You can turn around and go home. But if you want to know what's going on, the answer is here." He pointed straight ahead.

Diana drove the car through the gate. On the other side, she stopped and twisted around, watching through the rain-shrouded rear window at the gate sliding shut behind them. She turned and peered through the front windshield.

"We're almost there," Jake said.

Diana drove past what looked like the building's main entrance, now a padlocked door, and on around the corner. Jake opened the car window. Cold, damp air surged into the car, anchoring Diana's senses. She exhaled a puff of dragon's breath.

"Smell that?" Jake said.

Diana sniffed and noticed the air was tinged with sweetness that reminded her of an ice-cream shop.

"This was once a chocolate factory and that"—Jake indicated a massive white silo, about thirty feet in diameter and standing about eight stories tall; a metal ladder spiraled around the outside of it, ending in a small doorway two-thirds of the way up—"is where they used to store the chocolate.

"Is that cool or what?" Jake said. He rolled the window back up. "In warm weather the smell carries for miles. Kids used to say the water in the reservoir tasted like cocoa. It doesn't."

Above the hum of the car engine and the steady rain, Diana could hear water rushing. She continued driving slowly around the complex, and on the other side of the building was a body of water maybe a half mile wide, its surface dimpled like orange skin by falling rain. At the end nearest the silo, water cascaded over a dam.

"Park in there," Jake said, pointing to a covered bank of loading docks at the back of the building. The car rocked side to side as it rolled over brush that sprouted from holes in the cement approaches.

Already backed into one of the shadowy bays was a black limousine. Diana pulled in alongside it and shut down the engine.

"You want this?" Jake asked, handing her Daniel's driftwood walking stick.

She took it and got out of the car. The smell of mildew

and rotting leaves overwhelmed the chocolate. She touched the hood of the limo. It was warm, like it had been recently driven. Was that how Jake had gotten to Mill Village? One of his new partners drove him there? She wondered if this was the same limousine she'd seen cruising down her street. Was it the car that had blocked her into her driveway?

When Jake got out, he had her backpack and laptop. "I'm going to need all that?" she asked.

"Once you see the setup, you're going to want to stay."

As she slipped from between the cars, Jake fell in close behind her and ushered her up a few broad steps and onto a loading platform. A door along the back wall was propped open with a cinder block. He grabbed a flashlight that was sitting on a capped standpipe and turned on the beam. "You ready?"

Diana took a deep inhale of the chocolate-scented air.

"On belay," Jake said. It was what the belayer told a climber after he'd anchored the rope, the equivalent of *I'm ready and I've got your back.*

"Ready to climb," she said.

"Climb on." With a hand on Diana's back, Jake guided her inside.

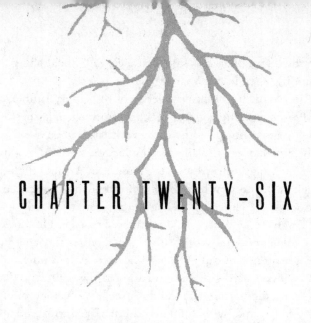

CHAPTER TWENTY-SIX

IANA'S HEART WAS BANGING IN HER CHEST AND SWEAT PRICKLED across her shoulders and neck. Fortunately, the flashlight seemed to grow brighter as she and Jake penetrated deeper into the building's basement corridor. The floor ramped upward and the rectangle of light—the doorway to the outside world— receded behind them.

Diana remembered following Jake and Daniel through a dark Swiss railway tunnel, a shortcut to the base of Waterfall Pitch that Daniel had discovered researching the climb on the Internet. As Jake's flashlight beam played across boarded-over windows and whitewashed cement walls covered with mold, she remembered how the lights of their helmet lamps had bobbed on the ground in front of them.

She'd been crazed eight hours later when she'd raced back alone through that same tunnel, desperate to find rescuers in time to save Daniel, terrified when she'd heard a rumble and seen the headlight of a fast-approaching train. Only just in time she'd found a recess in the tunnel wall. She'd clung there, screaming, as train cars roared past.

Afterward, in the heavy silence of the empty tunnel, she'd felt the first stirrings of that feeling of utter helplessness. That feeling had still been with her a week later when she'd reluctantly boarded an airplane for home. She'd sat in a window seat, clutching the armrest on the American Airlines flight from Zurich to Boston. When the flight attendant announced that the doors were closed, she'd begun to sweat.

"I want to get out," she'd whispered to Jake. He'd held her hand, told her not to worry. "No!" She'd pulled free and pressed the flight attendant call button. "I need to get out now!"

Passengers across the aisle had given them uneasy glances. When the flight attendant came to see what was wrong, Jake reassured her and by then Diana had managed to regain a semblance of calm. But when the plane started down the runway, her heart had begun to race. Her throat went so dry she couldn't swallow. As the plane had gained altitude, she'd sat there rigid, unable to breathe, imagining the engine stalling. In her mind's eye she'd seen the plane dropping like a rock, slamming into the ground, shattering like glass and spewing bodies.

"You feel out of control," Dr. Lightfoot had explained weeks later. "Anxiety is your body's natural response to danger. But now you're becoming conditioned to respond this way even when there's no real reason to be anxious."

It had been one of their first Skype video call sessions over the computer, and Dr. Lightfoot's quiet voice and compassionate expression had calmed her. Now she shuddered at the thought that someone might have been listening in, hearing everything she said and reading everything she typed into her computer.

Dr. Lightfoot had said, "You can't always stop yourself from losing it, but you're a very logical person. In some situations, recognizing what's happening and analyzing the situation may help you maintain control."

Dr. Lightfoot had been right. Logical analysis helped.

Now Diana tried to build a map in her mind of the mazelike path they'd followed as Jake guided her through the dark corridors that snaked through the basement of the old mill. As he led her through yet another passageway and up a stairway, she visualized the schematic she'd make to replicate this place in Other-World. In it, she envisioned two yellow dots—her own and Jake's—climbing the stairs. She'd feel calmer still if she knew where other yellow dots were lurking in the complex.

They emerged onto a landing. Jake held open a door to a stairwell so Diana could continue up. He kept a firm grip on her arm. After two flights, the stairs ended at an open metal door. She stepped through into a vast space, an entire floor of the mill building.

Jake closed the door and bolted it shut. Then he punched some numbers into a keypad mounted on the wall. A light on it began to blink yellow, and she heard a metallic click as the door locked. The light turned to a steady red. The door at the opposite end of the floor was closed, its keypad light red too.

She was locked in. Diana touched her jacket pockets. The GPS was in one, the cell phone in the other. Either of them would be able to pinpoint her location.

"What have you got in there?" Jake asked.

Diana reached into one of the pockets and pulled out her pills. She offered the container to Jake. He read the prescription label. "I didn't know you still needed these." He handed it back to her.

"So now you do." She shook some pills out into her palm. Jake watched as she placed one on the back of her tongue and swallowed. "Not everyone just bounces back the way you did."

"I . . ." He looked back at her, tense and tentative. Off balance. He watched as Diana poured the remaining pills back into the container and closed the lid. Then he seemed to shake himself out of it. Maybe she had some advantage—one that she had yet to understand.

Diana tried to focus on the space around her. Pipes and conduits crisscrossed overhead. The center of the floor was stacked with hulking pieces of rusted machinery along with a pile of defunct sinks and toilets.

The outside wall was a massive bank of multipaned windows. From the sound of rushing water, she wondered if she was near where she'd seen the cascade of water over the dam alongside the building. Rain pattered on the roof and rivulets dripped down the windows.

The far corner of the loft had been screened off with sheets of wallboard set into hinged wooden frames. Jake dropped her arm and Diana approached the sheltered area. She came to a halt when she saw what was beyond the wallboard screens. There was her four-poster Shaker-style bed, the one she and Daniel had bought together. It was made up with her own flowered sheets and white down comforter. In the high-ceilinged space, the bed looked like a piece of doll furniture. Next to it, on her grandmother's bedside table with its serpentine carved legs, was a vase containing a lavish burst of red roses. Jake tossed her backpack on the bed.

She stood there, stunned and shaking with mute fury. Jake had lured her out, invaded her home, and moved the furniture that he knew meant the most to her. She approached an unfinished bookcase that wasn't hers. The clothes neatly folded on its shelves were.

"Just because my things are here doesn't make it home," she said.

That's when she noticed a metal rack, standing in the corner. An empty plastic pouch hung from it, upside down. She went over to it and lifted the plastic tubing attached to the pouch. A spicy licorice smell filled her head and she remembered the tender spot on the back of Ashley's hand.

"What did you do to her?" she said.

"Nothing."

"Four days of nothing?"

"Just kept her quiet. Even you admit that's an improvement."

He could be such a smug bastard. "Why?"

"It was"—there was a pause, like Jake was carefully picking the word—"a mistake. A complication I didn't anticipate."

"She's not a complication? She's my sister."

"I know, I know. But I thought . . . I didn't realize . . . she looked just like—"

"Me." Diana finished the thought. She closed her eyes and let the realization sink in. This was her fault. She'd known that if she let her guard down, something terrible would happen. And then, without thinking, she'd dressed Ashley up as Nadia and launched her into a world that she knew was too dangerous to set foot in.

"Why can't she remember anything?" Diana asked.

"Rohypnol. It's a sedative that prevents memories from forming."

"I know what it is. You just happened to have it on you? Were you going to use that on me if I'd been there and didn't toddle along with you?"

He didn't bother to reply, and in his silence, the enormity of what he'd done sank in. "You kept my sister unconscious for four days?"

"I didn't want to hurt her, but it took me a while to figure out a way to get her home."

The hospital release forms. That explained the odd assortment of tests that never would have been run, the prescription with Pam's signature forged on it.

"So Pam doesn't have anything to do with this, does she?" Diana asked.

Jake dismissed the question with a pitying look.

Diana shivered. It had been such a practical solution, warehousing a human being until Jake had figured out how to throw her back. She scanned the walls and ceiling. Mounted in the corner she found what she was looking for, a pinpoint of red light. She waved at it.

"So where's Big Brother?" she asked.

"Exactly. That's why you're here," Jake said.

CHAPTER TWENTY-SEVEN

Jake disarmed the far door and led Diana out onto a landing. With a locked gate, blocking access to the stairway up, down the stairs was only one way out. She followed Jake down a flight, through a doorway, across a floor of the mill, and out into another stairwell. Back up a flight of stairs and down a long corridor, she lost track of where she was. She wondered if he was deliberately doubling back on himself.

Finally they reached a narrow upward-slanting corridor that ended in some crumbling concrete steps that led to a heavy steel door. She heard water rushing, and through one of the small windows set in the corridor wall, Diana could see the reservoir and dam.

"Careful." Jake indicated a plywood ramp that had been laid over uneven steps. He punched some numbers into another wall panel and the door clicked open.

"Here," he said, pulling the door wide.

The door was set in a three-foot-thick cement wall. A wave

of cool, chocolate-scented air wafted out. Diana knew immediately what lay just beyond—the silo. She hesitated, but Jake was behind her now, his hand at her back, pressing her forward and through the doorway. The chocolate smell grew stronger and turned bitter.

Diana scrabbled back as the floor—a metal grating—twanged when she stepped onto it. Below, through the openings in the grating, she could see several stories down to the bottom of the silo. Anxiety sputtered and flared in the pit of her stomach.

"It's okay," Jake said.

Cold air seeped upward and Diana folded her arms against the chill. Overhead, light trickled in through a panel of glass in the domed roof.

Jake hit a wall switch and spotlights, mounted on windowless walls of poured concrete, flooded the space with light. The interior was crammed with worktables with rolling office chairs pulled up to them and loaded with computer equipment. Cables snaked away and spaghettied on the floor, which was studded with electrical outlets.

"And talk about secure." Jake's hollow laugh seemed amplified in the space. He closed the door and keyed in a code to lock it.

She recognized the equipment on one of the tables. All of it was hers, set up in the same configuration she'd had at home, right down to the Post-its she'd stuck on the outside of a system box. He'd even brought her tulip chair. It was pulled up to the opposite side of the table.

Sitting on one of the tables was a gray cowboy hat. Diana thought of GROB. Her throat tightened. She'd connected with him, let him in, trusted him. Disappointment and humiliation burned. She still couldn't believe that GROB was Jake.

"Coffee?" Jake asked. He didn't wait for an answer, just went to the opposite wall where there was a sink and a makeshift counter, a slab of Formica-topped wood propped on sawhorse legs. On the counter sat a coffee grinder, and beside that a coffeepot, its light glowing.

Jake poured two cups, adding milk from the refrigerator under the counter. He came back and offered one to her.

Diana took the hot cup and cradled it in two hands. As she inhaled the bitter smell of chicory, her heart gave an extra beat. That was New Orleans style, just the way Daniel had liked it.

"This is what you wanted me to see?" She looked around again. It was pretty impressive. "Sure beats a semitrailer."

"By the way, we won the bid. Vault's a go."

It took a moment for her to put together what Jake was talking about. As if any of that mattered any longer.

"They want to meet with us tomorrow afternoon," Jake said. "I'll fly out early . . ." As he went on talking, he seemed so far away, like his voice was coming to her from deep in a wind tunnel. On an empty stomach—she hadn't eaten since that morning—the pill was kicking in fast.

It struck her as so odd that he still thought she'd just keep working with him. He was right about one thing—back in the early days when Gamelan was no more than a dream, Vault was just the kind of client she'd dreamed of having. But she couldn't go on engaging bigger and bigger clients, just to set them up to be victimized by the people behind Volganet.

Diana watched Jake set up her laptop on the table and plug it in.

"I'm not going to, you know," she said. He looked over at her. "I'd never, ever work with you and your new partners."

"New partners?" Jake narrowed his eyes.

"Volganet. Isn't it obvious?" she said.

"Diana, I'm sorry for everything we put you through. But it's not what you think."

"It's not? Then what is it?" She sipped coffee. The taste brought tears to her eyes. The last time she'd had coffee with chicory had been her last morning with Daniel. None of this would be happening if he were still here.

"Diana, trust me," Jake said. "I know you'll be surprised, but I hope you'll be pleased too. You'll understand, just as soon as . . ."

Diana followed his gaze up smooth silo walls that grew whiter and brighter as they rose toward the domed roof. About fifteen feet from the top was a small door, more of a hatch really. The metal spiral of stairs that she'd seen outside winding around the silo ended there. Inside there were no stairs, but there were U-shaped ends of rebars—steel bars, dark with rust—that stuck out of the concrete, at regular intervals.

A breeze stirred in the silo, and a sound, like the creaking of a rusty hinge, from overhead sent a chill down her spine. She squinted, shading her eyes as she tried to see past the bright spotlights shining down at her. Just beyond, the little doorway in the silo wall was open. A figure climbed through the opening and sat perched on the ledge.

"Hey, kiddo."

Electrical sparks shot through her. Fifteen months and two weeks—that's how long it had been since she'd heard that voice. It wasn't possible, but there he was, swinging his leg and holding on to the frame of the sill above his head. He let go with one hand and waved to her. Diana's stomach turned over and she gasped. But Daniel was relaxed, glued to his perch, as sure as an insect that gravity had no hold on him.

She heard a beeping sound, and whirled around just in time

to see the door to the silo close. The panel by the door blinked yellow, then steady red. Jake was gone.

Diana started to quake, she couldn't breathe, and that floaty feeling that briefly had buffered reality was gone. Her insides wrenched and her vision blurred. Her knees buckled under her as she reached for the tulip chair, but it slid away, overturning. Diana dropped to the floor.

As if he'd flown down, seconds later Daniel was crouched in front of her and holding her hand. It had to be a dream. She closed her eyes, willing herself to wake up. But still she felt his hand, holding hers. Smelled the tang of his sweat.

She opened her eyes. He looked older, thicker. Like Jake, his head was completely shaved.

"Oh God, is it really you?" she whispered. "How . . . ?" She could barely wrap her head around the questions that followed. How had he survived? How had he come back? How long had he been here? How could he have come back and not let her know?

When he brushed the hair back from her forehead and tucked a tendril behind her ear, it felt as if he left a trail of red-hot embers. He put his arms around her.

Daniel, Daniel, Daniel . . . He was alive.

"It's okay, it's okay . . ." He whispered the words in her ear.

And then she was crying. Deep sobs racked her body. Waves of agony overwhelmed her as the enormity of his deception washed over her. She tried to pull away but he held her tight in his arms.

Her throat closed, and she could barely get the words out. "You bastard. You lousy son of a bitch." She struggled to free herself. He'd let her believe that he was dead. Nothing could make that okay. "How could you let me . . . ?"

In a blind fury, funneling rage, confusion, and a backwash of grief, she drew back and tried to slap his face, her open hand connecting with the arm he'd raised as a shield. She tried again but he blocked the blow.

He reached out for her but she scrabbled back across the mesh floor. "Get away from me! How could you do—" When he closed in on her she pounded his chest with every ounce of strength she could muster.

He caught her wrist and held it.

She flailed, trying to free herself. "I hate you I hate you I hate you . . ."

He pulled her toward him.

"I . . . trusted . . . you." She spit the words out into his face.

He grabbed her other wrist. She tried to twist away but couldn't.

"And you . . . you . . ."

He held her until at last she went still. Time seemed to stop as he drew one of her hands to his mouth and kissed the tip of her thumb. Her index finger. She felt the warmth of his lips, his tongue.

He kissed each of the other fingers, one by one. Then her wrist, and she closed her eyes, her body vibrating with sensations she'd thought she'd never feel again.

When Diana opened her eyes, Daniel was looking directly at her. Slowly, without breaking eye contact, he kissed her, a long deep kiss. She remembered the soft fullness of his lips, the strength of his arms around her, how his very essence filled and overwhelmed her. She remembered how, in his embrace, the world outside simply ceased to exist.

CHAPTER TWENTY-EIGHT

Diana sat curled in Daniel's lap on the floor, feeling his warm breath in her ear. She reached up and touched the back of his neck, the hollow where the prickliness of his shaved head met soft skin. He let her draw her fingers across the familiar contours of his cheek, his sandpaper jaw, the puckered cleft in his chin.

"What happened?" she asked. "Why didn't you come back?"

"I can explain everything." He put his finger under her chin and gently raised her face to his. "Just give me a chance. I can explain."

"I'm listening."

A muscle worked in the corner of his jaw and he took a breath. "I don't know exactly what happened, but when I woke up in the hospital I had no idea who I was. They told me that I'd crawled out of the wilderness into a little village. I was in pretty bad shape. I'd been out there for days. I have no idea how I stayed alive or I how got there, but I did. They airlifted me to the nearest hospital. They said it was a miracle that I came through in one piece. Pretty much, anyway."

He splayed his fingers, showing her their scarred tips. "Frostbite," he said. "My toes too. The end of my nose. They were able to reconstruct it. I was very lucky. It could have been much worse.

"All I had on me was my driver's license. I was so raw and swollen, no one would have believed that the face on it was mine. Water had gotten under the laminate, and the name, address—most of the print on the license was illegible.

"I spent weeks in the hospital, months in rehab." He glanced down at her. "I started to walk again, but still I didn't know who I was or where I'd been. I kept coming back to that driver's license, holding it up to the light, examining it, trying to decipher the name. I had to guess at some of the letters. I Googled every possible permutation until finally I found my own death notice. I'd been dead for six months. It felt unreal.

"I tried to find out more about myself. Finally I found that ridiculous photograph of the three of us all dressed up for Halloween. Remember?"

Diana did. They'd started out thinking they'd go as the Three Musketeers and ended up as the Three Stooges. As Larry, Daniel had worn a flesh-colored bathing cap with teased-out steel wool glued around the sides and back. Jake had gotten a buzz cut so he could go as Curly. Diana as Moe wore a black wig with bangs down to the bridge of her nose. She'd practiced that sour, disgruntled Moe expression, fueled by a pugnacious chin. Daniel and Jake had drilled her on the routines, and for one drunken night, she'd completely gotten into what they found so hilarious about the slapstick shtick.

She'd broken down after that and actually watched some of the Three Stooges shorts. Soon she'd had enough. But it made her realize that for all the violence the knuckleheads inflicted on one another, they shared a genuine affection.

Daniel shifted Diana off his lap and helped her to her feet. Then he sat in one of the rolling office chairs. "Did we have a great time or what?" He tilted the chair back, crossing his arms and grinning at her. The familiarity of the pose took her breath away. "That photo of us, goofing around like that—it was the trigger. After that, things started coming back to me. Know what I remembered first? Before my parents, before my hometown, before anything else I remembered Toro, the black Lab we had when I was a kid. Memory's weird.

"Soon, more and more memories came back. But it was months before I could even think about what I was going to do next. By then, I'd started to remember what happened."

He went on, but Diana barely listened. *Pick, pick . . .* That was the sound she'd heard as she and Jake had waited on the icy ledge, their climbing ropes coiled on the ground. She'd tried to peer over the edge, but the wind had buffeted her, eager to bite any part of her that was exposed. She'd slipped her balaclava back on, crouched, and listened as Daniel sank his picks into the ice and drove in one crampon then another. She'd imagined him pushing and pulling his way up.

Then a moment of utter silence. She'd thought, *He's reached the second screw hold* as she waited for the sound of his ax and a reassuring shout that he was on the move again. Instead there had been a cry and a sickening thud.

Diana had scrambled to the edge of the outcropping, desperate to see what had happened and almost slipping over herself. Daniel's howl of despair had grown alternately fainter and louder as it bounced off frozen rock.

"Daniel!" Diana had screamed, the wind flinging the words back into her face.

Frantically, arm over arm, Jake had hauled up the climbing rope. From the end dangled an empty safety harness.

Afterward, after the search party returned with only his dented helmet, everyone had asked how this could have happened to an experienced climber. Theoretically it was impossible to fall out of a properly rigged safety harness. But it was even more impossible to survive the kind of fall Daniel would have taken.

She stared up the wall of the silo to the ledge on which Daniel had perched. He must have made the descent using the rebars. No ropes, no climbing harness. A single misstep would have been his last.

"Were you free climbing then too?" she asked, interrupting him. "Is that how you fell? Is that why you insisted on coming up last?"

He gave her a long look. "It was the Eiger." He spread his hands, that bad-boy charm still working for him. "How could I do it any other way?"

Diana knew. She'd always known. They had each rigged their own safety harnesses, and it had been the only explanation that made any sense. Daniel never buckled a safety belt on a roller coaster. Never encountered a railing he didn't climb over or an extreme sport he didn't relish. Canyon gliding. Parachuting. Bungee jumping. Skateboarding through the city, holding on to the bumpers of cars.

"How long have you been back?" she asked.

"December," he said.

That was four months ago. By then Diana had long ago moved into her mother's house. The new business was taking off.

"So Jake knew," Diana said. A statement, not a question.

"Not until I called him."

"But why didn't you get in touch with me?" Diana just stared at him, trying to fathom how he could have left her twisting in agony.

"Jake told me that you'd moved back home. Buried me in your mind. Collected the insurance. A million bucks." He whistled. "Exposed that health insurance scam. Awesome. It was what you'd dreamed about. You were already a legend. I couldn't just show up and pull the rug out from under you. I mean, it would have been a huge mess. You'd have had to return the insurance settlement."

Diana felt her mouth drop open. So he'd been doing her a favor, keeping her in the dark?

He went on. "I'd created a new identity for myself. It's a lot easier to do that abroad than it is here. When I got back to the States, Jake put me up. Then I found this place. But coming back turned out to be harder than I thought it would be. And it wasn't the same without you. But you'd grieved and gotten on with your life. I felt like I couldn't just show up." He reached over for the cowboy hat and put it on his head. "But I missed you. I had to see you."

Tears pricked in Diana's eyes. "As GROB?"

"I couldn't help myself. I guess that was selfish. But I knew we couldn't be together. I thought at least we could talk." He swallowed. "I thought that would give us both back part of what we'd lost."

She wanted to believe him. Really she did.

CHAPTER TWENTY-NINE

"SEE?" DANIEL SAID WHEN JAKE CAME BACK INTO THE SILO. "I told you there was no need to worry. She's not flipping out."

"So you knew Daniel survived," Diana said to Jake.

Jake gave her an uneasy look. Her calmness didn't deter him from rearming the door. "That's how it had to be. He was off the grid and needed to stay that way. You'd been so . . . unpredictable. We didn't know how you'd react, and Gamelan was getting established."

Back then, Jake had installed her network, set up her security systems. Redundancy, he'd told her. Every backup had to have a backup. It would have been easy for Jake to install the programs that monitored Diana's every move—video surveillance, keystroke logging, network intercepts. It was a model of redundancy.

"So keeping me in the dark—that was purely a business decision? Risk management, I suppose. You couldn't have me going off the deep end. Again."

Jake started to say something but Daniel put his hand on Jake's arm.

"Why the sudden change?" she added. "Why do you need me here now?"

"I know it feels sudden, but it's not. It's been building for a while. And Jake told you about Vault?" Daniel said.

"So what is the big freakin' deal about Vault?" she said. "The two of you can take it. Count me out."

Jake rolled his eyes at Daniel. It was his there-she-goes-again look.

"Why not?" Diana said.

Jake folded his arms across his chest. "Clients want you. You're Superwoman. The giant killer."

"The one with the squeaky-clean reputation," Daniel said.

"The one they trust," Jake said.

"What about your new partners, Volganet?"

At that, Jake barked a laugh. Daniel shot him a warning look.

"What?" Diana said.

Daniel said, "I promise you, there's no new partner."

"And strictly speaking, we don't need you to work with us either," Jake said.

Daniel rushed to add, "But it would be much better all around if you did."

Jake sat at one of the computers, typed something, then clicked the mouse a few times. A gigantic framed image sprang to life, projected across the silo's curved wall opposite them. It was OtherWorld, Diana's office, with Nadia standing in the middle of it. The avatar pivoted to face them. She was wearing her dark business suit.

"Welcome to the offices of Gamelan Security. I'm Nadia Varata." Jake spoke into a microphone and a voice balloon appeared over Nadia's head, but the voice that came from the computer sounded exactly like Diana's.

"Voice sim," Jake said. "It's come a long way. And in case you were thinking about sabotage, we took out a little insurance policy." He brought up a map. Typed and waited. He pointed to a green dot on the screen.

She stepped closer. It was a map of downtown. He zoomed in. The dot was at the same intersection as the Palm Court Hotel, where Ashley worked.

"It's a live feed," Jake said. "The location gets updated every five minutes, tracking the GPS signal in your sister's Black-Berry."

Diana touched the screen. Then she turned to look at Jake, then Daniel. Who were these men, neither of whom would return her gaze? "You'd kidnap her again?"

Jake said, "I can't promise what—"

"Cool it, would you, Jake?" Daniel said.

"I told you this wasn't going to work," Jake said. "She nearly blows away everything just when . . ." He shook his head. "Crap. It's all going to crap. All because of her."

"You're being a jerk," Daniel said.

"And you're being fool," Jake said. "Know what I think? I think it's time to pull the plug." He hit a switch and the pro-jected image went blank. "If she won't work with us, then we need to cut our losses."

His voice was cold, his jaw set. This was a side of Jake that Diana had never seen before. How far would he be willing to go to keep her from screwing up whatever business they were up to? And what had she done, she wondered, that had made it necessary to reel her in? She didn't buy for a minute that they needed any special expertise that she had.

"Not yet. That wasn't the plan," Daniel said.

Jake paced up and back, his footsteps vibrating across the mesh floor. "I don't care what we planned. It's time." He stopped. "Hell, it's past time. Abort the mission."

Diana's mind was racing. She didn't know what Jake meant, but his tone was ominous. Were they just playing good cop/bad cop? She wasn't nearly cool enough to tough it out.

"Hold on, hold on," she said, stepping between them. "Tomorrow, we have our meeting with Vault?" Jake and Daniel traded a look she couldn't read. "I'll play my part, I promise."

"Sure you will," Jake said.

"Have I ever not delivered on a promise?" Diana shot back at him.

"And after that?" Daniel said.

Both of them watched her, wary, waiting for her reply. "I . . . I can't lie," she said. "I don't know. We'll have to wait and see."

"At least she's being honest with us," Daniel said, addressing Jake.

"I still don't like it," Jake said.

"Don't mind him. He's a slow learner," Daniel said to Diana. "So are we good?"

Diana took a sip of the chicory-laced coffee that she'd left on a table, but it had gone cold. "For now," she said.

Over the rim of the cup, she watched Daniel. Just like that, he was back. It seemed impossible. Somewhere, beyond shock and surprise, she groped for her own emotions. Distrust. Confusion. And beneath that, dread. She knew there was another shoe that had yet to drop.

In a rush, Diana realized how isolated she'd become, a prisoner in both real and virtual worlds. Meanwhile, Ashley would be out there, sick with worry about what had happened to her.

"Hey, guys, if you don't want my sister to send out an alarm,

I'd better call her." She took her cell phone from her jacket pocket. "She's expecting me to call her from this phone, but it doesn't get any bars in here."

Jake gave her an uneasy look.

"Here," she said, offering Jake the phone. "You want to call her and tell her I'm okay?"

"Very funny," he said. "Okay, but make it short." He indicated the door to the outside corridor.

Four beeps and Jake had disarmed the door. He held it open so she could go past him, out over crumbling concrete steps and into the passage connecting to the main mill building.

She was halfway down the passageway when Jake called, "That's far enough."

Diana stepped to one of the small windows. Looking out, she could see that the rain had stopped, and the wind had died down so much that the surface of the water in the reservoir was glassy smooth.

"By the way," Jake said, "just so you know, there are security cameras everywhere." He indicated a camera that aimed into the corridor from over the door to the silo. "They can see in light or dark."

Diana turned her back to him. It wasn't until she went to dial that she realized her hands were shaking. She brought up recently placed calls, found Pam's number, and hit send. She waited through the message telling her that she had fifty-three minutes left in the prepaid account.

Pam picked up on the second ring. "Diana!" she said. Diana felt a rush of relief that Pam had recognized her number. "Where on earth—"

"Hey, *Ashley*," Diana said, cutting her off. "It's me."

There was dead silence on the other end. Diana pretended she was listening. As if in response, she said, "Yeah, well, I got to Mill Village and I thought he wasn't there but it turns out he was."

"Mill Village? Where the hell is that?" Pam whispered. "Are you okay?"

"Of course I'm not," she said, keeping her voice upbeat, hoping that Pam would tune out the emotion and hear the words. "Right. Staying with some old friends."

"Online friends?" Pam asked.

Diana laughed. "Yes, and no." She waited through a few beats of silence. "No, don't bother to pick up groceries for me this week. I could be here awhile." She laughed again. "Yeah, yeah, I'm taking notes and photos, twenty-four/seven, proof that I left the house."

"What do you want me to do?" Pam said. "Should I try and find you?"

"I'll let you know."

Jake gestured to her from the doorway to speed it up.

Diana raised her index finger, threw a couple of "uh-huhs" into the phone. Then: "Tomorrow morning, I'll be in touch. And, Ashley, Pam said she'd call. Could you two talk so I don't have to call her too? I've gotta go now. We'll talk soon."

"Tomorrow," Pam said. "I'll reach Ashley."

Diana hid a smile and disconnected the call.

"Did it sound as if she bought it?" Daniel said, coming out to her.

"Of course she bought it." Diana tried to keep her voice even as she tucked the cell phone into her pocket.

"Mission accomplished," Daniel said. "Are we still allowed to say that?" She let him wrap her in his arms. "You're as amazing as ever."

She rested her head on his shoulder and for a moment let

him support her weary body. She'd forgotten how good this felt. Despite his betrayal, she still ached for him.

"You know, there's one thing about this that bothers me," he said, pulling away.

"Right." She slipped the cell phone from her pocket and looked up at him. "This?"

"GPS signals. They can be tracked."

She looked down at the phone, possibly her last link to the outside world. "But if Ashley tries to call . . ."

"She won't. I faked my own death. How hard will it be to fake yours as well?"

She gave him a long look, like she was making up her mind. Only she was thinking how easy he thought it would be for her to let her sister think she was dead—after all, it had been no big deal for him to let Diana think he'd died.

"Do you trust me?" she asked. She'd learned about trust from Daniel. Trusting was the first and most essential step— you couldn't get betrayed if you didn't take it. "Actions speak, right?"

She dropped the cell phone on the floor, and ground it with her boot heel until the case cracked. Then she unlatched one of the windows in the corridor wall and held it open.

Daniel picked up the broken phone and smiled at her. He glanced past her at Jake, who was standing in the doorway to the silo. "I told you she'd be cool," he said. Then he reared back and tossed the phone out the window.

Diana watched it arc across the cloud-streaked sky and disappear. A few seconds later there was a splash as it landed in the reservoir.

LATER THAT NIGHT, DIANA WAS ALONE WITH DANIEL, BACK IN THE makeshift bedroom. She was ready to stop trying to stay awake. "I'm exhausted. You're not, are you?"

Daniel shrugged. She remembered now how he'd never seemed to run down the way normal people did. He could go flat out, wired and crackling with energy, for literally days on end. Then, practically midsentence, he'd collapse into the sleep of the dead.

"You still pull all-nighters?" she asked.

"Sure. You used to be able to do it too. All the time."

Jake had picked up pizzas for dinner. Once upon a time, she could've put away an entire pie. Now, after just two slices, the pepperoni started to taste like salted wax and the cheese felt as if it were hardening into a layer of sludge in her stomach.

"There are lots of things I used to be able to do."

Daniel picked her up and carried her to the bed. Once her bed. Before that, their bed. He set her down gently and lay down beside her.

She turned away from him. Daniel had told her that the red roses on the bedside table were "for new beginnings." More like betrayals and severed ties. Already some were losing petals and hanging their heads.

From outside she heard water rushing over the dam. In the corner of the sleeping alcove were a sink and toilet and a modular shower stall. A shelf was filled with most of the contents of Diana's home bathroom—her toothbrush and shampoos and soaps. So considerate of them.

Daniel nuzzled her neck.

"What do you think we're doing here?" she asked.

"Messing around, I hope." He nipped her ear. "Don't over-think it, babe." That was what he used to tell her when she froze up during a climb or hesitated during a combat sim. It was his equivalent of *May the force be with you.*

She curled tighter. Daniel put his arm around her waist and spooned behind her. He slipped his hand up under her shirt and she shuddered as he stroked her back.

"Remember that game we used to play?" he said, his breath warm on her neck.

In spite of herself, Diana closed her eyes and envisioned the letters as he traced them out. First *i*. Then a heart. Then a *u*. Again and again, his fingers like feather dusters traced the same pattern on the small of her back. His hand wandered down her hips and reached around to touch between her legs.

Part of her wanted to surrender—it would have been so easy, so natural. And what better way to cement his trust? But she couldn't. He'd let her believe he was dead. To protect the insurance settlement? She'd have returned the money in a heartbeat if it had meant having him back.

Instead, one by one, he and Jake had severed Diana's remaining links to the real world. Kidnapped—there was no other word for it—her sister. Sown distrust with her one friend, Pam, and leaving in her place a single false friend, GROB.

Daniel and Jake were stronger and undoubtedly smarter than she was. Her one advantage over them: she knew her own weaknesses. They both would insist that they didn't have any.

"You're right. I'm tired," she said. "And—" She rolled over to face him and grabbed his hands, feeling the coarseness of his fingertips where frostbite had supposedly eaten away the tips. "You can't just expect everything to go back the way it was. I've changed."

"You haven't changed. You're just trying to be something that you're not."

Diana hesitated. Could that possibly be true? Was she still the girl who'd fallen crazy in love with a wild man, who'd allowed herself to break nearly every rule she'd followed growing up?

"Look in my eyes," he said, squeezing her arm. "I'm the same guy."

"You're hurting me."

He loosened his grip. "Sorry. I'm out of practice."

"I'm still getting used to you being here at all," she said.

He rolled over on his back, put his hands behind his head, and stared at the ceiling. "I want things to be the way they were."

If wishes were fishes . . . She rested her head against his chest. "Suppose it doesn't work out. What happens then?"

He didn't say anything.

She sighed and closed her eyes. What was the point, anyway? Any promises extracted from Daniel would be empty ones. He said he loved her. Wanted to be with her. Couldn't stand another day without her. It was a nice story—one Daniel himself might even believe.

In her mind, she reconstructed the layout of the mill, two yellow spots glowing in this loftlike space where she and Daniel lay. They'd left Jake, still at work in the silo. She zoomed out, and farther out, until her mental map encompassed the entire state of Massachusetts. A pair of yellow spots glowed, one in Boston and one just south—Pam and Ashley. She hoped that by now they'd put together what each of them knew.

Diana focused on the steady *thub-dub* of Daniel's heart, and beyond that, on the constant sound of water flowing over the dam outside. Why was it so important to him that the three of them were working together again? The Three Musketeers. Three Stooges. Three mice, although she was the only one flying blind.

"Are you ready for the meeting with Vault?" Daniel asked.

"Is it tomorrow?" she asked.

She felt his body tense. "You know damned well it is. Jake is leaving here in the morning to catch a flight out of Manchester to BWI."

Diana propped herself up on an elbow and looked down at him. "No, I'm not ready."

"We have a deal," Daniel said.

"I still have work to do—"

"Jake's got the proposal."

"But it'll take some time to prepare a presentation for the kickoff. Why not postpone until later in the week?"

"It's not negotiable. The meeting is tomorrow afternoon."

"Why the rush?"

Daniel paused. "Because that's when they're expecting to meet with us. Gamelan built its reputation on delivering on what we promise."

Coming from him, that was too funny. Next, he'd be reciting the Boy Scout pledge.

"I may not have been there," Daniel said, "but I have been paying attention. This has to feel like business as usual."

"Business as usual." Diana sighed. As if that were something to aspire to. She laid her head down.

"You'll be ready?" he asked.

"I'll have to work on the presentation in the morning. I couldn't do a lick of work now if my life depended on it."

She edged away from him and closed her eyes. A few minutes later, she felt him slide off the bed. Heard his footsteps cross the room. She caught a glimpse of him, just before he slipped out the door.

Click. He'd pulled the door shut and she was alone again. She recognized the chirping sounds—he was keying in a code to lock the door. The blinking yellow turned to a steady red. Not to keep danger out, but to keep Diana in.

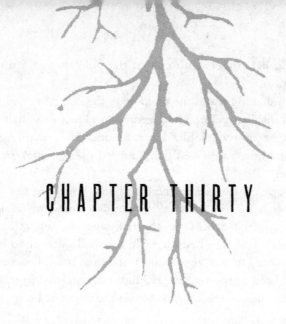

CHAPTER THIRTY

DIANA OPENED HER EYES WHAT FELT LIKE A MINUTE LATER BUT couldn't have been because it was pitch-dark. She sat bolt up-right up in the bed. The sound of rushing water seemed like it was roaring in her head and her heart pounded painfully against her rib cage. She tried to catch her breath.

Shapes came into focus and she remembered. She was in the mill. Shadows danced in the windows and the makeshift walls that surrounded her seemed flimsy, easily breached.

As she panted for air, the room seemed to spin. She curled into a ball. She shivered, as much from anxiety as from the cold, and her fingers tingled. She knew she was making herself sick, gulping air and hyperventilating.

Counting slowly and deliberately, she regained control of her breathing. The mound at the foot of the bed, dark against light bedding, turned out to be the leather jacket she'd or-dered from OtherWorld, the one Ashley had borrowed what seemed like a lifetime ago. She reached for it and pulled it to her. Dug her fingers into one of the pockets and found her medication.

With shaking hands she pried open the container and shook the pills into her palm. They seemed to glow in the half-light. There were just six left. She'd have to ration the remaining pills. She broke one, swallowed half, and fed the rest back into the container.

She put on the jacket, then lay back, bunching the pillow under her head. She counted the familiar items she could just make out in the dark. One, the tall, tapering post at the foot of her bed. Two, the bedside table that had once stood by her parents' bed. On that, the bouquet of wilted roses, her welcome home. Three, four—the tiny red lights that glowed from where she knew there were keypads beside the doors at both ends of the loft.

When her breathing had eased and the edges of her world had gone warm and slightly fuzzy, she resisted the pull of sleep. She stood and stepped to one of the windows. Four stories down, dull moonlight lit the mirrored surface of the still water that backed up behind the dam.

She crept to the edge of the wallboard screen and peered out. Under her bare feet, the uneven wide pine floorboards felt dry and splintery in places, worn smooth in others. Soundlessly she crossed from one end of the loft space to the other, trying each of the doors.

Returning to bed, she nearly tripped over a leg of the metal rack with its IV bag still hanging from it. A little red light glowed as, even now, a camera watched over where she now slept, where Ashley had been held unconscious for days. She recalled Jake's remark: *They can see in light or dark.* She imagined her own infrared image glowing fluorescent green and wondered if either of the two geniuses was aware of her movements. They'd thought that it was perfectly okay to keep her sister unconscious for days on end, just as long as they hadn't "hurt" her while they regrouped. When there was the mere possibility that plan B was going awry, Jake had been all too eager to "abort the mission"—as if in real life you could just reset your score to zero, or simply get up and leave the game.

Shaking with rage, Diana struck out. In slow motion, the metal rack toppled, rubber tubing flailing in the air like an angry snake. She grabbed a pillow from the bed and held it to her face, muffling a cry.

Had Daniel and Jake stayed up nights thinking up ways to bring her in? That limousine she'd seen on her street, like the one she'd seen parked in the mill's loading dock. The delivery van that had pulled into her driveway but hadn't delivered anything. Had those been them?

After Daniel's supposed death, she'd trusted Jake. He'd set up her computers. Her video surveillance. They shared the e-mail account and used its drafts folder as a drop for shared information. Jake had assured her that it was far safer to communicate that way than to broadcast messages across a network.

He had access to every mail message she sent. He could easily have discovered that she'd registered her avatar for the improv event at Copley Square. She'd been telling him she was feeling stronger, almost ready to venture out, so he would have been expecting her to do something like that.

She crept back into bed, shivering. Jake had been there, along with Ashley, to pull Diana back from the brink when she was wallowing in grief. When she still couldn't move on, he'd brought her news that Daniel's remains had been recovered. But he'd played her for a fool. He must have known that there was no way she could fly back to Switzerland with him. He hadn't gone to Switzerland alone; he hadn't gone there at all. She wondered whose ashes she had been given, or if there were any ashes at all in the urn he'd supposedly brought back along with documentation that was essential for Daniel to be declared legally dead so she could collect the insurance settlement.

That had been months before Daniel claimed he'd returned to the States. Was his tale of crawling to safety and recovered memory a fantasy too? She was determined to find out.

More important, why were they doing this—what was at stake now that made them risk exposure in order to bring her in? All she knew for sure was that instead of watching her back, all the while Jake had just been watching her.

Two could play that game. Diana spent the rest of the night awake and thinking. She ran scenarios for the next day through her head, doubling back from dead ends and branching to account for the unexpected. By morning she was exhausted and stiff with cold. If there was heat, she didn't know how to turn it on. The sky had turned light and she was still alone.

She headed to the makeshift bathroom. As she sat on the toilet, she eyed the modular shower stall. A hot shower would have been heaven, but she knew she'd never be able to let down her guard long enough to step naked into what looked like an upright coffin, especially not with that security camera staring down at her from the ceiling.

She snagged a washcloth and one of the pale blue towels stacked on the floor and sniffed them. A sponge bath would have to do.

Later, she dried off and put on clean underwear from a stack of neatly folded items that she recognized as her own. She put her jeans back on. It seemed easier to get into them. No wonder. For five days she'd barely eaten.

She found her fleece turtleneck pullover among the clothes folded in the little bookcase. Over that, she wore Nadia's leather jacket.

When she reemerged, the door to the passageway that connected to the silo stood ajar. She padded across the floor and peered out into the stairwell. On the floor were her red boots. When she went to pull them on, inside one of them she found a handwritten note: *Follow the tape.*

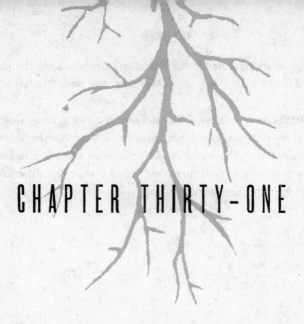

CHAPTER THIRTY-ONE

FOLLOW THE TAPE? SURE ENOUGH, A LINE OF DUCT TAPE HAD BEEN stuck to the floor on the landing, leading down the stairs. Overhead Diana spotted a small surveillance camera, tucked into a heavy beam and aimed at the doorway in which she was standing.

She pulled on the boots and stood, imagining herself in a video window on Daniel's computer screen. She tucked her trembling hands into her jacket pockets, feeling for her pills. She wasn't about to take more—she'd need every one of them, and besides, for what she had to do today, she needed to be extra sharp.

Running her hand along the wall to anchor herself, she followed the line of tape that ran down the stairs and through a doorway. It continued on across a floor of the mill and out into another stairwell. Up the stairway, through a corridor, and on she followed its circuitous path. Finally she came to the narrow, upward-slanted passageway that ended at the metal door to the silo. The surveillance camera over the doorway was pointed down at her.

Hesitantly, Diana tried the door. It wasn't locked, but it took all her strength to push it open. When she peered inside, she saw Daniel at one of the tables. He turned her way as a breeze swept through the doorway, and it felt as if a pair of hands were trying to pull the door shut.

"Hey, close it, would you?" he said.

Diana stepped into the silo. When she let the door go, it banged shut behind her. The air went still. She realized what had created the draft—the hatch far up the silo wall had been open too.

"So you finally woke up," he said.

He got up and walked past her to the door. He punched some numbers into the keypad on the wall, his back sheltering it from view, and the door lock clicked.

"Hungry?" he asked. Flint sparked in his dark eyes. "Got you a bacon-and-egg sandwich."

Diana closed her eyes and swallowed. Just what she needed to chase last night's greasy pizza.

"There's coffee too," he said. When he turned and pointed toward the counter, she saw he had a Bluetooth headset hooked over his ear.

"Thanks," Diana said.

The carafe in the coffeemaker was nearly empty. She poured herself the last cup and added some milk from the little refrigerator. She turned off the pot. Beside it sat a grease-stained bag. She touched it. Cold. She shuddered, imagining the congealed bacon on fat-saturated toast.

The first sip of coffee with a hint of chicory was bracing but bitter.

Daniel returned to the table and focused on the computer screen.

"You didn't come back last night," she said.

"You weren't exactly encouraging. Besides, there was a lot to do."

Diana wondered what he'd been working on, and whether he'd been working on it for the last ten hours straight. She assumed that Jake had left to catch his flight to Baltimore.

She leaned against the wall and sipped her coffee. "You know, months ago, when we first started working together, I was amazed at how easily Jake was able to find and close Neponset Hospital's security hole. It was almost like he was channeling you."

Daniel stopped typing but he didn't look over at her.

"How long have you been our silent partner?"

"Neponset Hospital." He yawned and rubbed his eyes. "Yeah, that was pretty slick, wasn't it?" He spread both arms, arched his back, and stretched.

"But Vault—they're a much bigger deal," she said. "I mean, they manage insurance coverage for virtually anyone who works for the federal government, past and present."

"Plus anyone incarcerated in a federal prison."

She whistled. "That's a lot of people. A lot of private information."

He swiveled to face her. "Information that the government has no business knowing, if you ask me."

"They must have paid a lot for that fancy new security system."

"Supposedly impossible to crack." Daniel grinned. "And then one of their employees goes and leaves his computer on a commuter train, a computer with a flash drive that never should have gotten out of the building. Got just what they deserved if you ask me." He winked at her. "Arrogance will be rewarded."

Those final words and the smirk that accompanied them were eerily familiar. Daniel had often used the phrase to underscore his contempt for his so-called enemies and the nobility behind the mayhem that he unleashed on them. He seemed oblivious to the irony, since his own arrogance easily matched that of the federal government and of corporations like Vault Security.

"So"—he yawned again—"welcome aboard. Have a seat." He indicated her white tulip chair, which was pulled up to one of the systems on a worktable beside his.

She sat and rolled closer to the screen. The log-in box for OtherWorld was already up. She typed in NADIA VARATA and her password and waited for home office to come into focus.

Instead, pixel by pixel, a replica of the interior of the silo materialized. Nadia, dressed in her signature black leather jacket and red cap, was sitting in the same tulip chair that Diana sat in at that moment, facing a table covered with computer equipment arranged only slightly differently from the machines in the real-world silo.

"We gave you a new home base. I hope you don't mind," Daniel said.

She didn't. They'd already demonstrated how they could control Nadia whenever they felt like it. But it was a timely and potent reminder of all the variables she'd need to take into account.

Diana maneuvered the mouse to angle the viewfinder. The interior of the silo had been replicated right down to the shading of the curved walls, from brown to white as they neared the roof, and the bent rebar ends sticking out of them. A little inset map of the space showed just one yellow dot—her avatar was alone in its virtual tower.

She quickly checked her inventories. Her libraries of "gestures," "sounds," and "clothing" seemed intact, but all of her "places" and "contact cards" had disappeared. Erased. Again, what she'd expected. Neither Daniel nor Jake would be so easily seduced by her promise to cooperate.

With a series of beeps, message after message popped onto her queue. She was surprised that Daniel and Jake hadn't disabled her communications. Uh-oh. A message from PWNED caught her eye. The subject line: "Re: Phew." Pam had sent it yesterday, after Diana had called her.

Pam's message began, *Got your message. So relieved to hear from you . . .*

Had Pam missed the point of her phone call? Diana gripped the mouse and shot a look over to Daniel. He seemed engrossed in his own work.

She quickly scanned the message, realizing that it wasn't a response to her call at all, but a reply to an electronic message appended at the bottom—a message supposedly from Diana, one that Jake or Daniel must have sent, reassuring Pam that Diana's trip to New Hampshire had gone well and she'd be there for a while longer. Diana could only hope that Pam wasn't fooled, and this response was her way of playing along.

She clicked reply. Her computer buzzed, like she'd entered a wrong answer, and up popped a box with the message, *Unable to complete*. She entered a query to see whether Pam was in-world at that moment. Another buzz. *Unable to complete*.

"Shit." She said it under her breath.

Daniel snorted. Diana choked, sure that he'd heard and realized what she was trying to do. But he was slumped in his chair, his eyes half closed and his mouth slack. His chin drifted down, down, and a moment later he jerked back alert. He snorted again and straightened, ran his hand back and forth over his mouth, and stared at the screen. A minute later, his head tipped to the side again.

Diana pushed away from the table. Her chair made a nasty sound as it scraped across the floor. Daniel jumped, and the little headset fell out of his ear. She walked over to him, picked it up, and handed it to him. Gently she put her hands on his shoulders.

He gave her a wary look that softened into a smile as she started to massage his shoulders, working her thumbs at the knots of tension in his trapezius muscles. He closed his eyes and rolled his head around.

"Mmmm. That feels good." He slipped the headset into his shirt pocket, closed his eyes, and breathed deeply.

She worked her way up and down in his neck and upper spine. Daniel's face went calm, the lines of tension disappearing from his forehead and jaw as her thumbs circled up into what would have been his hairline if he hadn't shaved his head. If he'd just let down his guard, he'd be dead asleep in seconds.

He grabbed her wrist. "What are you up to?"

"Idiot. You can see what I'm up to." She wrenched her arm free and rubbed her wrist. "I killed the coffee," she said. "You look like you could use another cup. I know I could."

Daniel started to get up but Diana put her hand firmly on his shoulder. "Let me," she said. He collapsed back into his chair.

She picked up his empty coffee cup and her own, still nearly full. "I think I remember how you like it. Good and strong."

Diana prayed that Daniel wouldn't follow her to the sink. When she got there, she turned on the water, and while it was running, she rinsed out Daniel's cup and pretended to rinse out her own. Meanwhile, she felt around in her pocket for her pills. With her thumb, she flipped open the lid of the container and emptied the remaining pills into the pocket.

She dumped out the last bit of coffee in the pot and rinsed it. Threw away the used coffee filter and replaced it with a new one. In the refrigerator's freezer compartment she found coffee beans. She ladled ten scoops into the coffee grinder. Her back shielding the grinder from Daniel's view, she slipped the pills from her pocket. There were five and a half left. She dropped all but one into the grinder.

"You remember the formula?" Daniel asked. He'd crossed the room silently and was standing right behind her.

Diana's heart stuttered. The little white pills seemed to glow among the nearly black beans.

"Of course I do," she said, quickly putting on the grinder's lid and pressing down to turn it on. Daniel put his hand over hers. *One, two, three* . . . She counted to herself, listening as the pitch of the grinding shifted higher and higher.

Daniel released his hand, but Diana kept hers pressed down and continued counting until she reached twenty. She couldn't afford any telltale white chunks to still be visible. When she removed the lid, the pills had disappeared into the fine, uniformly dark powder.

Daniel leaned close to the grinder and sniffed. "Ambrosia of the gods," he said.

He returned to his computer. While the coffee dripped through the filter, Diana stood behind him. He shifted to one side so she could see. It was a memo addressed to *Andrew.* Andrew Moore was Vault's head of IT. The subject line was "Recommendations." Daniel was building a numbered list, and he was up to number seven.

"You're giving them recommendations at a kickoff meeting?" she asked.

"Why not?"

"Because all we've done so far is gather background information, propose an approach, and cash their advance. Coming in day one with answers? Not a good idea."

"But it's obvious to anyone what they need to do."

"Not to anyone. Certainly not to them. They need to feel like you're listening. Your response has to seem agile, not off the shelf. It should grow out of their 'unique' "—Diana drew quote marks in the air—"'situation.' There's a reason we call what we do solutions. No one wants to pay a lot for the quick fix. Besides, it's about ownership. Give them a prescription up front? They'll feel like they could have gone to a wiki and gotten the same answers for free." She bent down, reaching for his keyboard. "May I?"

Daniel pushed away from the table, his arms folded across his chest.

"And—" At the top of the memo she highlighted TO: ANDREW. "This early in your relationship, don't assume you can use the COO's first name."

"Since when?"

"Since always. But that's a minor point." She scrolled through the document, stopped, and highlighted another line. "Never call what they do engineering." In another she highlighted *data storage*. "This is even worse. They like to think of themselves as software developers.' "

"You're kidding."

"Sweat the small stuff. Show that you know their marketing niche, what image they're trying to project. Believe me, it matters."

The coffeepot made slurping sounds as the last bit of water dripped through. Diana went over to it and filled Daniel's cup. She made sure he saw her add some fresh coffee to the top of her own unfinished cup. She turned to face him and took a sip, smiling as she did so.

"The main thing," she said, walking back to him and handing him his cup, "is this. We shouldn't be handing them answers at a first meeting. We should be listening." She bent over and read some more, shaking her head.

He got up, offering her his seat. "Go to it."

Diana took her time, revising what Daniel had written, watching out of the corner of her eye as he drank some coffee, then drank more.

"There." Finally, unable to stretch the task out any longer, she pushed away from the table. The page she'd been working on rolled off the printer. She handed it to Daniel.

"Discussion points?" he said, reading the heading. "That's slick."

"Short and sweet. Asking, not telling. Now take the main points and make them into a slide presentation and we're good to go."

"We need slides?" Daniel groaned.

"You want to control the meeting, don't you? Besides, that's what they expect. Oh, and you should use the Gamelan corporate style."

"We have a corporate style?"

"It's amazing what impresses people."

Daniel yawned and stretched. His eyes seemed to have gone flat, the spark of intensity dimmed.

"Why don't you take a break? I can do this stuff in my sleep, and you need to sleep." Diana carried the printout to her computer. As she walked, the paper seemed to flutter like a sail on a little boat floating across the room, and she felt detached and floaty. She'd had just enough of the Xanax-laced coffee to give her some buoyancy and a thin layer of separation between herself and her surroundings.

"Help yourself to more coffee." She tossed the words over her shoulder. "Our meeting's not for hours." She opened the Gamelan presentation template and began to reshape the memo.

A while later she glanced over at Daniel. She recognized the cow-skull logo on the Web site that he was looking at—Cult of the Dead Cow—the online meeting place for hackers worldwide. Daniel had been one of the founders of their Ninja Strike Force, the elitest of the elite.

Soon he was yawning again. *More coffee.* She tried to telegraph the thought.

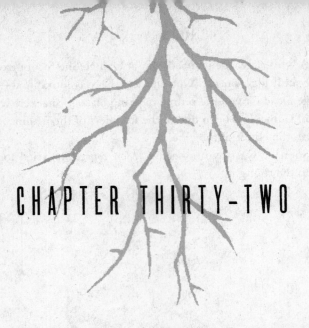

CHAPTER THIRTY-TWO

IANA TOOK HER TIME OVER THE PRESENTATION, FIDDLING AROUND
with transitions and special effects that she'd normally never
have messed with, stretching out what should have been a
thirty-minute job. Daniel stayed at Cult of the Dead Cow for
about a quarter of an hour. Then he opened a window with a
bright green background and boxes and lists—probably a system
management tool. After that he was in OtherWorld. He projected a combat sim on the curved silo wall. Diana had to turn
away to keep from feeling seasick at the 3-D effect. Finally he
pumped his fist and the gunfire and explosions stopped.

Then, for a while, there was just clicking and the odd *ding*
or *whoosh*. He was probably in e-mail. She heard him yawn. She
didn't look around when he got up to pour himself yet another
cup of coffee.

A little while later, Daniel leaned back in his chair, stretched
his legs out in front of him, and folded his arms across his chest.
He yawned and rubbed his face.

A few minutes later, he started to nod off, jerking awake and then subsiding. Finally he nodded off completely, tilting sideways. Diana waited. And waited.

She was about to get up when he gave a snort and sat up.

Diana pretended she was still working. Daniel had gone through more than half the pot of coffee. There should have been enough Xanax to make the average person comatose. But it would be a fatal mistake to consider Daniel average.

He sat forward, looked around, stretched and yawned, then settled back again. His eyes drifted shut and his head fell sideways. Full stop.

Diana waited, not daring to breathe. Daniel didn't stir. She cleared her throat. No response. She scraped her chair and coughed. Still he slept.

She walked over to him. With his mouth and his jaw slack, his face completely relaxed and unwired, Diana could see both the man she'd fallen in love with and the one he'd turned into. Then and always, he was so self-centered, so completely focused on whatever mission he'd set himself at a given moment, that he was willing to throw the people who loved him off a virtual cliff.

Once upon a time, Diana had let him mold her, shape her. If she'd been an apt pupil, then losing him wouldn't have broken her. But she'd allowed herself to depend on him to reflect back her very identity.

She looked around. He'd certainly found the perfect place from which to sow his brand of chaos. The mill was isolated, apparently abandoned, the silo like a bunker with its three-foot-thick walls.

She gazed up the wall, tracking a path connecting a rebar that was just a step up from the mesh floor to one just a few feet higher, to another one, and another, and on up to a rebar within easy reach of the hatch that led to the outside world. For any experienced climber, it wouldn't be a challenging ascent. No more difficult than the practice wall she'd once trained on—the "baby wall," Daniel had called it—after she'd mastered her terror of climbing it for the first time.

But climbing even a baby wall, alone and without a safety harness, was suicidal. Just imagining herself, halfway up and untethered, made her want to throw up. Besides, she had no intention of running away.

As she reached past Daniel for his laptop, she heard a sound. It was a faint but precise dinging, as if someone were tapping a key on a miniature xylophone.

Ding-ding-ding. Ding-ding-ding. It continued, irritating and persistent. Daniel twitched in his sleep. She hovered over him, trying to locate the source. Finally the sound stopped. That's when she noticed that a message-waiting alert was flashing on his screen. But that hadn't been where the sound itself originated.

Diana shifted the laptop over to the edge of his Daniel's worktable and pulled her chair up to it. She clicked on the alert.

The text message that popped open was from Jake. It was a short note, saying that his plane was leaving on time and he was waiting to board at Logan.

Diana replied the way she imagined Daniel would have done, with a simple "A-OK." Anything fancier and Jake might have realized that the reply hadn't been written by Daniel. She wanted to convey an impression of business as usual.

But what exactly was their "business as usual"? Compromising data—she got that. But then what? There had to be more to it.

She toggled through Daniel's open applications, pausing at a bright green network management screen. She stared at the network name at the top of the screen. Volganet. This was where data stolen from MedLogic had been copied. This was where her laptop kept trying to send GPS coordinates, betraying its location.

Damn them. They weren't working *with* Volganet. They *were* Volganet.

Diana scanned the screen and found a list of users with registered access to Volganet. She scrolled down through the more than thirty entries. JWILSON. BPACKER. PHREAK-ANOID. ACIDFI. MKATE. It was a mix of hacker handles and conventional user names.

There was SOK0S—that was Daniel. NADIAV was there too. Account status: LOCKED.

Next, she navigated through the hierarchies of files on Volganet. At the top level, directory names were short and cryptic. One that caught her eyes was ML. MedLogic? NH and UI. Those could be abbreviations for Neponset Hospital and Unity Insurance—Gamelan clients that had bolted the minute she'd gotten a lead on their hackers.

Diana drilled down, through folders within folders. She felt sick. She'd thought she was such a hotshot security consultant when, in fact, she'd been nothing more than a puppet, a front for Daniel and Jake. They'd taken advantage of the trust she'd built and used her as their Trojan horse. She'd given them unfettered access to these companies' systems, enabling them to help themselves . . . to what?

Opening some files at random, she found a bill for outpatient treatment; a medical history complete with name, address, and Social Security number; a DNA profile like the one stolen from MedLogic; a lab worker's personnel file; a cancer patient's treatment regimen; a script for Paxil.

Her gaze traveled from the computer screen to a pair of

servers that sat on the floor. They were good-size computers, about the size of mini-refrigerators, each with drawers stacked on top. Those would contain slots for hard drives, a data farm. All told, she guessed there'd be room for tens of thousands of gigabytes—much more than they needed for any business she'd thought they were in.

How long had she been acting the fool? The dates on some of the folders went back six months. That had been during the time when Daniel was still out of the country, or so he claimed. Was there even a single fact in his supposed time line that she could check?

The mill—the property sale had to have been registered. That she could confirm.

She brought up a map of New Hampshire. She found Mill Village, traced the Merrimack River a few miles north to where she guessed the mill was located. Most likely it was in Merrimack County.

She found the Merrimack County's online registry of deeds, created an account, and got as far as the inquiry screen. She set a range of 2008–2010 in the TRANSACTION DATE field. The only other piece of information she needed was LAST NAME.

She knew it was unlikely, but she tried Schechter, Daniel's last name. No match. Then she tried Jake's last name, Filgate. Back came a match for a Michele Filgate, but the property listed was on Main Street in Concord. Then she tried Wilson, then Packer, and on through the surnames she'd extracted from the list of system users.

Out of ideas, she tried typing in her own last name. *Bingo.* Diana Highsmith had purchased the four-acre parcel with three vacant industrial buildings for $1,660,000 on . . . Diana blinked . . . August 11, 2008.

Diana felt as if she'd been dropped, the air knocked out of

her. Daniel and Jake had used her identity to buy this property four months *before* her life had been shattered by Daniel's disappearance. They'd been planning, knowing that they'd need a bunker where Daniel could live off the grid.

Now she knew for sure what she'd been afraid to contemplate. There'd been no accident. Daniel hadn't been free-climbing without a harness. He hadn't been climbing at all. It was all a sham, orchestrated for her as an audience of one. She felt sick and angry, furious with herself. How could she have loved this man, trusted his friend? She was a complete fool.

Daniel must have started hiking back to civilization as soon as Diana had cleared the first ledge and was safely out of sight. He'd cried out from below and thrown his helmet into the crevasse. She might even have passed near him as she scrambled down, racing to base camp to bring help.

Had he felt even a twinge of regret or pity, or only relief at the baggage he'd shed and excitement at the new opportunities that were about to open up to him?

CHAPTER THIRTY-THREE

WHEN JAKE HAD BROUGHT HER THE URN, SUPPOSEDLY FROM SWITzerland and supposedly containing Daniel's ashes, Diana had finally stepped through a portal from before to after, from together to alone. Holding the urn, she'd realized that she'd never again feel Daniel's arms around her. Hear his ready laugh when she teased him. Watch pleasure suffuse his face as he enjoyed her body.

Now, looking at Daniel asleep in the chair, his face as tender and vulnerable as a child's in repose, she wondered if she'd ever really known him at all. If she had, she'd certainly lost him long before he catapulted himself out of her life.

Maybe he'd loved her—for five minutes. But longer than that? He couldn't love anyone but himself.

One thing was clear: Daniel had never intended to give up hacking. His offer to partner with her and go legit had been a setup designed to gull her into traveling to Switzerland in order to celebrate the transition. He and Jake had had other plans, and she was the witness they needed to make them happen. After that, she'd become the docile, blindfolded helpmate, the princess in the tower whom they needed to bring their plans to fruition.

What could have been worth the betrayal? As if Diana had finally asked the right question, the dinging sound started up again.

"Huh? What happened? Where's . . . ?" Daniel flailed, looking wildly around the room and tipping sideways, nearly falling out of his chair.

"Whoa, take it easy." Diana jumped up and grabbed his arm.

Ding-ding-ding. The sound seemed louder, and Diana spotted the source—barely visible in Daniel's pocket was the tip of the distinctive plastic arc of his Bluetooth receiver. It occurred to her that though cell phones didn't get a signal in the silo, his computer probably had a voice messaging program like Skype. He'd need a headset like the Bluetooth in order to hear and talk.

"Di?" Daniel looked at her, confused, his pupils dilated.

As she steadied him, she hooked the receiver and slid it from his pocket, folding it in her hand to muffle the sound. "You just fell asleep," she said.

"Jesus." Daniel tried to push himself to his feet but fell back, and all the while the damn thing kept dinging. She fumbled with the receiver until she found the button that turned off the sound and pressed it.

"What the hell's the matter with me? Feels like . . . feels like . . . I dunno . . ." His words slurred together. "Am I sick?" He touched his face. "My computer. Where . . . ?" He put his hands down in the empty spot on his desk where his keyboard should have been and sat there hunched over, his mouth hanging open.

"You're not sick. You were just exhausted. You fell asleep practically on top of your keyboard, so I moved it aside. See? It's right over here."

Daniel glanced over at it. "Log out. Need to log out," he muttered. "Need to . . . shut down."

"You already did that."

"Did I?"

"Remember? Right before you fell asleep. Come on. You need to lie down and rest."

She wasn't sure he'd heard her. But then he licked his lips and nodded.

She helped him sit on the floor. "You want to work all night, you should at least put a mattress or a couch in here," she said.

"Mmmm." He crossed his legs like a little kid sitting at a campfire. "Jake?"

"He's in Maryland. For the meeting with Vault?"

"Oh, yeah." He started to tip sideways. Stopped and looked at her. "What time is it?"

"We have plenty of time. The meeting's not for another couple of hours."

"But I need to . . ." Again he tried to push himself up. He was like the blow-up clown toy she'd once had that kept bobbing upright no matter how many times you smacked it down.

"I've got it under control. We'll be ready," Diana said.

"But . . ." He mumbled something unintelligible.

She knelt beside him and wrapped her arm around him. He smiled and gave her leg a weak squeeze. Rank, coffee-scented breath rose to meet her.

"You don't need to worry," she said. "I'm finishing up the presentation. Adding some material I researched. Enumerating the benefits and assessing the downside of doing nothing." She went on, making it up as she went, allowing her voice to rise and fall in a gentle rhythm like this was a bedtime story. "Don't worry about Jake. He's probably in the air. I checked. There's no weather to speak of in Baltimore. Looks like his plane is scheduled to land on time."

She went on and on, inventing status updates. Little by little she felt Daniel go limp. She eased him the rest of the way down onto the floor. He turned over and curled up. She took off her jacket, folded it, and slid it under his head.

Then she waited. Daniel's eyes were closed. His breathing evened out. When his computer beeped, she slowly got to her feet and went over to it. Another message-waiting alert had popped up on Daniel's screen. This time it was a voice mail.

She hooked the Bluetooth over her ear, turned it back on, and clicked open the message. "New message, marked 'urgent,' " said an electronic voice. A pause. Then: "Dr. Kennedy? This is Ashley Highsmith. You treated me at Neponset Hospital and left me your business card?" Ashley's voice sounded decidedly odd. Lighter and breathier. "I'm running a hundred-and-three-degree fever and"—she coughed and wheezed—"my chest aches." In the background, Diana heard a mockingbird singing. That had to be Pam's birdie clock. "My fingers and toes are swollen. Please. Call me." The phone number she left was Pam's.

When the message finished playing, a window popped up asking Diana if she wanted to return the call. She glanced quickly at Daniel. He was snoring. But before she could click yes, an e-mail message from Jake appeared. He'd sent it just seconds earlier, at 2:31 P.M. An hour and a half to go, just in time for him to get to Bethesda for the meeting. His message to Daniel began:

Plane delayed. Finally at BWI. Did u c? ^5!

On the next line was a link. Diana clicked and a news article came up.

> DNA evidence proves the impossible
> Federal law enforcement officials confirmed today that DNA collected from blood evidence at the scene of a recent bank robbery matches the DNA of a woman who died five years ago after undergoing a bone marrow transplant. When asked how this was possible, officials had no comment.

This was worthy of a high five? Diana read the rest of the article, then read it again, trying to wrap her head around the implications. Blood evidence at a crime scene matched a woman who'd died after undergoing a bone marrow transplant. How was that possible?

Diana rocked back in her chair. The implications were staggering. Every defense attorney in the country would be saving that news clip to read to their next jury, proof positive that DNA analysis was unreliable. Talk about instant reasonable doubt, and it could infect every case that involved DNA evidence. Daniel would have called it sabotage in defense of privacy.

Surely it was no coincidence that the file stolen from Med-Logic was a DNA profile, or that one of the files she'd opened on Volganet was a DNA profile too. Many of Gamelan's clients would have had DNA profiles of patients stored in their databases. How many of them had Jake and Daniel amassed?

Diana retraced her steps, looking for the DNA profile she'd found earlier. It didn't take long. In the same directory, there were hundreds and hundreds more.

Now she understood why Jake and Daniel had been desperate to ensure that Gamelan's relationship with their newest client got off to a smooth start. Working with Vault would give them access to thousands more profiles—Vault stored the health records of federal prisoners, civil servants, and elected officials. Anyone who'd had a DNA swab, or fertility treatment, or registered to donate a kidney or bone marrow. Possibly even elected officials whose DNA had been collected just in case their remains had to be identified.

Diana knew how easy it would be to alter the records in a DNA database, merrily swapping one person's profile for another's. Corrupt DNA databases—you'd only need to hit a couple—and you could upend Big Brother. To someone like Daniel, as the slogan went, that was priceless.

But with Daniel and Jake's usual thoughtless, scattershot approach, not every person who found himself implicated by DNA evidence would be dead. Innocent people would find themselves standing trial and others would get away with murder. And if the scheme was discovered, Diana would surely look as if she'd been partner to the conspiracy, if not the ringleader.

Now she understood why they'd had to bring her in. She'd given them no choice. The minute she'd intercepted that DNA profile from MedLogic, she'd outlived her usefulness. When she found Volganet, she was a hairsbreadth from figuring out what was going on. By bringing her in, Daniel must have thought he could control her. After all, she was isolated, alone. And she still had to be in love with him, didn't she?

Diana glanced down at Daniel. His eyelids quivered and his shoulders twitched. He was having a bad dream. Poor baby. But whatever was going on in his sleep, it was nothing compared to what he was going to wake up to.

She found the screen that had popped up and returned "Ashley's" call.

CHAPTER THIRTY-FOUR

ANIEL SLEPT ON. SIX HOURS LATER, WHEN DIANA WAVED A CUP
of unadulterated coffee under his nose, he finally blinked
awake. He sat up, groaning.

"Jesus. What happened? How long—?" He looked at his
watch. "Quarter to four. Christ. Is that all it is?"

"You told me to wake you for the meeting," Diana said.

Daniel looked at the coffee she offered him and winced,
but then took it and drank some. He glanced around. "We got
anything to eat?"

"There's that egg sandwich you got me this morning. It's a
little tired, but—"

"Nuke it. Nuking kills anything that can kill you."

"Interesting theory." She found the greasy paper bag and
stuffed it into the microwave. When she hit the switch, the light
came on, and the little carousel inside started turning. After
a bit, the odor of egg oozed out. Diana had been so busy, she

hadn't realized how hungry she was. She'd even have eaten that disgusting egg sandwich.

When she turned back, Daniel was staggering to his feet. "So, are we ready for the meeting?"

"We"—Diana paused—"are all set. Just waiting for Jake to e-mail me the coordinates and the pass code."

The microwave dinged. Diana opened it and handed Daniel the hot sandwich. He stared at it for a moment as if she'd handed him a dead frog. Then he opened a corner, sniffed, and took a bite.

Diana's stomach rumbled. God, she was hungry. She'd drunk most of the coffee milk and a PowerBar that she found, but that had been hours ago.

"If you want me to attend this meeting," she said, "then you'll have to unlock her." She jerked her thumb toward her computer, where Nadia stood in suspended animation in her business clothes in OtherWorld's re-creation of the mill's silo.

"Huh?"

"Nadia. She seems to be stuck in neutral."

"Oh, yeah. Sorry." Daniel shambled over to his worktable and glanced at the dark screen of his computer. He jiggled the mouse but nothing happened. Pressed the on button. The screen came to life. As he waited for it to boot up, his gaze traveled across the computer equipment on the table, down the cables to more equipment on the floor, as if checking that everything was the way he'd left it.

A beep brought him back. He swiped his index finger across the fingerprint reader attached to his laptop. When his desktop materialized he glanced at the bottom corner of the screen. "I can't believe it's so early. Feels like I slept for days."

"Oh? And what, exactly, does that feel like?" Diana asked.

Daniel grimaced. "Hey, I said I was sorry. Besides, drugging your sister was Jake's idea." As he scratched his head and yawned, Diana heard a barely audible electronic voice: "Hel-lo So-kay-oss. Wel-co-me ba—"

She'd inadvertently left the Bluetooth earpiece turned on in her pocket. Clearing her throat to cover the noise, she casually reached in and tapped the Bluetooth silent.

"Oh, yeah." Daniel fiddled at the computer for a few moments. "Liberate Nadia."

"Makes a good bumper sticker," Diana said.

Daniel scanned through the messages that had popped into his queue. "Here it is. Jake with the meeting coordinates," he said. "He copied you."

"Uh-oh. What's this?" She bent down and pretended to pick up the Bluetooth from the floor. "This yours? I almost stepped on it." She slid the little audio receiver onto the table.

Daniel barely glanced at it. "There. Reboot your system and you should be all set."

Diana settled at her computer and restarted it. She turned on the audio and slid the volume control louder. When she got back into OtherWorld as Nadia, messages streamed into her queue. She found the one supposedly from Jake, clicked it open, and pasted the coordinates for the Vault meeting into her transporter.

"Engage?" She looked over at Daniel.

Daniel laughed and pulled his chair up behind her, gave the screen a two-fingered salute. "Make it so."

Diana clicked go and the silo dissolved around her avatar. A moment later Nadia was hovering over a barren OtherWorld island. A box appeared and Diana typed in the pass code. A whirring sounded, then a click, like a safe opening. Clever touch.

Pixel by pixel, a meeting room rezzed around Nadia. The walls were the uneven dirt of an underground cave, but the table that Jake's avatar was seated at along with four other avatars, all in business suits, was a regulation conference table. There were two empty chairs. Diana sat Nadia in one of them.

In the real world of the silo, Daniel stooped behind her and draped an arm over her shoulders. "Here we go."

"All for one—" she whispered, looking up at him.

"One for all." He looked at her expectantly.

She smiled. "And every man for himself." She kissed him softly on the lips. *Game on.*

Then she pulled over the table microphone and spoke into it. "Nadia Varata."

One of the male avatars stood. She hovered the cursor over him, checking that this image was supposed to represent Andrew Moore, Vault's head of IT. "We're looking forward to working with you," Moore said.

He introduced the others and Diana wrote down the names and titles. Daniel returned to his own computer as she began delivering her presentation. She moved through it as quickly as she dared, lest Daniel zone out or fall asleep again before they got to the good part.

She had an odd sense of déjà vu. Nadia and the virtual Jake were working together just as they had for the last eight months, the pair of them a team making these new clients comfortable, lulling them into what would turn out to be a much more intimate relationship than they'd bargained for. Only this time, the clients wouldn't be the ones unpleasantly surprised.

She concluded her presentation with, "Bottom line: you need to know if your lost data is being traded or sold, and lock down your systems and procedures to prevent this kind of thing from recurring. We'd like to start right away."

"The sooner the better," Moore said. "This couldn't have come at a worse time. We're at a critical point in our sales cycle. If this gets out, the results will be disastrous. We want to get out in front of this and manage any fallout. But we need to know exactly what we're looking at."

"Excellent. Then we're on the same page," Diana said. "We'd like to come at this two ways. Detection and prevention. As soon as we get a copy of the data that was taken, we'll start tracking globally to see if it's out there. I understand you're concerned about security access codes as well and vulnerability in general. We can start penetration testing your network right away too. As soon as we finish with this meeting, if you like.

"One of the foremost experts in the world will be working with us on this." She glanced over to see if Daniel was listening. "It's possible that, within a few hours even, we'll have some answers for you. Then we'll be able to advise your staff on any changes that are needed."

"That's all well and good, but I'm concerned that—" Moore began, but he was interrupted. The audio feed sounded as if conversation was going on at the other end. "I'm sorry. Just a minute."

Although the avatars on the screen remained seated, Diana could hear muffled voices, then nothing, as if Moore had put his side on mute.

"Uh-oh." Diana made sure she said it loud enough so Daniel couldn't help hearing.

"What?" he said. "What's going on?"

"Shh. I think they're conferencing about something they don't want us to hear."

Daniel came over and stood behind her.

Finally the sound came back on. "Jim Lau," a voice said, and another male avatar, this one also dressed in a dark suit, his face a cliché from an Asian comic-book, materialized.

"That's their COO," she whispered up to Daniel.

"I know that," he shot back, his face tense. "I thought he wasn't going to be there."

"Jim?" A voice balloon appeared over Moore's head. "These are the folks from Gamelan Security. They're ready to get started."

"I'm sorry to have kept you in the dark," Lau said, his voice deep and resonant like someone who'd had radio training. "It was unavoidable. But there's been a development, and I wanted to bring you all the news myself because it's going to affect this project. You understand, the nondisclosure is in effect?"

"Of course," Diana said.

"No one's listening in on your end?" Lau asked.

She looked up at Daniel. He covered his ears, then his eyes, then his mouth. "Absolutely not," she said.

"All right, then. We've just received some disturbing news. I've been asked not to put anything in writing. To discuss it on a purely need-to-know basis. And you all need to know." He paused for a moment. "We've had a ransom demand."

Diana looked over at Daniel. He looked genuinely stunned.

"You sure it's for real?" she asked. "Because sometimes news of these kinds of . . . unfortunate events"—she didn't know what else to call leaving confidential corporate data on a commuter train—"can leak out. Someone might be trying to capitalize on the chatter."

"I'm afraid it's far more serious than that," Lau said. "We've been faxed a copy of one of the missing documents. It's genuine, all right. The demand is for ten million dollars. If we don't pay up in three days, they're threatening to sell the information to the highest bidder. I've had no choice but to call in the authorities. The data that was taken is highly sensitive. I can't go into detail, but suffice it to say that in the wrong hands, the results would reverberate to the highest levels of our government."

"Bogus," Daniel muttered under his breath. "Completely bogus."

Diana tensed, sweat beading on her upper lip. What was he thinking?

"Why isn't he saying anything?" Daniel continued. "He's just sitting there like a block of wood." Diana realized he meant Jake.

"That's the bad news," Lau continued. "But the good news is, precautions were taken to safeguard the data. Digital time bombs were embedded in the files, and when one of the files was opened, presumably to print the data that was faxed to us, a homing beacon was detonated. Right now, it's transmitting a signal. Agents are closing in on a location, as we speak."

"Agents?" Diana said.

"FBI."

Diana turned to Daniel. He'd gone pale. He stood, looking up into the domed roof of the silo, a hand cupped to his ear.

"What?" she whispered.

He shook his head.

Lau continued. "Tampering with federal data. It's a federal offense."

"Shit," Daniel said under his breath. He returned to his computer and brought up his network manager. "Can't believe . . . so stupid . . . idiot," he muttered. A moment later he was scrolling through log files.

Lau continued to speak but Diana wasn't listening. "Daniel, what are you looking for?"

He didn't respond. He just sat there, gaping at his computer screen.

Diana realized that Lau had stopped talking. Presumably he was waiting for her response. Fortunately, Daniel didn't appear to be paying close attention.

"So, how can we help?" she said.

"Go ahead with the security audit and penetration testing," Lau said. "But forget about tracking the stolen data. It's very important that you leave that alone. For now, at least. Understood?"

"Understood. We'll start testing right away."

"When do you think you'll have a report for us?"

"I'll need a meeting first with your in-house—"

"Jesus Christ," Daniel exploded.

"Pardon?" Lau said.

"Can you give me a moment?" Diana clapped a hand over the microphone, switched the sound input to mute, and froze the screen. She turned to Daniel. "Daniel, they can hear you."

He barely glanced over at her. He was scrolling through lists and opening files, swearing under his breath. "Shit. None of these files were here before. And now . . . Shit. Shit. Shit."

"Daniel!"

"Son of a bitch." He directed the word at his computer screen. "What the hell is going on?"

"Good question," she said. "You tell me. What in the hell *is* going on?"

Daniel was scrolling through network log files. He didn't even acknowledge her question.

Diana got up and went over to him. "Daniel!" she said, squeezing his shoulder.

He looked up, startled.

"Listen to me. This is just like what happened with my last client. Stolen data. Clients freaked out. I thought there might be a ransom demand, but I didn't have the evidence to prove it. Now we do."

A muscle in Daniel's jaw twitched. His gaze traveled from Diana to her computer screen, where the avatars from Vault and Jake waited in suspended animation, then returned to his own computer.

"Or," Diana continued, "is this making some kind of sense to you that I'm still not getting?"

Daniel didn't answer. He continued to gape at the network logs.

"Daniel?"

Finally he shook himself out of it. "Honestly? I don't know. This time I haven't even a clue."

"This time?" Diana said. "*This time?* Are we in this together or not?"

He gave her a dark look. "Diana, you're out of your depth. You have no idea what you're dealing with. Trust me on this."

Trust you? Right. "Well whatever it is, you're right about Jake. He's acting weird. He's just sitting there, like—"

Daniel narrowed his eyes and finished the thought. "Like he isn't really there."

Diana felt as if her heart had vaulted into her throat. Had he seen through the fantasy she'd so carefully constructed? She tried not to react.

"Exactly," she said.

"I don't like this," he said. "It feels . . . wrong. The whole thing feels wrong. End the meeting."

"But Vault—"

"Frankly, Vault and their security issues are not my biggest concern right now." A vein throbbed in his forehead. "End the meeting right now. It's a setup."

"You sound like me."

"Paranoid?" He looked up into the silo's domed roof again, tense and alert. "I'm never paranoid. I *know* I'm surrounded by the enemy."

This time Diana heard it too. The churning, low rumble of an engine. A car? A motorcycle? Daniel might even think it was choppers.

CHAPTER THIRTY-FIVE

DIANA COULD ALMOST SMELL HER OWN ANXIETY, SHARP AND PUN-
gent, like the inside of a tin can. When she unfroze the
screen, Jake's avatar continued to sit there like a department-
store dummy. But Daniel was beyond noticing. He was tabbing
through the mill's surveillance screens.

Diana did her best to stay in character and end the meeting
quickly. She transported Nadia home. Then she watched over
Daniel's shoulder as he checked the stills being fed by cameras
positioned inside and around the mill—the outer gate, hallways,
loft spaces, stairwells, the loading dock. There was nothing to
see. The final feed was pitch-black—the first-floor corridor with
the windows boarded over.

"Why don't you switch to infrared?" Diana said.

Daniel clicked the sun icon, turning it to a moon, and the
image changed. Now there were bright green mottled shapes,
the rough outlines of people.

"Shit. Who the hell . . . ?" Daniel said.

Two of the figures looked as if they were crouching. Just the top of a third was visible creeping beneath the camera. Another was captured midway up the steps. A fifth looked as if it was far away, just entering the corridor to the loading-dock platform.

When the image refreshed, there were only three figures.

"I don't understand how they're getting in," Daniel said. "That door is supposed to be locked. And if they broke in, there'd have been an alarm." He sprang to the wall of the silo and checked the keypad. "They've got the code." He gave her a long hard look.

"Daniel, I've got no access to the outside world. On top of that, I haven't got your security pass codes. What about this door?" She indicated the door to the silo. "Is it still armed?"

Daniel checked the door itself. "It is for now. But just to be sure . . ." He slid a metal bolt into the jamb.

"Who's got the pass codes?" Diana asked. "The alarm company?"

Daniel gave her a pitying look, and she added, "So, just you and Jake?"

The image refreshed again. Now there were two figures remaining in the loading dock, both of them on the platform.

"That means they must have gotten to Jake," Diana said.

Daniel's eyes went wide. He glanced at the door. Checked his watch. Turned back to the video screen. Now the loading dock was empty of human figures.

"They don't know where we are," he said, "but it won't take them long to figure it out."

"What in the hell is going on?" Diana asked.

The infrared camera showed the first-floor corridor empty. Daniel switched to the feed from the camera in the adjacent stairwell. Two figures, like black shadows, moved up the stairs.

"They're almost here. We don't have much time," he said.

"Daniel, who are *they*?" Diana asked. "And what are they looking for?"

Daniel hesitated. She could almost hear the question caroming back and forth in his mind: who to trust? That was the very question she'd asked at all the wrong times and come up with all the wrong answers.

Finally he said, "You heard what he said. Maybe it's the FBI. And if it is, then they're about to find what they're looking for." He looked over at the two computer servers.

"What they're looking for is on the hard drives?" she asked. He nodded.

"So delete the data. Haven't you got a kill switch built in here somewhere? A digital suicide bomb that will overwrite everything?"

Daniel blinked at her.

"Or we can pull the drives and shred them. Have you got a media shredder?"

But Daniel was looking at the first-floor camera again. More bright green figures were moving through the inky dark.

"Surely you must have anticipated something like this could happen," Diana said, though she knew the answer. As usual, there was no plan B, not for Daniel and Jake, masters of their little universe. They never believed that their plans could fail.

But with the likelihood of exposure staring him in the face, Daniel slumped in his chair. He rubbed his hand back and forth over his stubbly chin. "Christ. Years and years of planning. And then he can't wait a couple of more days?"

Years. Diana was beyond aching. She went over to him and took his hand. She turned the palm up. "And these?" She touched a mutilated fingertip. "It's not frostbite, is it?"

He waved his hands like the consummate magician that he was. "Anonymity. That's all I ever wanted. For me. For the world."

"But there was still DNA," Diana said. "Each person's unique identifier—"

"Linked, in a government database, with a name, an address, a Social Security number." Daniel finished the thought, shaking his head in disgust.

"So you decided to discredit DNA by, what, scrambling the databases?"

He went on, as if he hadn't heard her. "Only it doesn't stop there. It's never enough. Without anyone's permission, the government routinely tests the DNA of babies and stores it . . . indefinitely. And do you know what they're talking about now? Christ, in some places, it's already happening. Embedding GPS chips in newborns. Soon, every minute of every day, they'll know where you are.

"I knew I couldn't stop them. But every dragon has its vulnerable spot. I keep poking. Here. There. Slowing it down and slowing it down—"

"Hoping that sooner or later humanity comes to its senses?" Diana said.

Daniel's eyes glittered. "We're going after the computers on satellites next. GPS depends on their alignment."

"Every plane landing at Logan depends on their alignment," Diana said.

"Hey, you gotta break a few eggs . . . Don't you see? That's why we couldn't leave you out there. You were so close to figuring it out when we were so close to making it happen."

He was so casual, so matter-of-fact about it. Diana felt as if she'd been sucker-punched. But this was no time for pointless self-pity. "Guess I'm an A student," she said. "You taught me well. But why risk everything with ransom demands? You never used to care about money."

"I still don't. That ransom thing?" Daniel gave her a pained look. "That's Jake. But he's supposed to wait."

The security panel, just yards away from them, was beeping. Truly startled, Diana jumped to her feet. Someone was entering the code to the silo door. What in the hell was going on? Even if Jake's flight back was on time, he shouldn't be there yet. She'd counted on at least another hour.

"They're here already." Daniel backed away from the door.

Diana recovered quickly. "You need to get away before they get in. Take the data with you." She ran over to the computer servers and started pulling out hard disks, emptying the racks. Three. Five. Eight. Twelve of them—metal and plastic about as large as an oversize paperback book—littered the floor.

Daniel grabbed a backpack from under his worktable and began to stuff the media into it.

There was a long beep as the silo's electronic door latch released. The door gave a fraction but the bolt held it in place.

Daniel stuffed the last hard disk into the backpack. The zipper barely contained them all.

"Go." She pointed up toward the hatch high in the wall. "Hurry!"

The door vibrated as the person on the other side banged on it. Daniel strapped on the backpack and, without a moment's hesitation, started up the wall, springing from rebar to rebar like a mountain goat.

Go, go, go. Diana watched him as she backed up against the door.

"Let me in!" It was Jake. Thank God Daniel hadn't heard. Diana threw her weight against the door, slamming it shut and muting Jake's voice.

Diana had turned back the system clocks, adjusted Daniel's wristwatch, but she'd never expected Jake to arrive back at the mill two hours early. He must have caught an earlier flight home after what had been a routine meeting with Vault, hours ago, while Daniel was sound asleep and dead to the world.

"Hurry!" she shouted up to Daniel.

Halfway up, Daniel stopped and adjusted the backpack.

"What the hell is going on? Would you . . ."

Jake's muffled voice continued speaking as Diana shouted over it, "Daniel, are you okay? Be careful up there. You could easily slip and—"

"Diana, stop it! I've done this a million times. I'm not going to slip."

He climbed up to the hatch, reached over, and pulled it open.

With a mighty crash, the door was bashed in again, and in the silence that followed, Jake's voice rang out, loud and clear. "Daniel! Are you in there? Open the goddamn door!"

Diana froze. She moved away from the door, pointing at it and looking up at Daniel.

Daniel sat astride the ledge to the outside, one leg out, one leg in. "Jake?" he shouted.

"What the hell is going on in there?" Jake called back. "Hey, would you open the door?"

"Think about it," Diana said to Daniel, her voice a harsh whisper. "Ten minutes ago Jake was at a meeting in Bethesda. This can't be him. Not unless—"

"Not unless the meeting was a sham," Daniel said. "A setup. I knew it. But he couldn't . . . He wouldn't . . ."

"You said so yourself, his avatar was acting like Jake wasn't even there."

Daniel sat there for a moment, like he was trying to fit puzzle pieces together. Then he tossed the backpack outside and turned back to Diana. "Check camera seven. Now!"

It took her a moment to understand what he was asking her to do. She ran over to Daniel's computer and toggled through the surveillance feeds until she got to the video feed from the ceiling-mounted camera overlooking the landing outside the silo door. The fish-eye lens exaggerated size of the top of Jake's head.

"There's Jake," she said. "And there are two others. No, there are three of them."

"For chrissakes, would you let me in?" Jake's voice was barely audible.

"Who's out there with him?" Daniel said.

"Who's that out there with you?" Diana shouted through the door.

"What are you talking about? No one's out here with me. Open the goddamned door!"

Daniel looked down at her. He had one leg out and one leg in, a picture of indecision—an emotion she could never remember witnessing in him before. All he needed was a little nudge.

"You saw for yourself," Diana said. "At least six people entered the building. Now three of them are out in the hall with Jake." She glanced at the screen. "They're wearing dark jumpsuits and gloves. And they've got hoods pulled over their faces."

BAM. The door trembled with the impact. The surveillance still showed Jake rearing back, about to bash the door again with an ancient copper fire extinguisher. *BAM!*

"Go! Get out here," Diana cried up to Daniel. "They've got a battering ram. They'll break through any minute."

Diana cringed as the fire extinguisher crashed into the door again. The air inside the silo seemed to vibrate with the noise.

"Hurry!" she shouted. "This bolt's not going to hold much longer."

"Come with me," Daniel said.

At first she couldn't believe her ears. "What?"

"I said, come with me," Daniel shouted.

This hadn't been in the script either. "I can't. I mustn't. Daniel, you need me here to deal with these . . . these people."

Daniel leaned down and extended his arm to her. "Come on. I'm not leaving without you."

BAM. And a moment later, again. Soon the bolt would give and the door would fly open.

"Daniel, you have to go. Now. There's no time. And besides, I can't climb. It's impossible."

"That's ridiculous. Of course you can climb."

She took a step closer to the silo wall.

"Come on. Don't overthink it, babe."

She looked up, thirty feet overhead, to where Daniel was effortlessly perched.

"I'm not going," he said. "Not unless you come with me."

Before Diana realized she'd made the decision to do it, she was on the wall, grabbing hold of the U-shaped end of one of the rebars. She stepped up onto another one at knee height and pulled herself up.

If she'd been the invincible Nadia, she could have done this easily. Dressed as Nadia, she'd have had a better shot at it. But Nadia's leather jacket was on the floor where Daniel had been sleeping.

BAM. Then a clatter. She looked over, and though she couldn't see it, she knew that a screw had fallen from the bolt or door hinge.

"Diana! Come on!" Daniel said.

She craned her neck and looked up. He sat on the ledge, swinging his legs, perched there like a lost boy.

He stretched out his arm to her. "I love you."

The words struck her like dissonant chords. She swallowed tears. "You don't, you know. I'm not even sure you can."

Daniel looked at her, as if seeing her for the first time. "I need you."

There. That was more like it. Daniel had faked his own death, erased his fingerprints, embarked on a plan to discredit DNA. But he needed a partner with at least one foot in the real world in order to set the stage for the mayhem he intended to unleash next. She'd robbed him of Jake. She was his last hope.

Just focus on the moment, she told herself as she climbed up to the next rebar. Grabbed a higher handhold. Then climbed higher. And to the next and the next, until she was halfway up the wall.

Again there was a crash, then a metallic screech, as if a hinge had come loose.

Diana froze. She clung to the wall.

"Come on! You can do it," Daniel said. "You can do whatever you set your mind to."

She started up again. "I'm coming. Wait for me outside."

She looked up again and he was gone. When she reached the hatch, she heard Daniel outside, his footsteps on the metal platform at the top of the outside stairs. Waiting for her. Sure that she'd be by his side in moments.

"Sorry, Daniel," she whispered. "You're on your own this time."

She held on to a rebar with one hand, and with the other, she slammed the door to the hatch shut and drove the bolt home. Then she hung there for a moment, panting.

From the other side of the hatch she heard Daniel banging. "Diana!"

"Go!" she screamed. "They're here!"

There was another crash from below. "Daniel!" Jake's voice was so loud it sounded as if he was in the silo. Looking down, she could see that the door had buckled. It was seconds from giving way completely.

Diana took a tentative step down to a lower rebar. The tables and chairs and computer equipment looked so far away. She hung on, disoriented, as the world pinwheeled.

She couldn't lose it now. She had to center herself. Get a grip. *Don't overthink it, babe.*

She stared straight ahead at the plaster wall inches in front of her nose, at the dimples and irregularities in the surface that were invisible from below. She envisioned the rebars, above and below her, studding the wall at regular intervals. They were goals, and hitting them would trigger jingling coins like the ones in the first video games she'd played as a kid. Each one she triggered would increase her point count.

If . . . no, *when* she reached the floor, she'd finish liberating the princess from the clutches of the trolls.

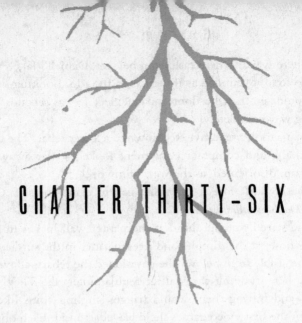

CHAPTER THIRTY-SIX

WHEN THE SILO DOOR BURST OPEN, DIANA WAS CROUCHED UNDER one of the tables. Her scream was genuine as the fire extinguisher went careening past her and bashed into the wall.

She'd had barely enough time to set all the system clocks back to the correct time and disarm all the doors in the complex. She'd sent Pam an urgent text message telling her to restore the live feeds from the mill's surveillance cameras. She needed to touch base with Ashley, but Jake's returning nearly two hours ahead of schedule had thrown everything off. Her only hope was to keep Jake guessing.

"Daniel!" Jake cried as he burst into the silo. He stopped in his tracks. "Daniel?" He turned in a full circle, finally spotting Diana cowering under the table.

"Jake?" Diana crept out. "You're alone? I thought . . . thank God it's only you." She stood, holding her hand to her throat and panting for breath. "I bolted the door. I was afraid—"

"Why the hell didn't you let me in?"

"I couldn't believe you'd be back so soon."

"I caught an earlier flight."

"I'm sorry. I thought it was a trick."

"A trick? Couldn't you hear me screaming? You crazy—"
He stopped and looked around. "Where's Daniel?"

"I thought you knew. He's long gone."

"What do you mean he's gone?"

"Left hours ago."

"Gone where?"

"I . . . I don't know. But he's not coming back. He said his
dream's been perverted. He's starting over. Clean. To do that,
he had to get away from me. From you."

The blood left Jake's face. "From me? No way."

"I'm just telling you what he said."

"He wouldn't just take off."

"See for yourself." She pointed to the systems on the floor.
"He took all the hard disks with him." Not that Daniel would
be able to use what was stored on them. Soon enough, he'd dis-
cover that all of the data had been encrypted.

Jake squatted by one of the servers and peered in at the
empty slots. "Where are they?"

Diana held out her hands. "I told you. Daniel took them."

"I don't believe you." Then his gaze swept the room. "Where
did you hide them?"

Diana sank down in her chair. As Jake tore through the
room, pulling open drawers and clearing shelves, she checked
the surveillance feeds. She switched all the exterior cameras to
night vision. The one overlooking the loading dock showed a
human figure. It was Daniel, getting into the Hummer.

Jake looked everywhere, even inside the little refrigerator.

"Really, they're not here," Diana said.

"It makes no sense. Why would he leave when . . . ?"

"When you're about to hit pay dirt?"

He gave her a cold stare. "Something like that."

Jake went over to his workstation and toggled through the security camera feeds. Diana watched, her heart in her throat. Her plans depended on help arriving on schedule.

"I told you. He's gone," she said.

Jake grabbed her upper arm. "What did you say to him?"

She wrenched free. She had to be careful not to overplay her hand. "I just pointed out the obvious. That you and Daniel have different goals. He's an idealist. And you . . . well, you're not."

"I do what it takes to get Daniel what he wants," Jake said. "It's not cheap, getting the wherewithal to save the world from Big Brother and all that shit that he's into. He's known that from the beginning."

"From the beginning. And when was it that you started planning all of this?" She indicated the space around them.

Jake looked at Diana, eyes narrowed. "Does it matter?"

"It matters to me."

He laughed. "Let's just say it's been a very long time."

"Whose idea was it for Daniel to fake his own death?"

"I know you want me to say it was my idea. But it wasn't." Jake laughed again in that not-funny way. "I warned him you'd never buy that lame story."

"He knew that I'd want to believe it."

He gave her a pitying smile. "Then I'm sorry to have to tell you this. The accident was Daniel's idea. You were there as a witness, and a means to an end after it."

Even though Diana had figured that out for herself, her heart wrenched when she heard Jake being so brutally and casually dismissive.

Jake went on. "His dream was to disappear, live off the grid, and, like the man said, sow chaos. To do that, he needed to sever his ties. Daniel's great at the vision thing. Not so good at tactics. So the details of the operation—that was more of a joint project."

"So the whole idea was to set me up as a front? Whose idea was it to use the trust I'd earned to hack my client's data?"

"I'm sure you can guess the answer to that. I don't give a shit about their frickin' data."

"Right. All you care about is fleecing them after the hack. That's your department."

"Accounts receivable." Jake brushed his fingers and thumb together. "You'd be surprised how much people are willing to pay to protect their reputations. Fortunately, less than it costs to finance this operation."

Diana said, "More than a million and a half, just to buy this place."

If Jake was surprised that she knew, he didn't show it. "Seemed like a bargain at the time. Still does."

"Must have set you back even more to make it livable."

"Fences. Plumbing. Wiring. Would you believe it costs more to blast potholes than it would have cost to build an access road, brand-new. Though in New Hampshire it's easy to find folks willing to do it off the books."

"Was it too risky to put the property in your own name? Certainly you couldn't put it in Daniel's."

"When people see that much cash, they don't ask questions. Besides, you gave me power of attorney."

"I must have been delusional."

"That and more. For months. Neither of us realized . . . we didn't anticipate how incapacitated you'd be." Was that a flicker of contrition? Jake looked away. "Yeah, that took us by surprise. Made things much more complicated than they needed to be."

As Jake glanced back over to where the missing hard disks

would have been, his fists clenched. Quickly Diana checked the outside surveillance feeds. Still nothing.

"You're actually a lot like Daniel," Jake went on. "You've got that idealistic, visionary thing going on but you don't want to get your hands dirty making it happen."

"So you got them dirty for me?"

Jake stared back at her. "Filthy. And just try proving that you didn't know what was going on. Your virtual fingerprints are everywhere. I made sure of that." He gave her an affable smile. "By the way, great meeting this afternoon. Excellent presentation. You had them eating out of our hands."

"Glad you enjoyed it. Because that's the last performance I'm going to give. It's over."

He held her gaze. "You think? This is my show, not yours. It goes on with or without Daniel and with or without you."

"But will it go on without *you*?" she said. Finally Jake blinked. "Because Daniel did one more thing before he ran off. He called the police. You're wanted for kidnapping. Assault. Extortion."

Jake's laugh sounded empty.

"You're lucky you caught an earlier flight," Diana went on. "The police were at the airport, waiting to arrest you when you got off the plane. Daniel didn't know you caught an earlier flight. They're on their way here right now."

"You're making that up." He grabbed Diana by the arm and hauled her over to where he could tab through the surveillance screens.

"You think so? Why don't you just stick around and find out?" She looked past him to the doorway, where the metal door hung from a single hinge.

Jake spun around. The doorway was empty. He squeezed her arm. "What the hell are you playing at? I told Daniel to cut his losses. Too bad he didn't—" He froze. Distant scuffling footsteps grew louder, more distinct.

Jake's fingers loosened on her arm as one police officer came into view. There was another one behind him. And another. Ashley brought up the rear.

Diana couldn't help smiling. Ashley was wearing the second outfit—Nadia's leather jacket and jeans. She rushed over to Diana and hugged her. Then she turned and pointed to Jake.

"That's him! That's the man who kidnapped me. He drugged me and held me here for a week. God knows what he did to me while I was unconscious."

"You crazy bitch," Jake said. "No one did anything to you while you were unconscious. And it wasn't me who kidnapped you."

"There's plenty of evidence," Diana said to the police officer in the lead, "upstairs in the other building. I can show you the place where my sister was held. The drugs she was given. There is surveillance footage that shows this man drugging her. And video that shows him grabbing her at Copley Square."

"I swear to God," Jake said, holding up his hands and backing away, "none of this was my idea. The man you want is Daniel Schechter." One of the officers grabbed his wrist and cuffed it, then turned him around and cuffed both hands behind his back.

Jake scowled at Diana. "Tell them. Tell them about Daniel. He was here. With us. This whole setup was his idea."

"If he was here, then his fingerprints would be," Diana said. "Go ahead," she said to one of the officers. "Dust the place. You'll find his." She jerked a thumb at Jake. "And you'll find mine. But I'm quite sure you won't find this person Daniel's."

Though she no longer needed a costume or an alternate identity to make her feel powerful and resilient, Diana grabbed

Nadia's jacket from the floor. She slipped it on. She loved that soft leather, and there was nothing quite like clothing that was custom made.

"Besides, how could Daniel Schechter have had anything to do with this? He's dead. Don't you remember?" she said, her gaze locked on Jake. "And I have his ashes to prove it."

CHAPTER THIRTY-SEVEN

A s Ashley drove home, Diana kept a tight grip on the door
handle. Unnerving as it had been driving a Hummer on I-93
North, riding along I-93 South in the middle of the night
in the Mini Cooper felt like zipping along at ground level in a
tin can.

She held Daniel's walking stick across her lap. The pine-
resiny essence wafted up. He was still out there. Somewhere.
She really didn't care where.

By the time they'd left the mill, police officers had im-
pounded all the surveillance and computer equipment, including Diana's laptop. They also seized the black limousine. The
Hummer, of course, had vanished along with Daniel.

Diana and Ashley had led the police to the floor where
Ashley had been held unconscious. They'd stood by watching
as investigators took pictures, lighting up the room in flashes
and gathering evidence. Ashley had watched, her arms crossed

over her chest, shivering, as investigators collected the IV bag with the tube and needle still attached.

"It feels so weird, standing here. Like an out-of-body experience," Ashley had said. She told Diana how bits and pieces, mostly visuals, were coming back to her. The rough-hewn beamed ceiling. The restraints—thick Velcro cuffs. The tube through which mind-numbing drugs had been forced into her body.

"You were very brave," Diana said, putting an arm around her sister.

"I was unconscious. How can you be brave when you're out cold?"

"Believe me. You were both."

After a pause, Ashley said, "What bastards."

"The worst."

Ashley and Diana had gone from the mill to New Hampshire State Police headquarters in Manchester, where they'd been questioned and given their statements. The district attorney assured them that Jake would be held while the investigation continued. He'd most likely be charged with assault and kidnapping, and depending on what investigators found, there could be charges of extortion and more.

As Ashley drove home along the nearly deserted stretch of I-93, she asked, "So how do you feel now?"

"I thought I'd feel more, I don't know, elation or something. Paying them back in kind." Diana stared out the window at the blur of trees that lined the road. "Instead, I guess I'm just sad. Disappointed that they weren't who I thought they were. Disappointed in myself that I was so willingly gulled. Disgusted, really." A sign on the side of the road, MASSACHUSETTS WELCOMES YOU, flew by. "Most of all, ready to move on."

"Sounds good to me," Ashley said, and flashed her a tired smile.

It was near dawn by the time they got back to Ashley's apartment. Ashley called in sick, and both she and Diana slept straight through the morning. That afternoon, Ashley drove Diana home. She parked in front of the little house where they'd grown up.

"We should probably call Mom," she said.

"It's Friday. She'll think something's wrong," Diana said.

"She already knows something's wrong."

Ashley got out of the car. Diana followed her to the front door. All it took was a turn of her house key to get inside. Except for a trail of dirt on the carpet that must have gotten tracked in when Jake and Daniel were moving her things, the living room looked untouched.

She raised the shades, then walked from room to room, letting in light. In her bedroom, she made a mental note—later she'd get out on Craigslist and find herself another bed. She never again wanted to see the one that she and Daniel had shared.

She stood in the doorway of her barren office and looked at the empty tables and shelves. The Peruvian wall hanging seemed like it was trying too hard. Maybe she'd get a Ping-Pong table. Or a cushy leather sectional couch and a mammoth TV screen. Or maybe not. The only thing she knew for sure was that Gamelan was officially out of business.

It seemed oddly comforting when the doorbell rang without the Klaxon going off first, with no monitor to show who was standing on her doorstep.

"I'll get it," Diana called to Ashley.

She returned to the front door and looked out through the

peephole. At first, it didn't look as if anyone was there. Then she saw a hand wave, and below that just the top of a head with white-white hair.

"Pam!" Diana pulled open the door and Pam's wheelchair whirred across the threshold.

"Okay, this is going to be a joint project," Pam said. "I brought the booze." She handed Diana a bottle of brandy. "We need three stiff shots."

Diana passed the bottle to Ashley. "Can you open this and do the honors?"

Ashley disappeared into the kitchen and came back with three juice glasses. She set them on the coffee table, pulled the cork from the bottle, and poured a few fingers of brandy into each glass.

"Too bad this won't fit into the fireplace as is," Diana said as she leaned Daniel's driftwood walking stick at an angle against the wall and brought her foot down. The wood cracked. She came down on it again and it broke into pieces.

Diana handed Pam and Ashley double sheets of newspaper and showed them how to roll it, tie it, and shred the ends. When they'd made a half-dozen newspaper logs and she'd nested them in the bottom of the fireplace, she gathered up the pieces of the walking stick and arranged them on top.

They were ready. Pam held a kitchen match. Ashley stood by the stereo system, waiting. When Diana nodded to her, she turned it on. As the first notes of Pachelbel's Canon filled the room, Pam struck the match on the brick fireplace surround and handed it to Diana. Diana touched the flame to a bit of newspaper fringe.

Ashley passed around the drinks, and together they watched the paper burn. It took a few minutes, but finally the dry wood caught. Then the fire burned hot and fast, white smoke curling up the chimney as, in the music, violins circled and soared.

Diana toasted the flames and sniffed her drink, then took a sip. The smoky tang of the brandy worked its way up the back of her throat and filled her head, as she hoped it would, over-whelming any last phantom sensation of pine resin.

Diana felt Ashley's hand on her shoulder. "You okay, hon?" Ashley asked.

"I am now, thanks to both of you."

"You're the one who pulled it off," Ashley said. "We just took orders."

Diana looked at Pam. "You did a great job. I got so caught up that I almost believed it myself when the COO started saying how he'd called the FBI."

"I borrowed my neighbor for that," Pam said. "He's an out-of-work voice-over actor. He doesn't usually get to ad-lib."

"If I weren't retiring, I'd want to hire him as my chief of operations," Diana said. "He did a brilliant job impersonating one."

She stepped to the mantel and took down the brass urn that supposedly contained Daniel's ashes. Ashley lit another match and held it as Diana rotated the urn so that the wax seal holding the lid in place melted. With a *pop*, it came free. She opened it and peered inside. The contents looked like nothing more sin-ister than pebbles and sand.

Diana set the urn on the brick fireplace threshold. With a brass shovel from her fireplace tool set, she scooped up the still-smoldering ashes from the walking stick and tipped them into the urn. She unfastened the leather cord from around her neck, slipped off one of the gold *D*s, and tossed that in too. Then she closed the urn and held it between her hands. She felt the last warmth seeping from the remaining embers but nothing else.

"So, when are we getting tickets?" Ashley asked.

"You taking a trip?" Pam asked.

"I thought we'd fly to Zurich," Ashley said. "What do you think, Di? First class? Get to the top the easy way. By train or lift, whatever. Scatter a few ashes?"

"You think they'll let me through airport security with this?" Diana said, indicating the urn. But as she looked down at it, she realized that it held nothing that mattered to her any longer. More than that, she didn't want to squander another ounce of energy looking back.

"Why waste a perfectly good trip to Europe on an asshole?" she said. "I have a much better idea."

She marched through the kitchen, opened the back door of the house, and stepped outside. There, alongside the door, were the dozens and dozens of stones she'd left, lined up like soldiers, each one marking another tentative foray into the outside world. She picked one up and dropped it into a pocket. It would be a keepsake, a reminder of a state of mind she vowed never to find herself in again. With a swing of her booted foot, she sent the rest of the stones flying into the grass.

She flipped open the lid of the nearby garbage can and dumped in the urn's contents. The urn made a satisfying thud as she tossed it in after.

"Good riddance," she said as she closed the lid.

Turn the page for an excerpt of
Hallie Ephron's previous book,

NEVER TELL A LIE.

Pregnant Woman Missing from Brush Hills

BRUSH HILLS, MA Police continue to search for clues in the disappearance of Melinda White, 33, who was last seen on Saturday. Authorities yesterday issued a bulletin describing the pregnant woman as "at risk" and a possible victim of foul play.

Ms. White, an administrative assistant with SoBo Realty, attended a yard sale in Brush Hills on Saturday morning and has not been seen since, police said. Her sister, Ruth White, of Naples, Florida, reported her missing on Monday.

"She calls me every day, and when I didn't hear from her, I knew that something was wrong," said Ruth White. She added that the close family was bearing the strain "as well as could be expected."

Brush Hills Police Detective Sergeant Albert Blanchard said authorities have no suspects in custody.

"We're trying to interview everyone that she knew and anyone who saw her on Saturday, but as far as leads to show us what happened—no," Blanchard said.

Anyone with information is asked to call the Brush Hills Police detective division.

1

Saturday, November 1

Rain or shine, that's what Ivy Rose had put in the yard-sale ad. What they'd gotten was a metallic gray sky and gusty winds. But the typical, contrary New England fall weather hadn't discouraged this crowd.

David moved aside the sawhorse that blocked the driveway, and buyers surged in. It seemed to Ivy that their Victorian ark tolerated the invasion the way a great white whale might float to the surface and permit birds to pick parasites off its back.

For three years Ivy had been oblivious to the dusty piles of junk left behind by elderly Paul Vlaskovic, the previous owner, a cadaverous fellow whom David referred to as Vlad. The clutter that filled their attic and basement might as well have existed in a parallel universe. Then, as sudden as a spring thunderstorm, the urge to expel what wasn't theirs had risen up in her until she could no longer stand it. *Out!* David had had the good grace, or maybe it was his instinct for self-preservation, not to blame it on hormones.

Ivy felt the baby's firm kick—no more moth-wing flutter. *Hello there, Sprout.* She rested her palms on her belly, for the moment solid as a rock. With just three weeks to go until she either gave birth or exploded, Ivy was supposed to be having contractions. Braxton Hicks. False labor. The revving of an engine, not quite juiced up enough to turn over.

She and David had reached the obsessing-about-a-name stage, and she wondered how many other soon-to-be parents had tossed around the name Braxton.

Viable, viable, viable. The word whispered itself over and over in her head. She'd married at twenty-four, and then it had taken five years to conceive. Three times she'd miscarried—the last time at twenty weeks, just when she'd thought it was safe to stop holding her breath.

David came up alongside her and put his arm around where she'd once had a waist. A fully pregnant belly was pretty astonishing, right up there with a prizewinning Hubbard squash.

"Hey, Stretch"—the nickname had taken on an entirely new connotation in these final months—"looks like we have ignition. Quite a crowd," he said. She shivered with pleasure as he pushed her hair to one side and nuzzled her neck.

Ivy loved the way David gave off the aroma of rich, loamy soil, the way his thatch of auburn hair seemed to go in twelve directions at once, and most of all the way his smile took over his face and crinkled his eyes. The broken nose he'd gotten playing college football, after surviving unscathed for two years as quarterback in high school, gave his sweet face character.

She was more what people called "interesting-looking"—dark soulful eyes, too long in the nose, and a mouth that was a bit too generous to be considered pretty. Most days she paid little attention to her looks. She rolled out of bed, brushed her teeth, ran a comb through long, thick, chestnut-colored hair, and got on with it.

"They think that because we have this great old house, we have great old stuff," Ivy said.

David twiddled an invisible cigar and Groucho Marxed his eyebrows at a pair of black telephones with rotary dials. "Little do they know . . ."

Ivy waved at a fellow yard-sale junkie, Ralph of the battered black Ford pickup, who was crouched over a box of electrical fixtures. Beside him, amid the tumult, stood Corinne Bindel, their elderly next-door neighbor, her bouffant too platinum and puffy to be real. Her arms were folded across the front of her brown tweed coat. The pained expression on her face said she couldn't imagine why anyone would pay a nickel for any of this junk.

"What do you say?" David asked. "After the dust settles, we set up some of the baby things?"

"Not yet," Ivy said. She rubbed the cobalt blue stone set in the hand-shaped silver good-luck charm that hung from a chain around her neck. The talisman had once been her grandmother's. She knew that it was silly superstition, but she wanted all of the baby things tucked away in the spare room until the baby arrived and had had each of her fingers and toes counted and kissed.

"Excuse me?" said a woman who peered at Ivy from under the brim of a Red Sox cap. She held a lime green Depression glass swan-shaped dish that had been in a box of wax fruit that mice had gotten to.

"You can have that for fifteen," Ivy said. "Not a chip or crack on it."

"Ivy?" The woman with cinnamon curls, streaked silvery blond, had a mildly startled look. "Don't remember me, do you?"

"I . . ." Ivy hesitated. There *was* something familiar about this woman who wore a cotton maternity top, patterned in blue cornflowers and yellow black-eyed Susans. Her hand, the nails polished pink and perfectly sculpted, rested on her own belly. Like Ivy, she was voluminously pregnant.

"Mindy White," the woman said. "Melinda back then."

Melinda White—the name conjured the memory of a chubby girl from elementary school. Frizzy brown hair, glasses, and a pasty complexion. It was hard to believe that this was the same person.

"Of course I remember you. Wow, don't you look great! And congratulations. Your first?" Ivy asked.

Melinda nodded and took a step closer. She smiled. Her once-crooked teeth were now straight and perfect. "Isn't this your first, too?"

Ivy avoided her probing look.

"I'm due Thanksgiving," Melinda said. "How 'bout you?"

"December," Ivy said. In fact, she was expecting a Thanksgiving baby, too. But Ivy had told everyone, even her best friend, Jody, that her due date was two weeks later. As the end approached, it would be enough to deal with just her and David agonizing over when she was going to go into labor and whether something would go wrong this time.

Melinda tilted her head and considered Ivy. "Happy marriage. Baby due any minute. You guys are so lucky. I mean, what more could you ask for?"

Kinehora was what Grandma Fay would have said to that, then spit to distract the evil eye. Ivy rubbed the amulet hanging around her neck.

Melinda's gaze shifted to the house. "And of course this fabulous Victorian. Let me know if you ever want to sell it. I work for a real estate agent."

"You collect Depression glass?" Ivy asked, indicating the swan.

"No, but my mother collects swans—or at least she used to. Would have snapped up this piece in a flash . . . but that was before"—Melinda tapped a half-empty Evian bottle to the side of her head—"Alzheimer's. She sold her house here in Brush Hills. Moved to Florida to live with my sister, Ruth. Remember Ruthie? Collects swans, too." The words came out in bursts, and Ivy felt as if a chugging locomotive were bearing down on her as Melinda stepped forward again, narrowing the gap between them to barely a forearm's length.

"This would be so perfect for her." Melinda admired the swan. "For Christmas. Or maybe her birthday. When my mother"—Melinda shifted a bulky white canvas tote bag higher on her shoulder and took a breath—"finally croaks, Ruthie will probably want the whole collection. You don't have a sister, or brother either, do you?"

She didn't wait for Ivy to answer. "Honestly, I didn't recognize this place. Used to come here all the time. We lived practically around the corner, and my mother, she worked for Mr. Vlaskovic. Sometimes. I remember playing jacks on the attic floor and eating red cherry Jell-O powder straight from the package." She pulled a face. "Refined sugar. Might as well be mainlining pure poison. What were we thinking? Have to be so careful now. Eating for two. You going to nurse?"

"I . . . uh . . ." The intimacy of the question startled Ivy. She checked her watch, hoping Melinda would take the hint.

"It's so much better for the baby," Melinda went on, oblivious. "Oh, God, do I sound like an ad for those crazy La Leche ladies or what?"

Over Melinda's shoulder, Ivy saw David talking with a woman who held a pair of brass sconces while four other people were crowded around him, arms loaded and waiting their turn. A young man with spiky black hair was examining the greatcoats hanging from a clothesline they'd strung under the porte cochere. The coats, which had been abandoned in a trunk in the basement, flapped in the stiff breeze like monstrous bat wings.

"Did you know that?" Melinda asked.

"Pardon?"

"They put corn syrup in baby formula," Melinda said. Her eyes Ivy recognized, small and intense.

"That doesn't sound good," Ivy said. Now Spiky Hair was trying on one of the greatcoats. "Hang on. I see someone over there looking at some coats. I don't want him to get away."

Ivy hurried off.

"Very dashing," she told the man. The black wool coat fit him perfectly. The mothball smell would disappear after a good dry cleaning. "Fifty dollars gets you all four of them."

The man examined the other coats. She expected him to haggle, but instead he drew his wallet from his pocket, peeled two twenties and a ten from a wad of bills, and handed them to her. He folded the coats over his arm and headed off.

Yes! Ivy pumped a fist in triumph. Then she stuffed the money into her apron pocket.

"Think he's a dealer?" It was Melinda. She'd come up behind Ivy.

Deep breath. With the baby's feet pressing up and into her diaphragm, Ivy was finding it harder to catch her breath.

"I always adored this house," Melinda said. "All those fireplaces. Great for playing hide-and-seek, so many hidden nooks and crannies." Melinda waited. Her inquisitive look felt like probing fingers.

Ivy remembered that Melinda's face had once been pudgy and soft, like if you poked her doughy cheek, it would leave an indentation.

"And those wonderful paint colors you picked," Melinda said. "You always had a great eye. I remember you were the first person at school to get a pair of Doc Martens."

Ivy's smile muscles were starting to wear. *Doc Martens?* She'd bought hers at the Garment District on the Dollar-A-Pound floor. She still had them, somewhere in the back of her closet. Should've thrown them into the yard sale along with the greatcoats.

Melinda's gaze drifted, her eyes dreamy. "Stirrup pants."

"Oh, God," Ivy said. "Can you believe we wore those?"

But Melinda hadn't worn stirrup pants. Her daily uniform had consisted of shapeless skirts and oversize sweaters. She'd eaten lunch alone in a corner of the high-school cafeteria and been herded to and from school by her mother. How utterly transformed Melinda seemed, with her manicured nails and stylish haircut. Slim. Outgoing and confident.

David swooped over. "Guess what," he said. "Someone wants to buy those red drapes." His look said, *Told you so!* "How about you go negotiate?"

"Hi, David. Long time no see," Melinda said. She jiggled her water bottle in the air and gazed up at him from beneath the bill of her cap.

"Hey there. How ya doin'?" David said, returning the greeting without a flicker of recognition.

Ivy excused herself. A balding man with a barrel chest and intense eyes caught in a tangle of gray eyebrows intercepted her. "You take ten bucks for this?" The black metal fan he held out to her could have done double duty as a bologna slicer. She'd marked it thirty, knowing that electric fans like it were going for fifty on the Internet.

"Twenty-five," she said.

He shrugged and handed her the money.

It had started to drizzle. Ivy glanced over at David. Melinda was saying something to him. He took a step back, looking completely poleaxed. Guess he remembered her after all.

Ivy looked down at her hand. She was holding a twenty and a five. That had been for the fan. She tucked the bills into her pocket.

Now, where had she been headed? Her mind had gone blank. Again.

Somewhere she'd read that women carrying girl babies suffered more short-term memory loss during pregnancy. Something about progesterone levels. If that was the case, then this was definitely a girl. Lately she'd been e-mailing herself reminders to read her to-do list. A week ago she'd even managed to lose her toothbrush.

The greatcoats were gone. Their neighbor, Mrs. Bindel, was reading their copy of the *Boston Globe*. Which wasn't for sale. David was still talking to Melinda and looking just as trapped as Ivy had felt earlier. A woman was shaking out one of the thick red silk brocade panels that had hung—

That was it! Now she remembered where she'd been headed. And she'd scoffed when David had insisted that someone would be willing to buy six sets of fringed drapes that had made the downstairs feel like a bordello or an Italian restaurant.

She went over to the woman, who had on a rock the size of an apricot pit. "We were hoping to get seventy-five for those." What the heck?

"I don't know." The woman pursed her lips. She rubbed the red silk brocade back and forth between thumb and forefinger, then lifted one of the tasseled edges to her nose and sniffed.

Ivy balled her fists and pressed them into the ache in the small of her back. "Actually, we'd take forty. One of them's a bit faded."

The drapery lady said nothing, just pouted at the fabric some more.

Another tap on her shoulder. "Ivy?" Melinda's fingers were wrapped around the glass swan's slender neck.

"You can have that, my treat," Ivy said. The words were pleasant, but the tone was snappish.

Melinda barely blinked. She tucked the swan dish into her canvas bag.

Ivy cleared a spot on the steps to the side door and sank down. She had heartburn, her morning OJ was repeating on her, she had to pee, and her ankles felt like overripe sausages about to burst their casings.

Thank God, David was on his way over.

"Did you see Theo?" he asked, an anxious look on his face. "I promised him one of those greatcoats."

"You should have told me to save him one. Was he here?"

"Just long enough to leave a campaign sign he wants us to put on the front lawn."

"Sorry, I sold every last—" Ivy closed her eyes as her abdominal muscles cramped.

David crouched alongside her. "You okay?" he said under his breath.

Ivy suppressed a burp. "Just tired."

David pulled over a cardboard box filled with 1960s *National Geographic*s and propped her feet on them.

"There's a guy looking for books," he said in his normal voice. "Wasn't there a box that we didn't put out?"

"If there is, it's still in the attic."

David started for the house. He paused midstep and turned back. "Hey, Mindy—want to see the inside?"

Mindy?

"Could I?" Melinda swung around. Her belly bumped into a card table, and a large mirror that had been leaning against the table leg began to topple forward. "Oh, my gosh!" she cried.

Ivy reached over and caught the mirror just before it hit the ground.

"I'm so sorry." Melinda had gone white. She bit her lip, and her face turned pinched. "I mean, what if—"

"It's okay," Ivy said. "Don't worry about it."

"You sure?"

"See?" Ivy set the mirror upright. "No damage done."

"Thank God," Melinda whispered.

"Really, it wouldn't have been a big deal."

"No big . . . ?" Melinda stooped alongside where Ivy was sitting. She gave Ivy a penetrating look as she placed one hand on Ivy's belly and the other on her own. Through her sweatshirt Ivy felt the pressure of Melinda's palm and the tips of those long pink fingernails against her taut skin. "Are you kidding? We don't need more bad luck, do we?"

Ivy felt her jaw drop.

Melinda stood and turned to David. "So did you keep the embossed leather wallpaper in the front hall? And that wonderful statue at the foot of the stairs?"

"You can see for yourself," David said. "Go ahead in. I'll give you the grand tour."

Melinda brushed past Ivy as she climbed the steps to the house. David rolled his eyes and followed.

Ivy rubbed her palms across her belly, trying to erase the feel of Melinda's handprint.

"Hey," Melinda said from the doorway.

Ivy turned.

Melinda mouthed the words, "See you," then turned and went inside, the screen door smacking shut behind her.

Ivy sincerely hoped not.